Nathaniel Hawthorne

Legends of the Province House, etc

Being second series of Twice-told tales

Nathaniel Hawthorne

Legends of the Province House, etc
Being second series of Twice-told tales

ISBN/EAN: 9783337174521

Printed in Europe, USA, Canada, Australia, Japan

Cover: Foto ©Andreas Hilbeck / pixelio.de

More available books at **www.hansebooks.com**

LEGENDS

OF THE

PROVINCE HOUSE,

ETC.

BEING SECOND SERIES OF

TWICE-TOLD TALES.

BY

NATHANIEL HAWTHORNE.

EDINBURGH:
WILLIAM PATERSON.
1883.

EDINBURGH:
PRINTED BY M'FARLANE AND ERSKINE,
ST JAMES SQUARE.

CONTENTS.

TWICE-TOLD TALES.

LEGENDS OF THE PROVINCE HOUSE.

I.

HOWE'S MASQUERADE.

ONE afternoon last summer, while walking along Washington Street, my eye was attracted by a sign-board
protruding over a narrow archway, nearly opposite the
Old South Church. The sign represented the front of a
stately edifice, which was designated as the "OLD
PROVINCE HOUSE, kept by Thomas Waite." I was
glad to be thus reminded of a purpose, long entertained,
of visiting and rambling over the mansion of the old
royal governors of Massachusetts; and entering the
arched passage, which penetrated through the middle
of a brick row of shops, a few steps transported me
from the busy heart of modern Boston into a small
and secluded court yard. One side of this space was
occupied by the square front of the Province House,
three stories high, and surmounted by a cupola, on
the top of which a gilded Indian was discernible, with
his bow bent and his arrow on the string, as if aiming at
the weathercock on the spire of the Old South. The
figure has kept this attitude for seventy years or more,
ever since good Deacon Drowne, a cunning carver of

wood, first stationed him on his long sentinel's watch over the city.

The Province House is constructed of brick, which seems recently to have been overlaid with a coat of light-colored paint. A flight of red freestone steps, fenced in by a balustrade of curiously wrought iron, ascends from the court yard to the spacious porch, over which is a balcony, with an iron balustrade of similar pattern and workmanship to that beneath. These letters and figures—16 P. S. 79—are wrought into the iron work of the balcony, and probably express the date of the edifice, with the initials of its founder's name. A wide door with double leaves admitted me into the hall or entry, on the right of which is the entrance to the bar room.

It was in this apartment, I presume, that the ancient governors held their levees, with vice-regal pomp, surrounded by the military men, the councillors, the judges, and other officers of the crown, while all the loyalty of the province thronged to do them honor. But the room, in its present condition, cannot boast even of faded magnificence. The panelled wainscot is covered with dingy paint, and acquires a duskier hue from the deep shadow into which the Province House is thrown by the brick block that shuts it in from Washington Street. A ray of sunshine never visits this apartment any more than the glare of the festal torches, which have been extinguished from the era of the revolution. The most venerable and ornamental object is a chimney-piece set round with Dutch tiles of blue-figured China, representing scenes from Scripture ; and, for aught I know, the lady of Pownall or Bernard may have sat beside this fire-place, and told her children the story of each blue tile. A bar in modern style, well replenished with decanters, bottles, cigar boxes, and network bags of lemons, and provided with a beer pump and a soda

fount, extends along one side of the room. At my
entrance, an elderly person was smacking his lips, with a
zest which satisfied me that the cellars of the Province
House still hold good liquor, though doubtless of other
vintages than were quaffed by the old governors. After
sipping a glass of port sangaree, prepared by the skilful
hands of Mr Thomas Waite, I besought that worthy
successor and representative of so many historic personages to conduct me over their time-honored mansion.

He readily complied; but, to confess the truth, I was
forced to draw strenuously upon my imagination, in
order to find aught that was interesting in a house which,
without its historic associations, would have seemed
merely such a tavern as is usually favored by the custom
of decent city boarders and old fashioned country gentlemen. The chambers, which were probably spacious in
former times, are now cut up by partitions, and sub-
divided into little nooks, each affording scanty room for
the narrow bed, and chair, and dressing table of a single
lodger. The great staircase, however, may be termed,
without much hyperbole, a feature of grandeur and
magnificence. It winds through the midst of the house
by flights of broad steps, each flight terminating in a
square landing-place, whence the ascent is continued
towards the cupola. A carved balustrade, freshly painted
in the lower stories, but growing dingier as we ascend,
borders the staircase with its quaintly twisted and intertwined pillars, from top to bottom. Up these stairs the
military boots, or perchance the gouty shoes, of many a
governor have trodden, as the wearers mounted to the
cupola, which afforded them so wide a view over their
metropolis and the surrounding country. The cupola is
an octagon, with several windows, and a door opening
upon the roof. From this station, as I pleased myself
with imagining, Gage may have beheld his disastrous
victory on Bunker Hill (unless one of the tri-mountains

intervened), and Howe have marked the approaches of
Washington's besieging army; although the buildings,
since erected in the vicinity, have shut out almost every
object, save the steeple of the Old South, which seems
almost within arm's length. Descending from the cupola,
I paused in the garret to observe the ponderous white-
oak framework, so much more massive than the frames
of modern houses, and thereby resembling an antique
skeleton. The brick walls, the materials of which were
imported from Holland, and the timbers of the mansion,
are still as sound as ever; but the floors and other
interior parts being greatly decayed, it is contemplated
to gut the whole, and build a new house within the
ancient frame and brick work. Among other incon-
veniences of the present edifice, mine host mentioned
that any jar or motion was apt to shake down the dust of
ages out of the ceiling of one chamber upon the floor of
that beneath it.

We stepped forth from the great front window into the
balcony, where, in old times, it was doubtless the custom
of the king's representative to show himself to a loyal
populace, requiting their huzzas and tossed-up hats with
stately bendings of his dignified person. In those days,
the front of the Province House looked upon the street ;
and the whole sight now occupied by the brick range of
stores, as well as the present court yard, was laid out in
grass plots, overshadowed by trees and bordered by a
wrought-iron fence. Now, the old aristocratic edifice
hides its time-worn visage behind an upstart modern
building ; at one of the back windows I observed some
pretty tailoresses, sewing, and chatting, and laughing,
with now and then a careless glance towards the
balcony. Descending thence, we again entered the bar
room, where the elderly gentleman above mentioned, the
smack of whose lips had spoken so favorably for Mr.
Waite's good liquor, was still lounging in his chair. He

seemed to be, if not a lodger, at least a familiar visitor of
the house, who might be supposed to have his regular
score at the bar, his summer seat at the open window,
and his prescriptive corner at the winter's fireside.
Being of a sociable aspect, I ventured to address him
with a remark, calculated to draw forth his historical
reminiscences, if any such were in his mind ; and it
gratified me to discover, that, between memory and
tradition, the old gentleman was really possessed of
some very pleasant gossip about the Province House.
The portion of his talk which chiefly interested me was
the outline of the following legend. He professed to
have received it at one or two removes from an eye-
witness ; but this derivation, together with the lapse of
time, must have afforded opportunities for many varia-
tions of the narrative ; so that, despairing of literal and
absolute truth, I have not scrupled to make such further
changes as seemed conducive to the reader's profit and
delight.

At one of the entertainments given at the Province
House, during the latter part of the siege of Boston,
there passed a scene which has never yet been satisfactorily explained. The officers of the British army,
and the loyal gentry of the province, most of whom were
collected within the beleagured town, had been invited
to a masked ball ; for it was the policy of Sir William
Howe to hide the distress and danger of the period, and
the desperate aspect of the siege, under an ostentation of
festivity. The spectacle of this evening, if the oldest
members of the provincial court circle might be believed,
was the most gay and gorgeous affair that had occurred
in the annals of the government. The brilliantly-lighted
apartments were thronged with figures that seemed to

have stepped from the dark canvas of historic portraits, or to have flitted forth from the magic pages of romance, or at least to have flown hither from one of the London theatres, without a change of garments. Steeled knights of the Conquest, bearded statesmen of Queen Elizabeth, and high-ruffled ladies of her court, were mingled with characters of comedy, such as a party-colored Merry Andrew, jingling his cap and bells ; a Falstaff, almost as provocative of laughter as his prototype ; and a Don Quixote, with a bean pole for a lance, and a pot lid for a shield.

But the broadest merriment was excited by a group of figures ridiculously dressed in old regimentals, which seemed to have been purchased at a military rag fair, or pilfered from some receptacle of the cast-off clothes of both the French and British armies.   Portions of their attire had probably been worn at the siege of Louisburg, and the coats of most recent cut might have been rent and tattered by sword, ball, or bayonet, as long ago as Wolfe's victory.   One of these worthies—a tall, lank figure, brandishing a rusty sword of immense longitude —purported to be no less a personage than General George Washington ; and the other principal officers of the American army, such as Gates, Lee, Putnam, Schuyler, Ward, and Heath, were represented by similar scarecrows.   An interview in the mock heroic style, between the rebel warriors and the British commander-in-chief, was received with immense applause, which came loudest of all from the loyalists of the colony. There was one of the guests, however, who stood apart, eyeing these antics sternly and scornfully, at once with a frown and a bitter smile.

It was an old man, formerly of high station and great repute in the province, and who had been a very famous soldier in his day.   Some surprise had been expressed, that a person of Colonel Joliffe's known whig principles,

though now too old to take an active part in the contest,
should have remained in Boston during the siege, and
especially that he should consent to show himself in the
mansion of Sir William Howe.   But thither he had
come, with a fair granddaughter under his arm ; and
there, amid all the mirth and buffoonery, stood this stern
old figure, the best sustained character in the masquerade, because so well representing the antique spirit of
his native land.   The other guests affirmed that Colonel
Joliffe's black puritanical scowl threw a shadow round
about him ; although, in spite of his sombre influence,
their gayety continued to blaze higher, like—(an ominous
comparison) — the flickering brilliancy of a lamp which
has but a little while to burn.   Eleven strokes, full half
an hour ago, had pealed from the clock of the Old South,
when a rumor was circulated among the company that
some new spectacle or pageant was about to be exhibited, which should put a fitting close to the splendid
festivities of the night.

"What new jest has your Excellency in hand?" asked
the Rev. Mather Byles, whose Presbyterian scruples had
not kept him from the entertainment.   "Trust me, sir, I
have already laughed more than beseems my cloth, at
your Homeric confabulation with yonder ragamuffin
General of the rebels.   One other such fit of merriment,
and I must throw off my clerical wig and band."

"Not so, good Doctor Byles," answered Sir William
Howe ; "if mirth were a crime, you had never gained
your doctorate in divinity.   As to this new foolery, I
know no more about it than yourself ; perhaps not so
much.   Honestly now, Doctor, have you not stirred up
the sober brains of some of your countrymen to enact a
scene in our masquerade?"

" Perhaps," slyly remarked the granddaughter of
Colonel Joliffe, whose high spirit had been stung by many
taunts against New England—"perhaps we are to have

a mask of allegorical figures. Victory, with trophies from Lexington and Bunker Hill—Plenty, with her over-flowing horn, to typify the present abundance in this good town—and Glory, with a wreath for his Excellency's brow."

Sir William Howe smiled at words which he would have answered with one of his darkest frowns, had they been uttered by lips that wore a beard. He was spared the necessity of a retort by a singular interruption. A sound of music was heard without the house, as if pro-ceeding from a full band of military instruments stationed in the street, playing not such a festal strain as was suited to the occasion ; but a slow funeral march. The drums appeared to be muffled, and the trumpets poured forth a wailing breath, which at once hushed the merri-ment of the auditors, filling all with wonder and some with apprehension. The idea occurred to many, that either the funeral procession of some great personage had halted in front of the Province House, or that a corpse, in a velvet-covered and gorgeously-decorated coffin, was about to be borne from the portal. After listening a moment, Sir William Howe called, in a stern voice, to the leader of the musicians, who had hitherto enlivened the entertainment with gay and lightsome melodies. The man was drum major to one of the British regiments.

"Dighton," demanded the general, "what means this foolery? Bid your band silence that dead march — or, by my word, they shall have sufficient cause for their lugubrious strains ! Silence it, sirrah !"

"Please your honor," answered the drum major, whose rubicund visage had lost all its color, "the fault is none of mine. I and my band are all here together ; and I question whether there be a man of us that could play that march without book. I never heard it but once before, and that was at the funeral of his late Majesty, King George the Second."

" Well, well ! " said Sir William Howe, recovering his composure—"it is the prelude to some masquerading antic. Let it pass."

A figure now presented itself, but among the many fantastic masks that were dispersed through the apartments, none could tell precisely from whence it came. It was a man in an old-fashioned dress of black serge, and having the aspect of a steward, or principal domestic in the household of a nobleman or great English landholder. This figure advanced to the outer door of the mansion, and throwing both its leaves wide open, withdrew a little to one side and looked back towards the grand staircase, as if expecting some person to descend. At the same time, the music in the street sounded a loud and doleful summons. The eye of Sir William Howe and his guests being directed to the staircase, there appeared, on the uppermost landing-place that was discernible from the bottom, several personages descending towards the door. The foremost was a man of stern visage, wearing a steeple-crowned hat and a skullcap beneath it ; a dark cloak, and huge wrinkled boots that came half way up his legs. Under his arm was a rolled-up banner, which seemed to be the banner of England, but strangely rent and torn ; he had a sword in his right hand, and grasped a bible in his left. The next figure was of milder aspect, yet full of dignity, wearing a broad ruff, over which descended a beard, a gown of wrought velvet, and a doublet and hose of black satin. He carried a roll of manuscript in his hand. Close behind these two came a young man of very striking countenance and demeanor, with deep thought and contemplation on his brow, and perhaps a flash of enthusiasm in his eye. His garb, like that of his predecessors, was of an antique fashion, and there was a stain of blood upon his ruff. In the same group with these, were three or four others, all men of dignity and evident command,

and bearing themselves like personages who were accustomed to the gaze of the multitude. It was the idea of the beholders, that these figures went to join the mysterious funeral that had halted in front of the Province House; yet that supposition seemed to be contradicted by the air of triumph with which they waved their hands, as they crossed the threshold and vanished through the portal.

"In the devil's name, what is this?" muttered Sir William Howe to a gentleman beside him; "a procession of the regicide judges of King Charles the martyr?"

"These," said Colonel Joliffe, breaking silence almost for the first time that evening—"these, if I interpret them aright, are the Puritan governors—the rulers of the old, original Democracy of Massachusetts. Endicott, with the banner from which he had torn the symbol of subjection, and Winthrop, and Sir Henry Vane, and Dudley, Haynes, Bellingham, and Leverett."

"Why had that young man a stain of blood upon his ruff?" asked Miss Joliffe.

"Because, in after years," answered her grandfather, "he laid down the wisest head in England upon the block, for the principles of liberty."

"Will not your Excellency order out the guard?" whispered Lord Percy, who, with other British officers, had now assembled round the General. "There may be a plot under this mummery."

"Tush! we have nothing to fear," carelessly replied Sir William Howe. "There can be no worse treason in the matter than a jest, and that somewhat of the dullest. Even were it a sharp and bitter one, our best policy would be to laugh it off. See—here come more of these gentry."

Another group of characters had now partly descended the staircase. The first was a venerable and white-bearded patriarch, who cautiously felt his way downward with a staff. Treading hastily behind him, and stretching forth his gauntleted hand as if to grasp the old man's shoulder, came a tall, soldier-like figure, equipped with a plumed cap of steel, a bright breast-plate, and a long sword, which rattled against the stairs. Next was seen a stout man, dressed in rich and courtly attire, but not of courtly demeanor; his gait had the swinging motion of a seaman's walk; and chancing to stumble on the staircase, he suddenly grew wrathful, and was heard to mutter an oath. He was followed by a noble-looking personage in a curled wig, such as are represented in the portraits of Queen Anne's time and earlier; and the breast of his coat was decorated with an embroidered star. While advancing to the door, he bowed to the right hand and to the left, in a very gracious and insinuating style; but as he crossed the threshold, unlike the early Puritan governors, he seemed to wring his hands with sorrow.

"Prithee, play the part of a chorus, good Doctor Byles," said Sir William Howe. "What worthies are these?"

"If it please your Excellency, they lived somewhat before my day," answered the doctor; "but doubtless our friend, the Colonel, has been hand and glove with them."

"Their living faces I never looked upon," said Colonel Joliffe, gravely; "although I have spoken face to face with many rulers of this land, and shall greet yet another with an old man's blessing, ere I die. But we talk of these figures. I take the venerable patriarch to be Bradstreet, the last of the Puritans, who was governor at ninety or thereabouts. The next is Sir Edmund Andros, a tyrant, as any New England schoolboy will tell you; and therefore the people cast him down from his high seat into a dungeon. Then comes Sir William Phipps, shepherd, cooper, sea captain, and governor—may many of his countrymen rise as high, from as low an origin ! Lastly, you saw the gracious Earl of Bellamont, who ruled us under King William."

" But what is the meaning of it all ?" asked Lord Percy.

" Now, were I a rebel," said Miss Joliffe, half aloud, " I might fancy that the ghosts of these ancient governors had been summoned to form the funeral procession of royal authority in New England."

Several other figures were now seen at the turn of the staircase. The one in advance had a thoughtful, anxious, and somewhat crafty expression of face ; and in spite of his loftiness of manner, which was evidently the result of an ambitious spirit and of long continuance in high stations, he seemed not incapable of cringing to a greater than himself. A few steps behind came an officer in a scarlet and embroidered uniform, cut in a fashion old enough to have been worn by the Duke of Marlborough. His nose had a rubicund tinge, which, together with the twinkle of his eye, might have marked him as a lover of the wine cup and good fellowship; notwithstanding which tokens, he appeared ill at ease, and often glanced around him, as if apprehensive of some secret mischief. Next came a portly gentleman, wearing a coat of shaggy cloth, lined with silken velvet ; he had sense, shrewdness, and humor in his face, and a folio volume under his arm ; but his aspect was that of a man vexed and tormented beyond all patience, and harassed almost to death. He went hastily down, and was followed by a dignified person, dressed in a purple velvet suit, with very rich embroidery ; his demeanor would have possessed much stateliness, only that a grievous fit of the gout compelled him to hobble from stair to stair, with contortions of face and body. When Doctor Byles beheld this figure on the staircase, he shivered as with an ague, but continued to watch him steadfastly, until the gouty gentleman had reached the threshold, made a gesture of anguish and despair, and vanished into the outer gloom, whither the funeral music summoned him.

"Governor Belcher!—my old patron!—in his very shape and dress!" gasped Doctor Byles. "This is an awful mockery!"

"A tedious foolery, rather," said Sir William Howe, with an air of indifference. "But who were the three that preceded him?"

"Governor Dudley, a cunning politician—yet his craft once brought him to a prison," replied Colonel Joliffe. "Governor Shute, formerly a colonel under Marlborough, and whom the people frightened out of the province; and learned Governor Burnet, whom the legislature tormented into a mortal fever."

"Methinks they were miserable men, these royal governors of Massachusetts," observed Miss Joliffe. "Heavens, how dim the light grows!"

It was certainly a fact that the large lamp which illuminated the staircase now burned dim and duskily: so that several figures, which passed hastily down the stairs and went forth from the porch, appeared rather like shadows than persons of fleshly substance. Sir William Howe and his guests stood at the doors of the contiguous apartments, watching the progress of this singular pageant, with various emotions of anger, contempt, or half-acknowledged fear, but still with an anxious curiosity. The shapes which now seemed hastening to join the mysterious procession, were recognized rather by striking peculiarities of dress, or broad characteristics of manner, than by any perceptible resemblance of features to their prototypes. Their faces, indeed, were invariably kept in deep shadow. But Dr. Byles, and other gentlemen who had long been familiar with the successive rulers of the province, were heard to whisper the names of Shirley, of Pownall, of Sir Francis Bernard, and of the well-remembered Hutchinson; thereby confessing that the actors, whoever they might be, in this spectral march of governors, had succeeded in putting on some distant portraiture of the real personages. As they vanished from the door, still did these shadows toss their arms into the gloom of night, with a dread expression of woe. Following the mimic representative of Hutchinson came a military figure, holding before his face the cocked hat which he had taken from his powdered head; but his epaulettes and other insignia of rank were those of a general officer; and something in his mien reminded the beholders of one who had recently been master of the Province House, and chief of all the land.

"The shape of Gage, as true as in a looking glass," exclaimed Lord Percy, turning pale.

"No, surely," cried Miss Joliffe, laughing hysterically; "it could not be Gage, or Sir William would have greeted his old comrade in arms! Perhaps he will not suffer the next to pass unchallenged."

"Of that be assured, young lady," answered Sir William Howe, fixing his eyes with a very marked expression upon the immovable visage of her grandfather. "I have long enough delayed to pay the ceremonies of a host to these departing guests. The next that takes his leave shall receive due courtesy."

A wild and dreary burst of music came through the open door. It seemed as if the procession, which had been gradually filling up its ranks, were now about to move, and that this loud peal of the wailing trumpets, and roll of the muffled drums, were a call to some loiterer to make haste. Many eyes, by an irresistible impulse, were turned upon Sir William Howe, as if it were he whom the dreary music summoned to the funeral of departed power.

" See !—here comes the last !" whispered Miss Joliffe, pointing her tremulous finger to the staircase.

A figure had come into view as if descending the stairs; although so dusky was the region whence it emerged, some of the spectators fancied that they had seen this human shape suddenly moulding itself amid the gloom. Downward the figure came, with a stately and martial tread, and reaching the lowest stair was observed to be a tall man, booted and wrapped in a military cloak, which was drawn up around the face so as to meet the flapped brim of a laced hat. The features, therefore, were completely hidden. But the British officers deemed that they had seen that military cloak before, and even recognized the frayed embroidery on the collar, as well as the gilded scabbard of a sword which protruded from the folds of the cloak, and glittered in a vivid gleam of light. Apart from these trifling particulars, there were characteristics of gait and bearing, which impelled the wondering guests to glance from the shrouded figure to Sir William Howe, as if to satisfy themselves that their host had not suddenly vanished from the midst of them.

With a dark flush of wrath upon his brow, they saw the General draw his sword and advance to meet the figure in the cloak before the latter had stepped one pace upon the floor.

" Villain, unmuffle yourself !" cried he. " You pass no farther !"

The figure, without blenching a hair's breadth from the sword which was pointed at his breast, made a solemn pause and lowered the cape of the cloak from about his face, yet not sufficiently for the spectators to catch a glimpse of it. But Sir William Howe had evidently seen enough. The sternness of his countenance gave place to a look of wild amazement, if not horror, while he recoiled several steps from the figure, and let

fall his sword upon the floor. The martial shape again
drew the cloak about his features and passed on ; but
reaching the threshold, with his back towards the spectators, he was seen to stamp his foot and shake his
clinched hands in the air. It was afterwards affirmed
that Sir William Howe had repeated that selfsame
gesture of rage and sorrow, when, for the last time, and
as the last royal governor, he passed through the portal
of the Province House.

"Hark !—the procession moves," said Miss Joliffe.

The music was dying away along the street, and its
dismal strains were mingled with the knell of midnight
from the steeple of the Old South, and with the roar of
artillery, which announced that the beleaguering army
of Washington had intrenched itself upon a nearer height
than before. As the deep boom of the cannon smote
upon his ear, Colonel Joliffe raised himself to the full
height of his aged form, and smiled sternly on the
British General.

"Would your Excellency inquire further into the
mystery of the pageant ?" said he.

"Take care of your gray head !" cried Sir William
Howe, fiercely, though with a quivering lip. "It has
stood too long on a traitor's shoulders !"

"You must make haste to chop it off, then," calmly
replied the Colonel ; "for a few hours longer, and not
all the power of Sir William Howe, nor of his master,
shall cause one of these gray hairs to fall. The empire
of Britain, in this ancient province, is at its last gasp
to-night ;—almost while I speak it is a dead corpse ;—
and methinks the shadows of the old governors are fit
mourners at its funeral !"

With these words Colonel Joliffe threw on his cloak,
and drawing his granddaughter's arm within his own,
retired from the last festival that a British ruler ever
held in the old province of Massachusetts Bay. It was

supposed that the Colonel and the young lady possessed some secret intelligence in regard to the mysterious pageant of that night. However this might be, such knowledge has never become general. The actors in the scene have vanished into deeper obscurity than even that wild Indian band who scattered the cargoes of the tea ships on the waves, and gained a place in history, yet left no names. But superstition, among other legends of this mansion, repeats the wondrous tale, that on the anniversary night of Britain's discomfiture, the ghosts of the ancient governors of Massachusetts still glide through the portal of the Province House. And, last of all, comes a figure shrouded in a military cloak, tossing his clinched hands into the air, and stamping his iron-shod boots upon the broad freestone steps, with a semblance of feverish despair, but without the sound of a foot-tramp.

When the truth-telling accents of the elderly gentleman were hushed, I drew a long breath and looked round the room, striving, with the best energy of my imagination, to throw a tinge of romance and historic grandeur over the realities of the scene. But my nostrils snuffed up a scent of cigar smoke, clouds of which the narrator had emitted by way of visible emblem, I suppose, of the nebulous obscurity of his tale. Moreover, my gorgeous fantasies were wofully disturbed by the rattling of the spoon in a tumbler of whisky punch, which Mr. Thomas Waite was mingling for a customer. Nor did it add to the picturesque appearance of the panelled walls, that the slate of the Brookline stage was suspended against them, instead of the armorial escutcheon of some far-descended governor. A stage driver sat at one of the windows, reading a penny paper of the day—the *Boston Times*—and presenting a figure which could nowise be

brought into any picture of "Times in Boston" seventy
or a hundred years ago.   On the window seat lay a
bundle, neatly done up in brown paper, the direction of
which I had the idle curiosity to read.   "Miss SUSAN
HUGGINS, at the PROVINCE HOUSE."   A pretty chamber-
maid, no doubt.   In truth, it is desperately hard work,
when we attempt to throw the spell of hoar antiquity
over localities with which the living world, and the day
that is passing over us, have aught to do.   Yet, as I
glanced at the stately staircase, down which the procession of the old governors had descended, and as I
emerged through the venerable portal, whence their
figures had preceded me, it gladdened me to be conscious
of a thrill of awe.   Then diving through the narrow
archway, a few strides transported me into the densest
throng of Washington Street.

II.

EDWARD RANDOLPH'S PORTRAIT.

THE old legendary guest of the Province House abode in my remembrance from midsummer till January. One idle evening, last winter, confident that he would be found in the snuggest corner of the bar room, I resolved to pay him another visit, hoping to deserve well of my country by snatching from oblivion some else unheard-of fact of history. The night was chill and raw, and rendered boisterous by almost a gale of wind, which whistled along Washington Street, causing the gaslights to flare and flicker within the lamps. As I hurried onward, my fancy was busy with a comparison between the present aspect of the street and that which it probably wore when the British Governors inhabited the mansion whither I was now going. Brick edifices in those times, were few, till a succession of destructive fires had swept, and swept again, the wooden dwellings and warehouses from the most populous quarters of the town. The buildings stood insulated and independent, not, as now, merging their separate existences into connected ranges, with a front of tiresome identity,—but each possessing features of its own, as if the owner's individual taste had shaped it,—and the whole presenting a picturesque irregularity, the absence of which is hardly compensated by any beauties of our modern architecture. Such a

scene, dimly vanishing from the eye by the ray of here
and there a tallow candle, glimmering through the small
panes of scattered windows, would form a sombre contrast to the street as I beheld it, with the gaslights
blazing from corner to corner, flaming within the shops,
and throwing a noonday brightness through the huge
plates of glass.

But the black, lowering sky, as I turned my eyes
upward, wore, doubtless, the same visage as when it
frowned upon the ante-revolutionary New Englanders.
The wintry blast had the same shriek that was familiar
to their ears. The Old South Church, too, still pointed
its antique spire into the darkness, and was lost between
earth and heaven ; and as I passed, its clock, which had
warned so many generations how transitory was their
lifetime, spoke heavily and slow the same unregarded
moral to myself. " Only seven o'clock," thought I. " My
old friend's legends will scarcely kill the hours 'twixt this
and bedtime."

Passing through the narrow arch, I crossed the court
yard, the confined precincts of which were made visible
by a lantern over the portal of the Province House. On
entering the bar room, I found, as I expected, the old
tradition monger seated by a special good fire of anthracite, compelling clouds of smoke from a corpulent
cigar. He recognized me with evident pleasure, for my
rare properties as a patient listener invariably make me
a favorite with elderly gentlemen and ladies of narrative
propensities. Drawing a chair to the fire, I desired mine
host to favor us with a glass apiece of whiskey punch,
which was speedily prepared, steaming hot, with a slice
of lemon at the bottom, a dark-red stratum of port wine
upon the surface, and a sprinkling of nutmeg strewn over
all. As we touched our glasses together, my legendary
friend made himself known to me as Mr. Bela Tiffany ;
and I rejoiced at the oddity of the name, because it gave

his image and character a sort of individuality in my
conception. The old gentleman's draught acted as a
solvent upon his memory, so that it overflowed with
tales, traditions, anecdotes of famous dead people, and
traits of ancient manners, some of which were childish
as a nurse's lullaby, while others might have been worth
the notice of the grave historian. Nothing impressed
me more than a story of a black, mysterious picture,
which used to hang in one of the chambers of the
Province House, directly above the room where we
were now sitting. The following is as correct a version
of the fact as the reader would be likely to obtain from
any other source, although, assuredly, it has a tinge of
romance approaching to the marvellous.

In one of the apartments of the Province House there
was long preserved an ancient picture, the frame of which
was as black as ebony, and the canvas itself so dark with
age, damp, and smoke, that not a touch of the painter's
art could be discerned. Time had thrown an impenetrable veil over it, and left to tradition and fable, and
conjecture, to say what had once been there portrayed.
During the rule of many successive governors, it had
hung, by prescriptive and undisputed right, over the
mantelpiece of the same chamber ; and it still kept its
place when Lieutenant Governor Hutchinson assumed
the administration of the province, on the departure of
Sir Francis Bernard.

The Lieutenant Governor sat, one afternoon, resting
his head against the carved back of his stately arm chair,
and gazing up thoughtfully at the void blackness of the
picture. It was scarcely a time for such inactive musing,
when affairs of the deepest moment required the ruler's
decision ; for, within that very hour Hutchinson had

received intelligence of the arrival of a British fleet,
bringing three regiments from Halifax to overawe the
insubordination of the people.   These troops awaited his
permission to occupy the fortress of Castle William and
the town itself.   Yet, instead of affixing his signature to
an official order, there sat the Lieutenant Governor, so
carefully scrutinizing the black waste of canvas, that his
demeanor attracted the notice of two young persons who
attended him.   One, wearing a military dress of buff, was
his kinsman, Francis Lincoln, the Provincial Captain of
Castle William ; the other, who sat on a low stool beside
his chair, was Alice Vane, his favorite niece.

She was clad entirely in white, a pale, ethereal
creature, who, though a native of New England, had
been educated abroad, and seemed not merely a stranger
from another clime, but almost a being from another
world.   For several years, until left an orphan, she had
dwelt with her father in sunny Italy, and there had
acquired a taste and enthusiasm for sculpture and paint-
ing, which she found few opportunities of gratifying in
the undecorated dwellings of the colonial gentry.   It was
said that the early productions of her own pencil
exhibited no inferior genius, though, perhaps, the rude
atmosphere of New England had cramped her hand, and
dimmed the glowing colors of her fancy.   But observing
her uncle's steadfast gaze, which appeared to search
through the mist of years to discover the subject of the
picture, her curiosity was excited.

"Is it known, my dear uncle," inquired she, "what
this old picture once represented?   Possibly, could it
be made visible, it might prove a masterpiece of some
great artist—else, why has it so long held such a conspicuous place?"

As her uncle, contrary to his usual custom (for he was
as attentive to all the humors and caprices of Alice as if
she had been his own best-beloved child), did not imme-

diately reply, the young Captain of Castle William **took** that office upon himself.

"This dark **old** square **of canvas, my** fair cousin," said he, "has been an heirloom in the Province House **from time** immemorial. As to the painter, I can tell you nothing ; but, if half the stories told of it be true, not **one** of the great Italian masters has ever produced so marvellous **a piece of work as that before you."**

Captain **Lincoln** proceeded to relate some of the strange **fables and fantasies, which, as it was** impossible to refute **them by ocular demonstration, had** grown to be articles **of popular belief, in reference to this old** picture. One of the **wildest, and at the same time the** best accredited **accounts, stated it to be an original and** authentic portrait **of the Evil One, taken at a witch** meeting near Salem ; **and that its strong and terrible** resemblance has been confirmed by several of the confessing wizards and witches, **at their trial, in open court.** It was likewise **affirmed that a familiar spirit, or demon,** abode behind **the blackness of the picture, and had** shown **himself, at seasons of public calamity, to more** than one **of the royal governors.** Shirley, **for instance,** had **beheld** this ominous apparition on the eve of General **Abercrombie's shameful and bloody defeat,** under the **walls of Ticonderoga.** Many of the servants of the Province House had caught glimpses of a visage frowning **down** upon them, **at morning or** evening twilight,—or in the depths of night, while **raking up the** fire that glimmered on the hearth beneath ; although, if any were bold enough to hold a torch before the picture, it would appear as **black and undistinguishable as ever.** The oldest inhabitant of Boston recollected **that his** father, in whose **days the portrait had not** wholly **faded out** of sight, had once looked **upon** it, **but** would never suffer himself to be **questioned as to** the face which was there represented. **In** connection with such stories, it was remarkable that over the top of the frame there were some ragged remnants of black silk, indicating that a veil had formerly hung down before the picture, until the duskiness of time had so effectually concealed it. But after all, it was the most singular part of the affair, that so many of the pompous governors of Massachusetts had allowed the obliterated picture to remain in the state chamber of the Province House.

"Some of these fables are really awful," observed Alice Vane, who had occasionally shuddered, as well as smiled, while her cousin spoke. "It would be almost worth while to wipe away the black surface of the canvas, since the original picture can hardly be so formidable as those which fancy paints instead of it."

"But would it be possible," inquired her cousin, "to restore this dark picture to its pristine hues?"

"Such arts are known in Italy," said Alice.

The Lieutenant Governor had roused himself from his abstracted mood, and listened with a smile to the conversation of his young relatives. Yet his voice had something peculiar in its tones, when he undertook the explanation of the mystery.

"I am sorry, Alice, to destroy your faith in the legends of which you are so fond," remarked he ; "but my antiquarian researches have long since made me acquainted with the subject of this picture—if picture it can be called—which is no more visible, nor ever will be, than the face of the long buried man whom it once represented. It was the portrait of Edward Randolph, the founder of this house, a person famous in the history of New England."

"Of that Edward Randolph," exclaimed Captain Lincoln, " who obtained the repeal of the first provincial charter, under which our forefathers had enjoyed almost democratic privileges ! He that was styled the arch-enemy of New England, and whose memory is still held in detestation as the destroyer of our liberties!"

"It was the same Randolph," answered Hutchinson, moving uneasily in his chair. "It was his lot to taste the bitterness of popular odium."

"Our annals tell us," continued the Captain of Castle William, "that the curse of the people followed this Randolph where he went, and wrought evil in all the subsequent events of his life, and that its effect was seen likewise in the manner of his death. They say, too, that the inward misery of that curse worked itself outward, and was visible on the wretched man's countenance, making it too horrible to be looked upon. If so, and if this picture truly represented his aspect, it was in mercy that the cloud of blackness had gathered over it."

"These traditions are folly to one who has proved, as I have, how little of historic truth lies at the bottom," said the Lieutenant Governor. "As regards the life and character of Edward Randolph, too implicit credence has been given to Dr. Cotton Mather, who—I must say it, though some of his blood runs in my veins—has filled our early history with old women's tales, as fanciful and extravagant as those of Greece or Rome."

"And yet," whispered Alice Vane, "may not such fables have a moral? And, methinks, if the visage of this portrait be so dreadful, it is not without a cause that it has hung so long in a chamber of the Province House. When the rulers feel themselves irresponsible, it were well that they should be reminded of the awful weight of a people's curse."

The Lieutenant Governor started, and gazed for a moment at his niece, as if her girlish fantasies had struck upon some feeling in his own breast, which all his policy or principles could not entirely subdue. He knew, indeed, that Alice, in spite of her foreign education, retained the native sympathies of a New England girl.

"Peace, silly child," cried he, at last more harshly than he had ever before addressed the gentle Alice. "The rebuke of a king is more to be dreaded than the clamor of a wild, misguided multitude. Captain Lincoln, it is decided. The fortress of Castle William must be occupied by the Royal troops. The two remaining regiments shall be billeted in the town, or encamped upon the Common. It is time, after years of tumult, and almost rebellion, that his majesty's government should have a wall of strength about it."

"Trust, sir—trust yet a while to the loyalty of the people," said Captain Lincoln; "nor teach them that they can ever be on other terms with British soldiers than those of brotherhood, as when they fought side by side through the French war. Do not convert the streets of your native town into a camp. Think twice before you give up old Castle William, the key of the province, into other keeping than that of true-born New Englanders."

"Young man, it is decided," repeated Hutchinson, rising from his chair. "A British officer will be in attendance this evening, to receive the necessary instructions for the disposal of the troops. Your presence also will be required. Till then, farewell.

With these words the Lieutenant Governor hastily left the room, while Alice and her cousin more slowly followed, whispering together, and once pausing to glance back at the mysterious picture. The Captain of Castle William fancied that the girl's air and mien were such as might have belonged to one of those spirits of fable— fairies, or creatures of a more antique mythology—who sometimes mingled their agency with mortal affairs, half in caprice, yet with a sensibility to human weal or woe. As he held the door for her to pass, Alice beckoned to the picture and smiled.

"Come forth, dark and evil Shape!" cried she. "It is thine hour!"

In the evening, Lieutenant Governor Hutchinson sat
in the same chamber where the foregoing scene had
occurred, surrounded by several persons whose various
interests had summoned them together. There were the
Selectmen of Boston, plain, patriarchal fathers of the
people, excellent representatives of the old puritanical
founders, whose sombre strength had stamped so deep an
impress upon the New England character. Contrasting
with these were one or two members of Council, richly
dressed in the white wigs, the embroidered waistcoats
and other magnificence of the time, and making a somewhat ostentatious display of courtier-like ceremonial. In
attendance, likewise, was a major of the British army,
awaiting the Lieutenant Governor's orders for the landing
of the troops, which still remained on board the transports.
The Captain of Castle William stood beside Hutchinson's
chair, with folded arms, glancing rather haughtily at the
British officer, by whom he was soon to be superseded
in his command. On a table, in the centre of the chamber,
stood a branched silver candlestick, throwing down the
glow of half a dozen wax lights upon a paper apparently
ready for the Lieutenant Governor's signature.

Partly shrouded in the voluminous folds of one of the
window curtains, which fell from the ceiling to the floor, was
seen the white drapery of a lady's robe. It may appear
strange that Alice Vane should have been there at such a
time ; but there was something so childlike, so wayward,
in her singular character, so apart from ordinary rules,
that her presence did not surprise the few who noticed it.
Meantime, the chairman of the Selectmen was addressing to the Lieutenant Governor a long and solemn protest
against the reception of the British troops into the town.

"And if your Honor," concluded this excellent, but
somewhat prosy old gentleman, " shall see fit to persist
in bringing these mercenary sworders and musketeers
into our quiet streets, not on our heads be the responsi-

bility. Think, sir, while there is yet time, that if one drop of blood be shed, that blood shall be an eternal stain upon your Honor's memory. You, sir, have written with an able pen the deeds of our forefathers. The more to be desired is it, therefore, that yourself should deserve honorable mention, as a true patriot and upright ruler, when your own doings shall be written down in history."

"I am not insensible, my good sir, to the natural desire to stand well in the annals of my country," replied Hutchinson, controlling his impatience into courtesy, "nor know I any better method of attaining that end than by withstanding the merely temporary spirit of mischief, which, with your pardon, seems to have infected elder men than myself. Would you have me wait till the mob shall sack the Province House, as they did my private mansion? Trust me, sir, the time may come when you will be glad to flee for protection to the King's banner, the raising of which is now so distasteful to you."

"Yes," said the British major, who was impatiently expecting the Lieutenant Governor's orders. "The demagogues of this Province have raised the devil, and cannot lay him again. We will exorcise him, in God's name and the King's."

"If you meddle with the devil, take care of his claws!" answered the Captain of Castle William, stirred by the taunt against his countrymen.

"Craving your pardon, young sir," said the venerable Selectman, "let not an evil spirit enter into your words. We will strive against the oppressor with prayer and fasting, as our forefathers would have done. Like them, moreover, we will submit to whatever lot a wise Providence may send us,—always after our own best exertions to amend it."

"And there peep forth the devil's claws!" muttered

Hutchinson, who well understood the nature of Puritan submission. " This matter shall be expedited forthwith. When there shall be a sentinel at every corner, and a court of guard before the town house, a loyal gentleman may venture to walk abroad. What to me is the outcry of a mob, in this remote province of the realm? The King is my master, and England is my country ! Upheld by their armed strength, I set my foot upon the rabble, and defy them !"

He snatched a pen, and was about to affix his signature to the paper that lay on the table, when the Captain of Castle William placed his hand upon his shoulder. The freedom of the action, so contrary to the ceremonious respect which was then considered due to rank and dignity, awakened general surprise, and in none more than in the Lieutenant Governor himself. Looking angrily up, he perceived that his young relative was pointing his finger to the opposite wall. Hutchinson's eye followed the signal; and he saw, what had hitherto been unobserved, that a black silk curtain was suspended before the mysterious picture, so as completely to conceal it. His thoughts immediately recurred to the scene of the preceding afternoon ; and, in his surprise, confused by indistinct emotions, yet sensible that his niece must have had an agency in this phenomenon, he called loudly upon her.

" Alice !—come hither, Alice !"

No sooner had he spoken than Alice Vane glided from her station, and pressing one hand across her eyes, with the other snatched away the sable curtain that concealed the portrait. An exclamation of surprise burst from every beholder ; but the Lieutenant Governor's voice had a tone of horror.

" By Heaven," said he, in a low, inward murmur, speaking rather to himself than to those around him, " if the spirit of Edward Randolph were to appear among us

3   **12**

from the place of torment, he could not wear more of the terrors of hell upon his face !"

"For some wise end," said the aged Selectman, solemnly, "hath Providence scattered away the mist of years that had so long hid this dreadful effigy. Until this hour no living man hath seen what we behold !"

Within the antique frame, which so recently had enclosed a sable waste of canvas, now appeared a visible picture, still dark, indeed, in its hues and shadings, but thrown forward in strong relief. It was a half-length figure of a gentleman in a rich, but very old-fashioned dress of embroidered velvet, with a broad ruff and a beard, and wearing a hat, the brim of which overshadowed his forehead. Beneath this cloud the eyes had a peculiar glare, which was almost lifelike. The whole portrait started so distinctly out of the background, that it had the effect of a person looking down from the wall at the astonished and awe-stricken spectators. The expression of the face, if any words can convey an idea of it, was that of a wretch detected in some hideous guilt, and exposed to the bitter hatred, and laughter, and withering scorn, of a vast surrounding multitude. There was the struggle of defiance, beaten down and overwhelmed by the crushing weight of ignominy. The torture of the soul had come forth upon the countenance. It seemed as if the picture, while hidden behind the cloud of immemorial years, had been all the time acquiring an intenser depth and darkness of expression, till now it gloomed forth again, and threw its evil omen over the present hour. Such, if the wild legend may be credited, was the portrait of Edward Randolph, as he appeared when a people's curse had wrought its influence upon his nature.

"'Twould drive me mad — that awful face !" said Hutchinson, who seemed fascinated by the contemplation of it.

" Be warned, then !" whispered Alice. " He trampled on a people's rights. Behold his punishment—and avoid a crime like his !"

The Lieutenant Governor actually trembled for an instant ; but, exerting his energy—which was not, however, his most characteristic feature—he strove to shake off the spell of Randolph's countenance.

" Girl !" cried he, laughing bitterly, as he turned to Alice, " have you brought hither your painter's art—your Italian spirit of intrigue—your tricks of stage effect— and think to influence the councils of rulers and the affairs of nations by such shallow contrivances? See here !"

"Stay yet a while," said the Selectman, as Hutchinson again snatched the pen ; "for if ever mortal man received a warning from a tormented soul, your Honor is that man !"

"Away !" answered Hutchinson fiercely. "Though yonder senseless picture cried 'Forbear !' — it should not move me !"

Casting a scowl of defiance at the pictured face (which seemed, at that moment, to intensify the horror of its miserable and wicked look), he scrawled on the paper, in characters that betokened it a deed of desperation, the name of Thomas Hutchinson. Then, it is said he shuddered, as if that signature had granted away his salvation.

" It is done," said he ; and placed his hand upon his brow.

" May Heaven forgive the deed," said the soft, sad accents of Alice Vane, like the voice of a good spirit flitting away.

When morning came there was a stifled whisper through the household, and spreading thence about the town, that the dark, mysterious picture had started from the wall, and spoken face to face with Lieutenant Governor Hutchinson. If such a miracle had been wrought, however, no traces of it remained behind ; for, within the antique frame, nothing could be discerned, save the impenetrable cloud, which had covered the canvas since the memory of man. If the figure had, indeed, stepped forth, it had fled back, spirit-like, at the daydawn, and hidden itself behind a century's obscurity. The truth probably was, that Alice Vane's secret for restoring the hues of the picture had merely effected a temporary renovation. But those who, in that brief interval, had beheld the awful visage of Edward Randolph, desired no second glance, and ever afterwards trembled at the recollection of the scene, as if an evil spirit had appeared visibly among them. And as for Hutchinson, when, far over the ocean, his dying hour drew on, he gasped for breath, and complained that he was choking with the blood of the Boston Massacre ; and Francis Lincoln, the former Captain of Castle William, who was standing at his bedside, perceived a likeness in his frenzied look to that of Edward Randolph. Did his broken spirit feel, at that dread hour, the tremendous burden of a People's curse ?

At the conclusion of this miraculous legend, I inquired of mine host whether the picture still remained in the chamber over our heads ; but Mr. Tiffany informed me that it had long since been removed, and was supposed to be hidden in some out-of-the-way corner of the New England Museum. Perchance some curious antiquary may light upon it there, and, with the assistance of Mr. Howorth, the picture cleaner, may supply a not un- necessary proof of the authenticity of the facts here set down. During the progress of the story a storm had been gathering abroad, and raging and rattling so loudly in the upper regions of the Province House, that it seemed as if all the old governors and great men were running riot above stairs, while Mr. Bela Tiffany babbled of them below. In the course of generations, when many people have lived and died in an ancient house, the whistling of the wind through its crannies, and the creaking of its beams and rafters, become strangely like the tones of the human voice, or thundering laughter, or heavy footsteps treading the deserted chambers. It is as if the echoes of half a century were revived. Such were the ghostly sounds that roared and murmured in our ears, when I took leave of the circle round the fireside of the Province House, and plunging down the door steps, fought my way homeward against a drifting snow storm.

III.

LADY ELEANORE'S MANTLE.

MINE excellent friend, the landlord of the Province House, was pleased, the other evening, to invite Mr. Tiffany and myself to an oyster supper. This slight mark of respect and gratitude, as he handsomely observed, was far less than the ingenious tale-teller, and I, the humble note-taker of his narratives, had fairly earned, by the public notice which our joint lucubrations had attracted to his establishment. Many a cigar had been smoked within his premises — many a glass of wine, or more potent aqua vitæ, had been quaffed — many a dinner had been eaten by curious strangers, who, save for the fortunate conjunction of Mr. Tiffany and me, would never have ventured through that darksome avenue, which gives access to the historic precincts of the Province House. In short, if any credit be due to the courteous assurances of Mr. Thomas Waite, we . had brought his forgotten mansion almost as effectually into public view as if we had thrown down the vulgar range of shoe shops and dry goods stores, which hides its aristocratic front from Washington Street. It may be unadvisable, however, to speak too loudly of the increased custom of the house, lest Mr. Waite should find it difficult to renew the lease on so favorable terms as heretofore.

Being thus welcomed as benefactors, neither Mr.
Tiffany nor myself felt any scruple in doing full justice to
the good things that were set before us. If the feast
were less magnificent than those same panelled walls
had witnessed, in a by-gone century — if mine host
presided with somewhat less of state, than might have
befitted a successor of the royal Governors—if the
guests made a less imposing show than the bewigged,
and powdered, and embroidered dignitaries, who erst
banqueted at the gubernatorial table, and now sleep
within their armorial tombs on Copp's Hill, or round
King's Chapel—yet never, I may boldly say, did a
more comfortable little party assemble in the Province
House, from Queen Anne's days to the Revolution.
The occasion was rendered more interesting by the
presence of a venerable personage, whose own actual
reminiscences went back to the epoch of Gage and Howe,
and even supplied him with a doubtful anecdote or two
of Hutchinson. He was one of that small, and now all
but extinguished class, whose attachment to royalty, and
to the colonial institutions and customs that were connected with it, had never yielded to the democratic
heresies of after times. The young queen of Britain has
not a more loyal subject in her realm—perhaps not one
who would kneel before her throne with such reverential
love—as this old grandsire, whose head has whitened
beneath the mild sway of the Republic, which still, in his
mellower moments he terms a usurpation. Yet prejudices so obstinate have not made him an ungentle or
impracticable companion. If the truth must be told, the
life of the aged loyalist has been of such a scrambling
and unsettled character—he has had so little choice of
friends, and been so often destitute of any—that I doubt
whether he would refuse a cup of kindness with either
Oliver Cromwell or John Hancock; to say nothing of
any democrat now upon the stage. In another paper of

this series, I may perhaps give the reader a closer glimpse of his portrait.

Our host, in due season, uncorked a bottle of Madeira, of such exquisite perfume and admirable flavor, that he surely must have discovered it in an ancient bin, down deep beneath the deepest cellar, where some jolly old butler stored away the Governor's choicest wine, and forgot to reveal the secret on his death bed. Peace to his red-nosed ghost, and a libation to his memory! This precious liquor was imbibed by Mr. Tiffany with peculiar zest : and, after sipping the third glass, it was his pleasure to give us one of the oddest legends which he had yet raked from the storehouse, where he keeps such matters. With some suitable adornments from my own fancy, it ran pretty much as follows.

Not long after Colonel Shute had assumed the government of Massachusetts Bay, now nearly a hundred and twenty years ago, a young lady of rank and fortune arrived from England, to claim his protection as her guardian. He was her distant relative, but the nearest who had survived the gradual extinction of her family ; so that no more eligible shelter could be found for the rich and high-born lady Eleanore Rochcliffe, than within the Province House of a transatlantic colony. The consort of Governor Shute, moreover, had been as a mother to her childhood, and was now anxious to receive her, in the hope that a beautiful young woman would be exposed to infinitely less peril from the primitive society of New England, than amid the artifices and corruptions of a court. If either the Governor or his lady had especially consulted their own comfort, they would probably have sought to devolve the responsibility on other hands ; since, with some noble and splendid traits of character, Lady Eleanore was remarkable for a harsh,

unyielding pride, a haughty consciousness of her hereditary and personal advantages, which made her almost
incapable of control. Judging from many traditionary
anecdotes, this peculiar temper was hardly less than a
monomania ; or, if the acts which it inspired were those
of a sane person, it seemed due from Providence that
pride so sinful should be followed by as severe a
retribution. That tinge of the marvellous, which is
thrown over so many of these half-forgotten legends,
has probably imparted an additional wildness to the
strange story of Lady Eleanore Rochcliffe.

The ship in which she came passenger had arrived
at Newport, whence Lady Eleanore was conveyed to
Boston in the Governor's coach, attended by a small
escort of gentlemen on horseback. The ponderous
equipage, with its four black horses, attracted much
notice as it rumbled through Cornhill, surrounded by
the prancing steeds of half a dozen cavaliers, with swords
dangling to their stirrups and pistols at their holsters.
Through the large glass windows of the coach, as it
rolled along, the people could discern the figure of Lady
Eleanore, strangely combining an almost queenly stateliness with the grace and beauty of a maiden in her teens.
A singular tale had gone abroad among the ladies of the
province, that their fair rival was indebted for much of
the irresistible charm of her appearance to a certain
article of dress—an embroidered mantle—which had
been wrought by the most skilful artist in London, and
possessed even magical properties of adornment. On
the present occasion, however, she owed nothing to
the witchery of dress, being clad in a riding habit of
velvet, which would have appeared stiff and ungraceful
on any other form.

The coachman reined in his four black steeds, and the
whole cavalcade came to a pause in front of the contorted
iron balustrade that fenced the Province House from the

public street. It was an awkward coincidence, that the
bell of the Old South was just then tolling for a funeral;
so that, instead of a gladsome peal with which it was
customary to announce the arrival of distinguished
strangers, Lady Eleanore Rochcliffe was ushered by
a doleful clang, as if calamity had come embodied in her
beautiful person.

"A very great disrespect!" exclaimed Captain Langford, an English officer, who had recently brought
despatches to Governor Shute. "The funeral should
have been deferred, lest Lady Eleanore's spirits be
affected by such a dismal welcome."

"With your pardon, sir," replied Doctor Clarke, a
physician, and a famous champion of the popular party,
"whatever the heralds may pretend, a dead beggar must
have precedence of a living queen. King Death confers
high privileges."

These remarks were interchanged while the speakers
waited a passage through the crowd, which had gathered
on each side of the gateway, leaving an open avenue to
the portal of the Province House. A black slave in
livery now leaped from behind the coach, and threw open
the door; while at the same moment Governor Shute
descended the flight of steps from his mansion, to assist
Lady Eleanore in alighting. But the Governor's stately
approach was anticipated in a manner that excited
general astonishment. A pale young man, with his black
hair all in disorder, rushed from the throng, and pros-
trated himself beside the coach, thus offering his person
as a footstool for Lady Eleanore Rochcliffe to tread
upon. She held back an instant; yet with an expression as if doubting whether the young man were
worthy to bear the weight of her footstep, rather than
dissatisfied to receive such awful reverence from a
fellow-mortal.

"Up, sir," said the Governor, sternly, at the same

time lifting his cane over the intruder. "What means the Bedlamite by this freak?"

"Nay," answered Lady Eleanore playfully, but with more scorn than pity in her tone, "your Excellency shall not strike him. When men seek only to be trampled upon, it were a pity to deny them a favor so easily granted—and so well deserved!"

Then, though as lightly as a sunbeam on a cloud, she placed her foot upon the cowering form, and extended her hand to meet that of the Governor. There was a brief interval, during which Lady Eleanore retained this attitude; and never, surely, was there an apter emblem of aristocracy and hereditary pride, trampling on human sympathies and the kindred of nature, than these two figures presented at that moment. Yet the spectators were so smitten with her beauty, and so essential did pride seem to the existence of such a creature, that they gave a simultaneous acclamation of applause.

"Who is this insolent young fellow?" inquired Captain Langford, who still remained beside Doctor Clarke. "If he be in his senses, his impertinence demands the bastinado. If mad, Lady Eleanore should be secured from further inconvenience by his confinement."

"His name is Jervase Helwyse," answered the Doctor— "a youth of no birth or fortune, or other advantages, save the mind and soul that nature gave him; and being secretary to our colonial agent in London, it was his misfortune to meet this Lady Eleanore Rochcliffe. He loved her—and her scorn has driven him mad."

"He was mad so to aspire," observed the English officer.

"It may be so," said Doctor Clarke, frowning as he spoke. "But I tell you, sir, I could well nigh doubt the justice of the Heaven above us, if no signal humilation overtake this lady, who now treads so haughtily into yonder mansion. She seeks to place herself above

the sympathies of our common nature, which envelops
all human souls. See, if that nature do not assert its
claim over her in some mode that shall bring her level
with the lowest!"

"Never!" cried Captain Langford, indignantly —
"neither in life, nor when they lay her with her
ancestors."

Not many days afterwards the Governor gave a ball
in honor of Lady Eleanore Rochcliffe. The principal
gentry of the colony received invitations, which were
distributed to their residences, far and near, by messengers on horseback, bearing missives sealed with all the
formality of official despatches. In obedience to the
summons, there was a general gathering of rank,
wealth, and beauty; and the wide door of the Province
House had seldom given admittance to more numerous
and honorable guests than on the evening of Lady
Eleanore's ball. Without much extravagance of eulogy,
the spectacle might even be termed splendid; for,
according to the fashion of the times, the ladies shone in
rich silks and satins, outspread over wide-projecting
hoops; and the gentlemen glittered in gold embroidery,
laid unsparingly upon the purple, or scarlet, or sky-blue
velvet, which was the material of their coats and waistcoats. The latter article of dress was of great importance, since it enveloped the wearer's body nearly to the
knees, and was perhaps bedizened with the amount of
his whole year's income, in golden flowers and foliage.
The altered taste of the present day—a taste symbolic of
a deep change in the whole system of society—would
look upon almost any of those gorgeous figures as ridiculous; although that evening the guests sought their
reflections in the pier glasses, and rejoiced to catch their
own glitter amid the glittering crowd. What a pity that
one of the stately mirrors has not preserved a picture of
the scene, which, by the very traits that were so transitory

might have taught us much that would be worth knowing and remembering !

Would, at least, that either painter or mirror could convey to us some faint idea of a garment, already noticed in this legend—the Lady Eleanore's embroidered mantle—which the gossips whispered was invested with magic properties, so as to lend a new and untried grace to her figure each time that she put it on ! Idle fancy as it is, this mysterious mantle has thrown an awe around my image of her, partly from its fabled virtues, and partly because it was the handiwork of a dying woman, and, perchance, owed the fantastic grace of its conception to the delirium of approaching death.

After the ceremonial greetings had been paid, Lady Eleanore Rochcliffe stood apart from the mob of guests, insulating herself within a small and distinguished circle, to whom she accorded a more cordial favor than to the general throng. The waxen torches threw their radiance vividly over the scene, bringing out its brilliant points in strong relief; but she gazed carelessly, and with now and then an expression of weariness or scorn, tempered with such feminine grace, that her auditors scarcely perceived the moral deformity of which it was the utterance. She beheld the spectacle not with vulgar ridicule, as disdaining to be pleased with the provincial mockery of a court festival, but with the deeper scorn of one whose spirit held itself too high to participate in the enjoyment of other human souls. Whether or no the recollections of those who saw her that evening were influenced by the strange events with which she was subsequently connected, so it was that her figure ever after recurred to them as marked by something wild and unnatural; although, at the time, the general whisper was of her exceeding beauty, and of the indescribable charm which her mantle threw around her. Some close observers, indeed, detected a feverish flush and alternate paleness of countenance, with a corresponding flow and revulsion of spirits, and once or twice a painful and helpless betrayal of lassitude, as if she were on the point of sinking to the ground. Then, with a nervous shudder, she seemed to arouse her energies, and threw some bright and playful, yet half-wicked sarcasm into the conversation. There was so strange a characteristic in her manners and sentiments, that it astonished every right-minded listener; till looking in her face, a lurking and incomprehensible glance and smile perplexed them with doubts both as to her seriousness and sanity. Gradually, Lady Eleanore Rochcliffe's circle grew smaller, till only four gentlemen remained in it. These were Captain Langford, the English officer before mentioned; a Virginian planter, who had come to Massachusetts on some political errand; a young Episcopal clergyman, the grandson of a British Earl; and lastly, the private secretary of Governor Shute, whose obsequiousness had won a sort of tolerance from Lady Eleanore.

At different periods of the evening the liveried servants of the Province House passed among the guests, bearing huge trays of refreshments, and French and Spanish wines. Lady Eleanore Rochcliffe, who refused to wet her beautiful lips even with a bubble of Champagne, had sunk back into a large damask chair, apparently overwearied either with the excitement of the scene or its tedium; and while, for an instant, she was unconscious of voices, laughter, and music, a young man stole forward, and knelt down at her feet. He bore a salver in his hand, on which was a chased silver goblet, filled to the brim with wine, which he offered as reverentially as to a crowned queen, or rather with the awful devotion of a priest doing sacrifice to his idol. Conscious that some one touched her robe, Lady Eleanore started, and unclosed her eyes upon the pale, wild features and dishevelled hair of Jervase Helwyse.

" Why do you haunt me thus?" said she, in a languid tone, but with a kindlier feeling than she ordinarily permitted herself to express. " They tell me that I have done you harm."

" Heaven knows if that be so," replied the young man solemnly. " But, Lady Eleanore, in requital of that harm, if such there be, and for your own earthly and heavenly welfare, I pray you to take one sip of this holy wine, and then to pass the goblet round among the guests. And this shall be a symbol that you have not sought to withdraw yourself from the chain of human sympathies — which whoso would shake off must keep company with fallen angels."

" Where has this mad fellow stolen that sacramental vessel?" exclaimed the Episcopal clergyman.

This question drew the notice of the guests to the silver cup, which was recognized as appertaining to the communion plate of the Old South Church ; and, for aught that could be known, it was brimming over with the consecrated wine.

" Perhaps it is poisoned," half whispered the Governor's secretary.

" Pour it down the villain's throat!" cried the Virginian, fiercely.

" Turn him out of the house!" cried Captain Langford, seizing Jervase Helwyse so roughly by the shoulder that the sacramental cup was overturned, and its contents sprinkled upon Lady Eleanore's mantle. " Whether knave, fool, or Bedlamite, it is intolerable that the fellow should go at large."

" Pray, gentlemen, do my poor admirer no harm," said Lady Eleanore, with a faint and weary smile. " Take him out of my sight, if such be your pleasure ; for I can find in my heart to do nothing but laugh at him— whereas, in all decency and conscience, it would become me to weep for the mischief I have wrought !"

But while the bystanders were attempting to lead away the unfortunate young man, he broke from them, and with a wild, impassioned earnestness, offered a new and equally strange petition to Lady Eleanore. It was no other than that she should throw off the mantle, which, while he pressed the silver cup of wine upon her, she had drawn more closely around her form, so as almost to shroud herself within it.

"Cast it from you!" exclaimed Jervase Helwyse, clasping his hands in an agony of entreaty. "It may not yet be too late! Give the accursed garment to the flames!"

But Lady Eleanore, with a laugh of scorn, drew the rich folds of the embroidered mantle over her head, in such a fashion as to give a completely new aspect to her beautiful face, which — half hidden, half revealed — seemed to belong to some being of mysterious character and purposes.

"Farewell, Jervase Helwyse!" said she. "Keep my image in your remembrance, as you behold it now."

"Alas, lady!" he replied, in a tone no longer wild, but sad as a funeral bell. "We must meet shortly, when your face may wear another aspect — and that shall be the image that must abide within me."

He made no more resistance to the violent efforts of the gentlemen and servants, who almost dragged him out of the apartment, and dismissed him roughly from the iron gate of the Province House. Captain Langford, who had been very active in this affair, was returning to the presence of Lady Eleanore Rochcliffe, when he encountered the physician, Doctor Clarke, with whom he had held some causal talk on the day of her arrival. The Doctor stood apart, separated from Lady Eleanore by the width of the room, but eyeing her with such keen sagacity, that Captain Langford involuntarily gave him credit for the discovery of some deep secret.

"You appear to be smitten, after all, with the charms of this queenly maiden," said he, hoping thus to draw forth the physician's hidden knowledge.

"God forbid !" answered Doctor Clarke, with a grave smile ; "and if you be wise you will put up the same prayer for yourself. Woe to those who shall be smitten by this beautiful Lady Eleanore ! But yonder stands the Governor—and I have a word or two for his private ear. Good night !"

He accordingly advanced to Governor Shute, and addressed him in so low a tone that none of the by-standers could catch a word of what he said ; although the sudden change of his Excellency's hitherto cheerful visage betokened that the communication could be of no agreeable import. A very few moments afterwards, it was announced to the guests that an unforeseen circumstance rendered it necessary to put a premature close to the festival.

The ball at the Province House supplied a topic of conversation for the colonial metropolis, for some days after its occurrence, and might still longer have been the general theme, only that a subject of all-engrossing interest thrust it, for a time, from the public recollection. This was the appearance of a dreadful epidemic, which, in that age, and long before and afterwards, was wont to slay its hundreds and thousands, on both sides of the Atlantic. On the occasion of which we speak, it was distinguished by a peculiar virulence, insomuch that it has left its traces—its pit marks, to use an appropriate figure—on the history of the country, the affairs of which were thrown into confusion by its ravages. At first, unlike its ordinary course, the disease seemed to confine itself to the higher circles of society, selecting its victims from among the proud, the well born and the wealthy, entering unabashed into stately chambers, and lying down with the slumberers in silken beds. Some of the most distinguished guests of the Province House—even those whom the haughty Lady Eleanore Rochcliffe had deemed not unworthy of her favor—were stricken by this fatal scourge. It was noticed, with an ungenerous bitterness of feeling, that the four gentlemen—the Virginian, the British officer, the young clergyman, and the Governor's secretary—who had been her most devoted attendants on the evening of the ball, were the foremost on whom the plague stroke fell. But the disease, pursuing its onward progress, soon ceased to be exclusively a prerogative of aristocracy. Its red brand was no longer conferred, like a noble's star, or an order of knighthood. It threaded its way through the narrow and crooked streets, and entered the low, mean, darksome dwellings, and laid its hand of death upon the artisans and laboring classes of the town. It compelled rich and poor to feel themselves brethren, then; and stalking to and fro across the Three Hills, with a fierceness which made it almost a new pestilence, there was that mighty conqueror—that scourge and horror of our forefathers—the Small Pox!

We cannot estimate the affright which this plague inspired of yore, by contemplating it as the fangless monster of the present day. We must remember, rather, with what awe we watched the gigantic footsteps of the Asiatic cholera, striding from shore to shore of the Atlantic, and marching like destiny upon cities far remote, which flight had already half depopulated. There is no other fear so horrible and unhumanizing, as that which makes man dread to breathe Heaven's vital air, lest it be poison, or to grasp the hand of a brother or friend, lest the gripe of pestilence should clutch him. Such was the dismay that now followed in the track of the disease, or ran before it throughout the town. Graves were hastily dug, and the pestilential relics as hastily covered, because the dead were enemies of the living, and strove to draw them headlong, as it were, into their own dismal pit. The public councils were suspended, as if mortal wisdom might relinquish its devices, now that an unearthly usurper had found his way into the ruler's mansion. Had an enemy's fleet been hovering on the coast, or his armies trampling on our soil, the people would probably have committed their defence to that same direful conqueror, who had wrought their own calamity, and would permit no interference with his sway. This conqueror had a symbol of his triumphs. It was a blood-red flag, that fluttered in the tainted air, over the door of every dwelling into which the Small Pox had entered.

Such a banner was long since waving over the portal of the Province House; for thence, as was proved by tracking its footsteps back, had all this dreadful mischief issued. It had been traced back to a lady's luxurious chamber—to the proudest of the proud—to her that was so delicate, and hardly owned herself of earthly mould— to the haughty one, who took her stand above human sympathies—to Lady Eleanore! There remained no room for doubt, that the contagion had lurked in that gorgeous mantle, which threw so strange a grace around her at the festival. Its fantastic splendor had been conceived in the delirious brain of a woman on her death bed, and was the last toil of her stiffening fingers, which had interwoven fate and misery with its golden threads. This dark tale, whispered at first, was now bruited far and wide. The people raved against the Lady Eleanore, and cried out that her pride and scorn had evoked a fiend, and that, between them both, this monstrous evil had been born. At times, their rage and despair took the semblance of grinning mirth; and whenever the red flag of the pestilence was hoisted over another, and yet another door, they clapped their hands and shouted through the streets, in bitter mockery: "Behold a new triumph for the Lady Eleanore!"

One day, in the midst of these dismal times, a wild figure approached the portal of the Province House, and folding his arms, stood contemplating the scarlet banner, which a passing breeze shook fitfully, as if to fling abroad the contagion that it typified. At length, climbing one of the pillars by means of the iron balustrade, he took down the flag, and entered the mansion, waving it above his head. At the foot of the staircase he met the Governor, booted and spurred, with his cloak drawn around him, evidently on the point of setting forth upon a journey.

"Wretched lunatic, what do you seek here?" exclaimed Shute, extending his cane to guard himself from contact. "There is nothing here but Death. Back—or you will meet him!"

"Death will not touch me, the banner-bearer of the pestilence!" cried Jervase Helwyse, shaking the red flag aloft. "Death, and the Pestilence, who wears the aspect of the Lady Eleanore, will walk through the streets to-night, and I must march before them with this banner!"

"Why do I waste words on the fellow?" muttered the Governor, drawing his cloak across his mouth. "What matters his miserable life, when none of us are sure of twelve hours' breath? On, fool, to your own destruction!"

He made way for Jervase Helwyse, who immediately ascended the staircase, but, on the first landing-place, was arrested by the firm grasp of a hand upon his shoulder. Looking fiercely up, with a madman's impulse to struggle with, and rend asunder his opponent, he found himself powerless beneath a calm, stern eye, which possessed the mysterious property of quelling frenzy at its height. The person whom he had now encountered was the physician, Doctor Clarke, the duties of whose sad profession had led him to the

Province House, where he was an infrequent guest in more prosperous times.

"Young man, what is your purpose?" demanded he.

"I seek the Lady Eleanore," answered Jervase Helwyse, submissively.

"All have fled from her," said the physician. "Why do you seek her now? I tell you, youth, her nurse fell death-stricken on the threshold of that fatal chamber. Know ye not, that never came such a curse to our shores as this lovely Lady Eleanore?—that her breath has filled the air with poison?—that she has shaken pestilence and death upon the land, from the folds of her accursed mantle?"

"Let me look upon her!" rejoined the mad youth, more wildly. "Let me behold her, in her awful beauty, the regal garments of the pestilence! She and Death sit on a throne together. Let me kneel down before them!"

"Poor youth!" said Doctor Clarke; and, moved by a deep sense of human weakness, a smile of caustic humor curled his lip even then. "Wilt thou still worship the destroyer, and surround her image with fantasies the more magnificent, the more evil she has wrought? Thus man doth ever to his tyrants! Approach, then! Madness, as I have noted, has that good efficacy, that it will guard you from contagion—and perchance its own cure may be found in yonder chamber."

Ascending another flight of stairs, he threw open a door, and signed to Jervase Helwyse that he should enter. The poor lunatic, it seems probable, had cherished a delusion that his haughty mistress sat in state, unharmed herself by the pestilential influence, which, as by enchantment, she scattered round about her. He dreamed, no doubt, that her beauty was not dimmed, but brightened into superhuman splendor. With such anticipations, he stole reverentially to the door at which the physician stood, but paused upon the threshold, gazing fearfully into the gloom of the darkened chamber.

"Where is the Lady Eleanore?" whispered he.

"Call her," replied the physician.

"Lady Eleanore!—Princess!—Queen of Death!" cried Jervase Helwyse, advancing three steps into the chamber. "She is not here! There on yonder table, I behold the sparkle of a diamond which once she wore upon her bosom. There"—and he shuddered—"there hangs her mantle, on which a dead woman embroidered a spell of dreadful potency. But where is the Lady Eleanore?"

Something stirred within the silken curtains of a canopied bed; and a low moan was uttered, which, listening intently, Jervase Helwyse began to distinguish as a woman's voice, complaining dolefully of thirst. He fancied, even, that he recognized its tones.

"My throat!—my throat is scorched," murmured the voice. "A drop of water!"

"What thing art thou?" said the brain-stricken youth, drawing near the bed and tearing asunder its curtains. "Whose voice hast thou stolen for thy murmurs and miserable petitions, as if Lady Eleanore could be conscious of mortal infirmity? Fie! Heap of diseased mortality, why lurkest thou in my lady's chamber?"

"O, Jervase Helwyse," said the voice—and as it spoke, the figure contorted itself, struggling to hide its blasted face—"look not now on the woman you once loved! The curse of Heaven hath stricken me, because I would not call man my brother, nor woman sister. I wrapped myself in PRIDE as in a MANTLE, and scorned the sympathies of nature; and therefore has nature made this wretched body the medium of a dreadful sympathy. You are avenged—they are all avenged—Nature is avenged—for I am Eleanore Rochcliffe!"

The malice of his mental disease, the bitterness

lurking at the bottom of his heart, mad as he was, for a blighted and ruined life, and love that had been paid with cruel scorn, awoke within the breast of Jervase Helwyse. He shook his finger at the wretched girl, and the chamber echoed, the curtains of the bed were shaken with his outburst of insane merriment.

"Another triumph for the Lady Eleanore!" he cried. "All have been her victims! Who so worthy to be the final victim as herself?"

Impelled by some new fantasy of his crazed intellect, he snatched the fatal mantle, and rushed from the chamber and the house. That night, a procession passed, by torchlight, through the streets, bearing in the midst the figure of a woman, enveloped with a richly-embroidered mantle; while in advance stalked Jervase Helwyse, waving the red flag of the pestilence. Arriving opposite the Province House, the mob burned the effigy, and a strong wind came and swept away the ashes. It was said, that, from that very hour, the pestilence abated, as if its sway had some mysterious connection, from the first plague stroke to the last, with Lady Eleanore's Mantle. A remarkable uncertainty broods over that unhappy lady's fate. There is a belief, however, that, in a certain chamber of this mansion, a female form may sometimes be duskily discerned, shrinking into the darkest corner, and muffling her face within an embroidered mantle. Supposing the legend true, can this be other than the once proud Lady Eleanore?

———

Mine host, and the old loyalist, and I, bestowed no little warmth of applause upon this narrative, in which we had all been deeply interested; for the reader can scarcely conceive how unspeakably the effect of such a tale is heightened, when, as in the present case, we may repose perfect confidence in the veracity of him who tells it. For my own part, knowing how scrupulous is Mr Tiffany to settle the foundation of his facts, I could not have believed him one whit the more faithfully, had he professed himself an eye-witness of the doings and sufferings of poor Lady Eleanore. Some sceptics, it is true, might demand documentary evidence, or even require him to produce the embroidered mantle, forgetting that—Heaven be praised—it was consumed to ashes. But now the old loyalist, whose blood was warmed by the good cheer, began to talk, in his turn, about the traditions of the Province House, and hinted that he, if it were agreeable, might add a few reminiscences to our legendary stock. Mr. Tiffany, having no cause to dread a rival, immediately besought him to favor us with a specimen ; my own entreaties, of course, were urged to the same effect ; and our venerable guest, well pleased to find willing auditors, awaited only the return of Mr. Thomas Waite, who had been summoned forth to provide accommodations for several new arrivals. Perchance the public—but be this as its own caprice and ours shall settle the matter—may read the result in another Tale of the Province House.

IV.

OLD ESTHER DUDLEY.

OUR host having resumed the chair, he, as well as Mr. Tiffany and myself, expressed much eagerness to be made acquainted with the story to which the loyalist had alluded. That venerable man first of all saw fit to moisten his throat with another glass of wine, and then, turning his face towards our coal fire, looked steadfastly for a few moments into the depths of its cheerful glow. Finally, he poured forth a great fluency of speech. The generous liquid that he had imbibed, while it warmed his age-chilled blood, likewise took off the chill from his heart and mind, and gave him an energy to think and feel, which we could hardly have expected to find beneath the snows of fourscore winters. His feelings, indeed, appeared to me more excitable than those of a younger man ; or, at least, the same degree of feeling manifested itself by more visible effects, than if his judgment and will had possessed the potency of meridian life. At the pathetic passages of his narrative, he readily melted into tears. When a breath of indignation swept across his spirit, the blood flushed his withered visage even to the roots of his white hair ; and he shook his clinched fist at the trio of peaceful auditors, seeming to fancy enemies in those who felt very kindly towards the desolate old soul. But ever and anon, sometimes in the midst of his most earnest talk, this ancient person's intellect would wander vaguely, losing its hold of the matter in hand, and groping for it amid misty shadows. Then would he cackle forth a feeble laugh, and express a doubt whether his wits—for by that phrase it pleased our ancient friend to signify his mental powers—were not getting a little the worse for wear.

Under these disadvantages, the old loyalist's story required more revision to render it fit for the public eye, than those of the series which have preceded it; nor should it be concealed, that the sentiment and tone of the affair may have undergone some slight, or perchance more than slight metamorphosis, in its transmission to the reader through the medium of a thorough-going democrat. The tale itself is a mere sketch, with no involution of plot, nor any great interest of events, yet possessing, if I have rehearsed it aright, that pensive influence over the mind, which the shadow of the old Province House flings upon the loiterer in its court yard.

The hour had come—the hour of defeat and humiliation—when Sir William Howe was to pass over the threshold of the Province House, and embark with no such triumphal ceremonies as he once promised himself, on board the British fleet. He bade his servants and military attendants go before him, and lingered a moment in the loneliness of the mansion, to quell the fierce emotions that struggled in his bosom as with a death throb. Preferable, then, would he have deemed his fate, had a warrior's death left him a claim to the narrow territory of a grave, within the soil which the King had given him to defend. With an ominous perception that, as his departing footsteps echoed adown the staircase, the sway of Britain was passing forever from New

England, he smote his clinched hand on his brow, and cursed the destiny that had flung the shame of a dismembered empire upon him.

"Would to God," cried he, hardly repressing his tears of rage, "that the rebels were even now at the doorstep! A blood stain upon the floor should then bear testimony that the last British ruler was faithful to his trust."

The tremulous voice of a woman replied to his exclamation.

"Heaven's cause and the King's are one," it said. "Go forth, Sir William Howe, and trust in Heaven to bring back a Royal Governor in triumph."

Subduing at once the passion to which he had yielded only in the faith that it was unwitnessed, Sir William Howe became conscious that an aged woman, leaning on a gold-headed staff, was standing betwixt him and the door. It was old Esther Dudley, who had dwelt almost immemorial years in this mansion until her presence seemed as inseparable from it as the recollections of its history. She was the daughter of an ancient and once eminent family, which had fallen into poverty and decay, and left its last descendant no resource save the bounty of the King, nor any shelter except within the walls of the Province House. An office in the household, with merely nominal duties, had been assigned to her as a pretext for the payment of a small pension, the greater part of which she expended in adorning herself with an antique magnificence of attire. The claims of Esther Dudley's gentle blood were acknowledged by all the successive Governors; and they treated her with the punctilious courtesy which it was her foible to demand, not always with success, from a neglectful world. The only actual share which she assumed in the business of the mansion, was to glide through its passages and public chambers late at night, to see that the servants had dropped no fire from their

flaring torches, nor left embers crackling and blazing on
the hearths.   Perhaps it was this invariable custom of
walking her rounds in the hush of midnight, that caused
the superstition of the times to invest the old woman
with attributes of awe and mystery ; fabling that she had
entered the portal of the Province House, none knew
whence, in the train of the first Royal Governor, and
that it was her fate to dwell there till the last should have
departed.   But Sir William Howe, if he ever heard this
legend, had forgotten it.

"Mistress Dudley, why are you loitering here?"
asked he, with some severity of tone.   "It is my
pleasure to be the last in this mansion of the King."

"Not so, if it please your Excellency," answered the
time-stricken woman.   "This roof has sheltered me long.
I will not pass from it until they bear me to the tomb of
my forefathers.   What other shelter is there for old
Esther Dudley, save the Province House or the grave?"

"Now Heaven forgive me!" said Sir William Howe
to himself.   "I was about to leave this wretched old
creature to starve or beg.   Take this, good Mistress
Dudley," he added, putting a purse into her hands,
"King George's head on these golden guineas is sterling
yet, and will continue so, I warrant you, even should
the rebels crown John Hancock their king.   That purse
will buy a better shelter than the Province House can
now afford."

"While the burden of life remains upon me, I will
have no other shelter than this roof," persisted Esther
Dudley, striking her staff upon the floor, with a gesture
that expressed immovable resolve.   "And when your
Excellency returns in triumph, I will totter into the
porch to welcome you."

"My poor old friend!" answered the British General,
—and all his manly and martial pride could no longer
restrain a gush of bitter tears.   "This is an evil hour

for you and me. The province which the King intrusted to my charge is lost. I go hence in misfortune—perchance in disgrace — to return no more. And you, whose present being is incorporated with the past— who have seen Governor after Governor in stately pageantry ascend these steps—whose whole life has been an observance of majestic ceremonies, and a worship of the King—how will you endure the change? Come with us ! Bid farewell to a land that has shaken off its allegiance, and live still under a Royal government at Halifax."

" Never, never ! " said the pertinacious old dame. " Here will I abide ; and King George shall still have one true subject in his disloyal province."

" Beshrew the old fool ! " muttered Sir William Howe, growing impatient of her obstinacy, and ashamed of the emotion into which he had been betrayed. " She is the very moral of old-fashioned prejudice, and could exist nowhere but in this musty edifice. Well, then, Mistress Dudley, since you will needs tarry, I give the Province House in charge to you. Take this key, and keep it safe until myself, or some other Royal Governor, shall demand it of you."

Smiling bitterly at himself and her, he took the heavy key of the Province House, and delivering it into the old lady's hands, drew his cloak around him for departure. As the General glanced back at Esther Dudley's antique figure, he deemed her well fitted for such a charge, as being so perfect a representative of the decayed past— of an age gone by, with its manners, opinions, faith, and feelings, all fallen into oblivion or scorn—of what had once been a reality, but was now merely a vision of faded magnificence. Then Sir William Howe strode forth, smiting his clinched hands together, in the fierce anguish of his spirit ; and old Esther Dudley was left to keep watch in the lonely Province House, dwelling there

with memory; and if Hope ever seemed to flit around
her, still it was Memory in disguise.

The total change of affairs that ensued on the departure
of the British troops did not drive the venerable lady
from her stronghold.   There was not, for many years
afterwards, a Governor of Massachusetts; and the magis-
trates, who had charge of such matters, saw no objection
to Esther Dudley's residence in the Province House,
especially as they must otherwise have paid a hireling
for taking care of the premises, which with her was a
labor of love.   And so they left her the undisturbed
mistress of the old historic edifice.   Many and strange
were the fables which the gossips whispered about her,
in all the chimney corners of the town.   Among the
time-worn articles of furniture that had been left in the
mansion, there was a tall, antique mirror, which was
well worthy of a tale by itself, and perhaps may hereafter
be the theme of one.   The gold of its heavily-wrought
frame was tarnished, and its surface so blurred, that the
old woman's figure, whenever she passed before it, looked
indistinct and ghost-like.   But it was the general belief
that Esther could cause the Governors of the overthrown
dynasty, with the beautiful ladies who had once adorned
their festivals, the Indian chiefs who had come up to the
Province House to hold council or swear allegiance, the
grim Provincial warriors, the severe clergyman—in short,
all the pageantry of gone days—all the figures that ever
swept across the broad plate of glass in former times—
she could cause the whole to reappear, and people the
inner world of the mirror with shadows of old life.   Such
legends as these, together with the singularity of her
isolated existence, her age, and the infirmity that each
added winter flung upon her, made Mistress Dudley the
object both of fear and pity ; and it was partly the result
of either sentiment, that, amid all the angry license of the
times, neither wrong nor insult ever fell upon her unpro-

tected head. Indeed, there was so much haughtiness in her demeanor towards intruders, among whom she reckoned all persons acting under the new authorities, that it was really an affair of no small nerve to look her in the face. And to do the people justice, stern republicans as they had now become, they were well content that the old gentlewoman, in her hoop petticoat and faded embroidery, should still haunt the palace of ruined pride and overthrown power, the symbol of a departed system, embodying a history in her person. So Esther Dudley dwelt, year after year, in the Province House, still reverencing all that others had flung aside, still faithful to her King, who, so long as the venerable dame yet held her post, might be said to retain one true subject in New England, and one spot of the empire that had been wrested from him.

And did she dwell there in utter loneliness? Rumor said, not so. Whenever her chill and withered heart desired warmth, she was wont to summon a black slave of Governor Shirley's from the blurred mirror, and send him in search of guests who had long ago been familiar in those deserted chambers. Forth went the sable messenger, with the starlight or the moonshine gleaming through him, and did his errand in the burial ground, knocking at the iron doors of tombs, or upon the marble slabs that covered them, and whispering to those within : "My mistress, old Esther Dudley, bids you to the Province House at midnight." And punctually as the clock of the Old South told twelve, came the shadows of the Olivers, the Hutchinsons, the Dudleys, all the grandees of a by-gone generation, gliding beneath the portal into the well-known mansion, where Esther mingled with them as if she likewise were a shade. Without vouching for the truth of such traditions, it is certain that Mistress Dudley sometimes assembled a few of the stanch, though crestfallen old tories, who had lingered in the rebel town during those days of wrath and tribulation. Out of a cobwebbed bottle, containing liquor that a royal Governor might have smacked his lips over, they quaffed healths to the King, and babbled treason to the Republic, feeling as if the protecting shadow of the throne were still flung around them. But, draining the last drops of their liquor, they stole timorously homeward, and answered not again, if the rude mob reviled them in the street.

Yet Esther Dudley's most frequent and favored guests were the children of the town. Towards them she was never stern. A kindly and loving nature, hindered elsewhere from its free course by a thousand rocky prejudices, lavished itself upon these little ones. By bribes of gingerbread of her own making, stamped with a royal crown, she tempted their sunny sportiveness beneath the gloomy portal of the Province House, and would often beguile them to spend a whole play day there, sitting in a circle round the verge of her hoop petticoat, greedily attentive to her stories of a dead world. And when these little boys and girls stole forth again from the dark mysterious mansion, they went bewildered, full of old feelings that graver people had long ago forgotten, rubbing their eyes at the world around them as if they had gone astray into ancient times, and become children of the past. At home, when their parents asked where they had loitered such a weary while, and with whom they had been at play, the children would talk of all the departed worthies of the Province, as far back as Governor Belcher, and the haughty dame of Sir William Phipps. It would seem as though they had been sitting on the knees of these famous personages, whom the grave had hidden for half a century, and had toyed with the embroidery of their rich waistcoats, or roguishly pulled the long curls of their flowing wigs. "But Governor Belcher has been dead this many a year," would the mother say to her little boy. "And did you really see him at the

Province House?" "O, yes, dear mother! yes!" the half-dreaming child would answer. "But when old Esther had done speaking about him he faded away out of his chair." Thus, without affrighting her little guests, she led them by the hand into the chambers of her own desolate heart, and made childhood's fancy discern the ghosts that haunted there.

Living so continually in her own circle of ideas, and never regulating her mind by a proper reference to present things, Esther Dudley appears to have grown partially crazed. It was found that she had no right sense of the progress and true state of the Revolutionary war, but held a constant faith that the armies of Britain were victorious on every field, and destined to be ultimately triumphant. Whenever the town rejoiced for a battle won by Washington, or Gates, or Morgan, or Greene, the news, in passing through the door of the Province House, as through the ivory gate of dreams, became metamorphosed into a strange tale of the prowess of Howe, Clinton, or Cornwallis. Sooner or later, it was her invincible belief, the colonies would be prostrate at the footstool of the King. Sometimes she seemed to take for granted that such was already the case. On one occasion, she startled the town's people by a brilliant illumination of the Province House, with candles at every pane of glass, and a transparency of the King's initials and a crown of light, in the great balcony window. The figure of the aged woman, in the most gorgeous of her mildewed velvets and brocades, was seen passing from casement to casement, until she paused before the balcony, and flourished a huge key above her head. Her wrinkled visage actually gleamed with triumph, as if the soul within her were a festal lamp.

"What means this blaze of light? What does old Esther's joy portend?" whispered a spectator. "It is frightful to see her gliding about the chambers,

5   12

and rejoicing there without a soul to bear her company."

"It is as if she were making merry in a tomb," said
another.

"Pshaw! It is no such mystery," observed an old
man, after some brief exercise of memory. "Mistress
Dudley is keeping jubilee for the King of England's
birthday."

Then the people laughed aloud, and would have thrown
mud against the blazing transparency of the King's crown
and initials, only that they pitied the poor old dame, who
was so dismally triumphant amid the wreck and ruin of
the system to which she appertained.

Oftentimes it was her custom to climb the weary staircase that wound upward to the cupola, and thence strain
her dimmed eyesight seaward and countryward, watching
for a British fleet, or for the march of a grand procession,
with the King's banner floating over it. The passengers
in the street below would discern her anxious visage,
and send up a shout—"When the golden Indian on the
Province House shall shoot his arrow, and when the
cock on the Old South spire shall crow, then look for a
Royal Governor again!"—for this had grown a byword
through the town. And at last, after long, long years,
old Esther Dudley knew, or perchance she only dreamed,
that a Royal Governor was on the eve of returning to
the Province House, to receive the heavy key which Sir
William Howe had committed to her charge. Now it
was the fact, that intelligence bearing some faint analogy
to Esther's version of it, was current among the town's
people. She set the mansion in the best order that her
means allowed, and arraying herself in silks and tarnished gold, stood long before the blurred mirror to
admire her own magnificence. As she gazed, the gray
and withered lady moved her ashen lips, murmuring half
aloud, talking to shapes that she saw within the mirror,

to shadows of her own fantasies, to the household friends of memory, and bidding them rejoice with her, and come forth to meet the Governor. And while absorbed in this communion, Mistress Dudley heard the tramp of many footsteps in the street, and looking out of the window, beheld what she construed as the Royal Governor's arrival.

"O, happy day! O, blessed, blessed hour!" she exclaimed. "Let me but bid him welcome within the portal, and my task in the Province House, and on earth, is done!"

Then with tottering feet, which age and tremulous joy caused to tread amiss, she hurried down the grand staircase, her silks sweeping and rustling as she went, so that the sound was as if a train of spectral courtiers were thronging from the dim mirror. And Esther Dudley fancied, that as soon as the wide door should be flung open, all the pomp and splendor of by-gone times would pace majestically into the Province House, and the gilded tapestry of the past would be brightened by the sunshine of the present. She turned the key—withdrew it from the lock—unclosed the door—and stepped across the threshold. Advancing up the court yard appeared a person of most dignified mien, with tokens, as Esther interpreted them, of gentle blood, high rank, and long-accustomed authority, even in his walk and every gesture. He was richly dressed, but wore a gouty shoe, which, however, did not lessen the stateliness of his gait. Around and behind him were people in plain civic dresses, and two or three war-worn veterans, evidently officers of rank, arrayed in a uniform of blue and buff. But Esther Dudley, firm in the belief that had fastened its roots about her heart, beheld only the principal personage, and never doubted that this was the long-looked-for Governor, to whom she was to surrender up her charge. As he approached, she involun-

tarily sank down on her knees, and tremblingly held
forth the heavy key.

"Receive my trust! take it quickly!" cried she; "for
methinks Death is striving to snatch away my triumph.
But he comes too late. Thank Heaven for this blessed
hour! God save King George!"

"That, Madam, is a strange prayer to be offered up
at such a moment," replied the unknown guest of the
Province House, and courteously removing his hat, he
offered his arm to raise the aged woman. "Yet, in
reverence for your gray hairs and long-kept faith, Heaven
forbid that any here should say you nay. Over the
realms which still acknowledge his sceptre, God save
King George!"

Esther Dudley started to her feet, and hastily clutch-
ing back the key, gazed with fearful earnestness at the
stranger; and dimly and doubtfully, as if suddenly
awakened from a dream, her bewildered eyes half recognized his face. Years ago, she had known him among
the gentry of the province. But the ban of the King
had fallen upon him! How, then, came the doomed
victim here? Proscribed, excluded from mercy, the
monarch's most dreaded and hated foe, this New England merchant had stood triumphantly against a king-
dom's strength; and his foot now trod upon humbled
Royalty, as he ascended the steps of the Province House,
the people's chosen Governor of Massachusetts.

"Wretch, wretch that I am!" muttered the old woman,
with such a heart-broken expression, that the tears gushed
from the stranger's eyes. "Have I bidden a traitor welcome? Come, Death! come quickly!"

"Alas, venerable lady!" said Governor Hancock,
lending her his support with all the reverence that a
courtier would have shown to a queen. "Your life has
been prolonged until the world has changed around you.
You have treasured up all that time has rendered worth-

less—the principles, feelings, manners, modes of being and acting, which another generation has flung aside— and you are a symbol of the past. And I, and these around me—we represent a new race of men—living no longer in the past, scarcely in the present—but projecting our lives forward into the future. Ceasing to model ourselves on ancestral superstitions, it is our faith and principle to press onward, onward ! Yet," continued he, turning to his attendants, "let us reverence, for the last time, the stately and gorgeous prejudices of the tottering Past !"

While the Republican Governor spoke, he had continued to support the helpless form of Esther Dudley ; her weight grew heavier against his arm ; but at last, with a sudden effort to free herself, the ancient woman sank down beside one of the pillars of the portal. The key of the Province House fell from her grasp, and clanked against the stone.

"I have been faithful unto death," murmured she. "God save the King !"

"She hath done her office !" said Hancock, solemnly. "We will follow her reverently to the tomb of her ancestors ; and then, my fellow-citizens, onward — onward ! We are no longer children of the Past !"

As the old loyalist concluded his narrative, the enthusiasm which had been fitfully flashing within his sunken eyes, and quivering across his wrinkled visage, faded away, as if all the lingering fire of his soul were extinguished. Just then, too, a lamp upon the mantelpiece threw out a dying gleam, which vanished as speedily as it shot upward, compelling our eyes to grope for one another's features by the dim glow of the hearth. With such a lingering fire, methought, with such a dying gleam, had the glory of the ancient system vanished from the Province House, when the spirit of old Esther Dudley took its flight. And now, again, the clock of the Old South threw its voice of ages on the breeze, knolling the hourly knell of the Past, crying out far and wide through the multitudinous city, and filling our ears, as we sat in the dusky chamber, with its reverberating depth of tone. In that same mansion—in that very chamber—what a volume of history had been told off into hours, by the same voice that was now trembling in the air. Many a Governor had heard those midnight accents, and longed to exchange his stately cares for slumber. And as for mine host, and Mr. Bela Tiffany, and the old loyalist, and me, we had babbled about dreams of the past, until we almost fancied that the clock was still striking in a bygone century. Neither of us would have wondered, had a hoop-petticoated phantom of Esther Dudley tottered into the chamber, walking her rounds in the hush of midnight, as of yore, and motioned us to quench the fading embers of the fire, and leave the historic precincts to herself and her kindred shades. But as no such vision was vouchsafed, I retired unbidden, and would advise Mr. Tiffany to lay hold of another auditor, being resolved not to show my face in the Province House for a good while hence—if ever.

WHAT a singular moment is the first one, when you have hardly begun to recollect yourself, after starting from midnight slumber? By unclosing your eyes so suddenly, you seem to have surprised the personages of your dream in full convocation round your bed, and catch one broad glance at them before they can flit into obscurity. Or, to vary the metaphor, you find yourself, for a single instant, wide awake in that realm of illusions, whither sleep has been the passport, and behold its ghostly inhabitants and wondrous scenery, with a perception of their strangeness, such as you never attain while the dream is undisturbed. The distant sound of a church clock is borne faintly on the wind. You question with yourself, half seriously, whether it has stolen to your waking ear from some gray tower, that stood within the precincts of your dream. While yet in suspense, another clock flings its heavy clang over the slumbering town, with so full and distinct a sound, and such a long murmur in the neighboring air, that you are certain it must proceed from the steeple at the nearest corner. You count the strokes—one—two, and there they cease, with a booming sound, like the gathering of a third stroke within the bell.

If you could choose an hour of wakefulness out of the whole night, it would be this. Since your sober bedtime, at eleven, you have had rest enough to take off the pressure of yesterday's fatigue ; while before you, till the sun comes from "far Cathay" to brighten your window, there is almost the space of a summer night; one hour to be spent in thought, with the mind's eye half shut, and two in pleasant dreams, and two in that strangest of enjoyments, the forgetfulness alike of joy and woe. The moment of rising belongs to another period of time, and appears so distant, that the plunge out of a warm bed into the frosty air cannot yet be anticipated with dismay. Yesterday has already vanished among the shadows of the past; to-morrow has not yet emerged from the future. You have found an intermediate space, where the business of life does not intrude; where the passing moment lingers, and becomes truly the present; a spot where Father Time, when he thinks nobody is watching him, sits down by the wayside to take breath. O that he would fall asleep, and let mortals live on without growing older!

Hitherto you have lain perfectly still, because the slightest motion would dissipate the fragments of your slumber. Now, being irrevocably awake, you peep through the half-drawn window curtain, and observe that the glass is ornamented with fanciful devices in frostwork, and that each pane presents something like a frozen dream. There will be time enough to trace out the analogy, while waiting the summons to breakfast. Seen through the clear portion of the glass, where the silvery mountain peaks of the frost scenery do not ascend, the most conspicuous object is the steeple; the white spire of which directs you to the wintry lustre of the firmament. You may almost distinguish the figures on the clock that has just told the hour. Such a frosty sky, and the snow-covered roofs, and the long vista of the frozen street, all white, and the distant water hardened into rock, might make you shiver, even under four blankets and a woollen comforter. Yet look at that one glorious star! Its beams are distinguishable from all the rest, and actually cast the shadow of the casement on the bed, with a radiance of deeper hue than moonlight, though not so accurate an outline.

You sink down and muffle your head in the clothes, shivering all the while, but less from bodily chill than the bare idea of a polar atmosphere. It is too cold even for the thoughts to venture abroad. You speculate on the luxury of wearing out a whole existence in bed, like an oyster in its shell, content with the sluggish ecstasy of inaction, and drowsily conscious of nothing but delicious warmth, such as you now feel again. Ah! that idea has brought a hideous one in its train. You think how the dead are lying in their cold shrouds and narrow coffins, through the drear winter of the grave, and cannot persuade your fancy that they neither shrink nor shiver, when the snow is drifting over their little hillocks, and the bitter blast howls against the door of the tomb. That gloomy thought will collect a gloomy multitude, and throw its complexion over your wakeful hour.

In the depths of every heart, there is a tomb and a dungeon, though the lights, the music, and revelry above may cause us to forget their existence, and the buried ones, or prisoners whom they hide. But sometimes, and oftenest at midnight, these dark receptacles are flung wide open. In an hour like this, when the mind has a passive sensibility, but no active strength; when the imagination is a mirror, imparting vividness to all ideas, without the power of selecting or controlling them; then pray that your griefs may slumber, and the brotherhood of remorse not break their chain. It is too late! A funeral train comes gliding by your bed, in which Passion and Feeling assume bodily shape, and things of the mind become dim spectres to the eye. There is your earliest Sorrow, a pale young mourner, wearing a sister's likeness to first love, sadly beautiful, with a hallowed sweetness in her melancholy features, and grace in the flow of her sable robe. Next appears a shade of ruined

loveliness, with dust among her golden hair, and her
bright garments all faded and defaced, stealing from
your glance with drooping head, as fearful of reproach ;
she was your fondest Hope, but a delusive one ; so call
her Disappointment now. A sterner form succeeds, with
a brow of wrinkles, a look and gesture of iron authority ;
there is no name for him unless it be Fatality, an emblem
of the evil influence that rules your fortunes ; a demon
to whom you subjected yourself by some error at the
outset of life, and were bound his slave forever, by once
obeying him. See ! those fiendish lineaments graven
on the darkness, the writhed lip of scorn, the mockery
of that living eye, the pointed finger, touching the sore
place in your heart ! Do you remember any act of
enormous folly, at which you would blush, even in the
remotest cavern of the earth? Then recognize your
Shame.

Pass, wretched band ! Well for the wakeful one, if,
riotously miserable, a fiercer tribe do not surround him,
the devils of a guilty heart, that holds its hell within
itself. What if Remorse should assume the features of
an injured friend? What if the fiend should come in
woman's garments, with a pale beauty amid sin and
desolation, and lie down by your side? What if he
should stand at your bed's foot, in the likeness of a corpse,
with a bloody stain upon the shroud? Sufficient without
such guilt is this nightmare of the soul ; this heavy,
heavy sinking of the spirits ; this wintry gloom about the
heart ; this indistinct horror of the mind, blending itself
with the darkness of the chamber.

By a desperate effort, you start upright, breaking from
a sort of conscious sleep, and gazing wildly round the
bed, as if the fiends were any where but in your haunted
mind. At the same moment, the slumbering embers on
the hearth send forth a gleam which palely illuminates
the whole outer room, and flickers through the door of

the bed chamber, but cannot quite dispel its obscurity.
Your eye searches for whatever may remind you of the
living world. With eager minuteness, you take note of
the table near the fireplace, the book with an ivory knife
between its leaves, the unfolded letter, the hat and the
fallen glove. Soon the flame vanishes, and with it
the whole scene is gone, though its image remains an
instant in your mind's eye, when darkness has swal-
lowed the reality. Throughout the chamber there is
the same obscurity as before, but not the same gloom
within your breast. As your head falls back upon the
pillow, you think—in a whisper be it spoken—how
pleasant, in these night solitudes, would be the rise
and fall of a softer breathing than your own, the slight
pressure of a tenderer bosom, the quiet throb of a purer
heart, imparting its peacefulness to your troubled one, as
if the fond sleeper were involving you in her dream.

Her influence is over you, though she have no existence
but in that momentary image. You sink down in a
flowery spot, on the borders of sleep and wakefulness,
while your thoughts rise before you in pictures, all
disconnected, yet all assimilated by a pervading glad-
someness and beauty. The wheeling of gorgeous
squadrons, that glitter in the sun, is succeeded by
the merriment of children round the door of a school
house, beneath the glimmering shadow of old trees,
at the corner of a rustic lane. You stand in the sunny
rain of a summer shower, and wander among the sunny
trees of an autumnal wood, and look upward at the
brightest of all rainbows, over-arching the unbroken
sheet of snow, on the American side of Niagara. Your
mind struggles pleasantly between the dancing radiance
round the hearth of a young man and his recent bride,
and the twittering flight of birds in spring, about their
new-made nest. You feel the merry bounding of a ship
before the breeze ; and watch the tuneful feet of rosy

girls, as they twine their last and merriest dance, in a splendid ball room ; and find yourself in the brilliant circle of a crowded theatre, as the curtain falls over a light and airy scene.

With an involuntary start, you seize hold on consciousness, and prove yourself but half awake, by running a doubtful parallel between human life and the hour which has now elapsed. In both you emerge from mystery, pass through a vicissitude that you can but imperfectly control, and are borne onward to another mystery. Now comes the peal of the distant clock, with fainter and fainter strokes as you plunge farther into the wilderness of sleep. It is the knell of a temporary death. Your spirit has departed, and strays like a free citizen among the people of a shadowy world, beholding strange sights, yet without wonder and dismay. So calm, perhaps, will be the final change ; so undisturbed, as if among familiar things, the entrance of the soul to its Eternal home !

THE VILLAGE UNCLE.

AN IMAGINARY RETROSPECT.

COME! another log upon the hearth. True, our little parlor is comfortable, especially here, where the old man sits in his old arm chair; but on Thanksgiving night the blaze should dance higher up the chimney, and send a shower of sparks into the outer darkness. Toss on an armful of those dry oak chips, the last relics of the Mermaid's knee timbers, the bones of your namesake, Susan. Higher yet, and clearer be the blaze, till our cottage windows glow the ruddiest in the village, and the light of our household mirth flash far across the bay to Nahant. And now, come, Susan, come, my children, draw your chairs round me, all of you. There is a dimness over your figures! You sit quivering indistinctly with each motion of the blaze, which eddies about you like a flood, so that you all have the look of visions, or people that dwell only in the firelight, and will vanish from existence, as completely as your own shadows, when the flame shall sink among the embers. Hark! let me listen for the swell of the surf; it should be audible a mile inland, on a night like this. Yes; there I catch the sound, but only an uncertain murmur, as if a good way down over the beach; though, by the almanac, it is high tide at eight o'clock, and the billows must now be dashing within thirty yards of our door. Ah! the old man's ears are failing him; and so is his eyesight,

and perhaps his mind; else you would not all be so
shadowy, in the blaze of the Thanksgiving fire.

How strangely the past is peeping over the shoulders
of the present! To judge by my recollections, it is
but a few moments since I sat in another room; yonder
model of a vessel was not there, nor the old chest of
drawers, nor Susan's profile and mine, in that gilt frame;
nothing, in short, except this same fire, which glimmered
on books, papers, and a picture, and half discovered my
solitary figure in a looking glass. But it was paler than
my rugged old self, and younger, too, by almost half a
century. Speak to me, Susan; speak, my beloved ones;
for the scene is glimmering on my sight again, and as it
brightens you fade away. O, I should be loath to lose
my treasure of past happiness, and become once more
what I was then; a hermit in the depths of my own
mind; sometimes yawning over drowsy volumes, and
anon a scribbler of wearier trash than what I read; a
man who had wandered out of the real world and got
into its shadow, where his troubles, joys, and vicissitudes
were of such slight stuff, that he hardly knew whether
he lived, or only dreamed of living. Thank Heaven,
I am an old man now, and have done with all such
vanities.

Still this dimness of mine eyes! Come nearer, Susan,
and stand before the fullest blaze of the hearth. Now
I behold you illuminated from head to foot, in your
clean cap and decent gown, with the dear lock of gray
hair across your forehead, and a quiet smile about your
mouth, while the eyes alone are concealed by the red
gleam of the fire upon your spectacles. There, you
made me tremble again! When the flame quivered,
my sweet Susan, you quivered with it, and grew indistinct, as if melting into the warm light, that my last
glimpse of you might be as visionary as the first was,
full many a year since. Do you remember it? You

stood on the little bridge, over the brook, that runs across King's Beach into the sea. It was twilight; the waves rolling in, the wind sweeping by, the crimson clouds fading in the west, and the silver moon brightening above the hill; and on the bridge were you, fluttering in the breeze like a sea bird that might skim away at your pleasure. You seemed a daughter of the viewless wind, a creature of the ocean foam and the crimson light, whose merry life was spent in dancing on the crests of the billows, that threw up their spray to support your footsteps. As I drew nearer, I fancied you akin to the race of mermaids, and thought how pleasant it would be to dwell with you among the quiet coves, in the shadow of the cliffs, and to roam along secluded beaches of the purest sand, and when our northern shores grew bleak, to haunt the islands, green and lonely, far amid summer seas. And yet it gladdened me, after all this nonsense, to find you nothing but a pretty young girl, sadly perplexed with the rude behavior of the wind about your petticoats.

Thus I did with Susan as with most other things in my earlier days, dipping her image into my mind and coloring it of a thousand fantastic hues, before I could see her as she really was. Now, Susan, for a sober picture of our village! It was a small collection of dwellings that seemed to have been cast up by the sea, with the rockweed and marine plants that it vomits after a storm, or to have come ashore among the pipe staves and other lumber, which had been washed from the deck of an eastern schooner. There was just space for the narrow and sandy street between the beach in front, and a precipitous hill that lifted its rocky forehead in the rear, among a waste of juniper bushes and the wild growth of a broken pasture. The village was picturesque in the variety of its edifices, though all were rude. Here stood a little old hovel, built, perhaps, of

driftwood, there a row of boat houses, and beyond them
a two-story dwelling of dark and weather-beaten aspect,
the whole intermixed with one or two snug cottages
painted white, a sufficiency of pigsties, and a shoemaker's
shop. Two grocery stores stand opposite each other in
the centre of the village. These were the places of
resort at their idle hours, of a hardy throng of fishermen,
in red baize shirts, oil-cloth trousers, and boots of brown
leather covering the whole leg ; true seven-league boots,
but fitter to wade the ocean than walk the earth. The
wearers seemed amphibious, as if they did but creep out
of salt water to sun themselves ; nor would it have been
wonderful to see their lower limbs covered with clusters
of little shellfish, such as cling to rocks and old ship
timber over which the tide ebbs and flows. When their
fleet of boats was weather-bound, the butchers raised
their price, and the spit was busier than the frying pan ;
for this was a place of fish, and known as such, to all the
country round about ; the very air was fishy, being
perfumed with dead sculpins, hardheads, and dogfish,
strewn plentifully on the beach. You see, children, the
village is but little changed since your mother and I
were young.

How like a dream it was, when I bent over a pool of
water, one pleasant morning, and saw that the ocean had
dashed its spray over me and made me a fisherman !
There were the tarpauling, the baize shirt, the oil-cloth
trousers and seven-league boots, and there my own
features, but so reddened with sunburn and sea breezes,
that methought I had another face, and on other
shoulders too. The seagulls and the loons, and I, had
now all one trade ; we skimmed the crested waves and
sought our prey beneath them, the man with as keen
enjoyment as the birds. Always, when the east grew
purple, I launched my dory, my little flat-bottomed skiff,
and rowed cross-handed to Point Ledge, the Middle

Ledge, or, perhaps, beyond Egg Rock; often, too, did I
anchor off Dread Ledge, a spot of peril to ships unpiloted;
and sometimes spread an adventurous sail and tracked
across the bay to South Shore, casting my lines in sight
of Scituate. Ere nightfall, I hauled my skiff high and
dry on the beach, laden with red rock cod, or the white-
bellied ones of deep water; haddock bearing the black
marks of Saint Peter's fingers near the gills; the long-
bearded hake, whose liver holds oil enough for a midnight lamp; and now and then a mighty halibut, with a
back broad as my boat. In the autumn, I toled and
caught those lovely fish, the mackerel. When the wind
was high,—when the whale boats anchored off the Point,
nodded their slender masts at each other, and the dories
pitched and tossed in the surf,—when Nahant Beach was
thundering three miles off, and the spray broke a hundred feet in air, round the distant base of Egg Rock,—
when the brimful and boisterous sea threatened to tumble
over the street of our village,—then I made a holiday
on shore.

Many such a day did I sit snugly in Mr. Bartlett's
store, attentive to the yarns of uncle Parker; uncle to
the whole village by right of seniority, but of southern
blood, with no kindred in New England. His figure is
before me now, enthroned upon a mackerel barrel; a
lean old man, of great height, but bent with years, and
twisted into an uncouth shape by seven broken limbs;
furrowed also, and weather-worn, as if every gale, for
the better part of a century, had caught him somewhere
on the sea. He looked like a harbinger of tempest; a
shipmate of the Flying Dutchman. After innumerable
voyages aboard men-of-war and merchantmen, fishing
schooners and chebacco boats, the old salt had become
master of a handcart, which he daily trundled about the
vicinity, and sometimes blew his fish horn through the
streets of Salem. One of uncle Parker's eyes had been

blown out with gunpowder, and the other did but glimmer in its socket. Turning it upward as he spoke, it was his delight to tell of cruises against the French, and battles with his own shipmates, when he and an antagonist used to be seated astride of a sailor's chest, each fastened down by a spike nail through his trousers, and there to fight it out. Sometimes he expatiated on the delicious flavor of the hagden, a greasy and goose-like fowl, which the sailors catch with hook and line on the Grand Banks. He dwelt with rapture on an interminable winter at the Isle of Sables where he had gladdened himself, amid polar snows, with the rum and sugar saved from the wreck of a West India schooner. And wrathfully did he shake his fist as he related how a party of Cape Cod men had robbed him and his companions of their lawful spoil, and sailed away with every keg of old Jamaica, leaving him not a drop to drown his sorrow. Villains they were, and of that wicked brotherhood who are said to tie lanterns to horses' tails, to mislead the mariner along the dangerous shores of the Cape.

Even now, I seem to see the group of fishermen, with that old salt in the midst. One fellow sits on the counter, a second bestrides an oil barrel, a third lolls at his length on a parcel of new cod lines, and another has planted the tarry seat of his trousers on a heap of salt, which will shortly be sprinkled over a lot of fish. They are a likely set of men. Some have voyaged to the East Indies or the Pacific, and most of them have sailed in Marblehead schooners to Newfoundland; a few have been no farther than the Middle Banks, and one or two have always fished along the shore ; but, as uncle Parker used to say, they have all been christened in salt water, and know more than men ever learn in the bushes. A curious figure, by way of contrast, is a fish dealer from far-up country, listening with eyes wide open, to narratives that might startle Sinbad the sailor. Be it well with you, my brethren! Ye are all gone, some to your graves ashore, and others to the depths of ocean ; but my faith is strong that ye are happy ; for whenever I behold your forms, whether in dream or vision, each departed friend is puffing his long nine, and a mug of the right black strap goes round from lip to lip.

But where was the mermaid in those delightful times? At a certain window near the centre of the village, appeared a pretty display of gingerbread men and horses, picture books and ballads, small fish hooks, pins, needles, sugar plums, and brass thimbles, articles on which the young fishermen used to expend their money from pure gallantry. What a picture was Susan behind the counter! A slender maiden, though the child of rugged parents, she had the slimmest of all waists, brown hair curling on her neck, and a complexion rather pale, except when the sea breeze flushed it. A few freckles became beauty spots beneath her eyelids. How was it, Susan, that you talked and acted so carelessly, yet always for the best, doing whatever was right in your own eyes, and never once doing wrong in mine, nor shocked a taste that had been morbidly sensitive till now? And whence had you that happiest gift of brightening every topic with an unsought gayety, quiet but irresistible, so that even gloomy spirits felt your sunshine, and did not shrink from it? Nature wrought the charm. She made you a frank, simple, kind-hearted, sensible, and mirthful girl. Obeying nature, you did free things without indelicacy, displayed a maiden's thoughts to every eye, and proved yourself as innocent as naked Eve.

It was beautiful to observe how her simple and happy nature mingled itself with mine. She kindled a domestic fire within my heart, and took up her dwelling there, even in that chill and lonesome cavern, hung round with glittering icicles of fancy. She gave me warmth of feeling while the influence of my mind made her contemplative.

I taught her to love the moonlight hour, when the expanse of the encircled bay was smooth as a great mirror and slept in a transparent shadow ; while beyond Nahant, the wind rippled the dim ocean into a dreamy brightness, which grew faint afar off, without becoming gloomier. I held her hand and pointed to the long surf wave, as it rolled calmly on the beach in an unbroken line of silver ; we were silent together, till its deep and peaceful murmur had swept by us. When the Sabbath sun shone down into the recesses of the cliffs, I led the mermaid thither, and told her that those huge, gray, shattered rocks, and her native sea, that raged forever like a storm against them, and her own slender beauty in so stern a scene, were all combined into a strain of poetry. But on the Sabbath eve, when her mother had gone early to bed, and her gentle sister had smiled and left us, as we sat alone by the quiet hearth, with household things around, it was her turn to make me feel, that here was a deeper poetry, and that this was the dearest hour of all. Thus went on our wooing, till I had shot wild fowl enough to feather our bridal bed, and the Daughter of the Sea was mine.

I built a cottage for Susan and myself, and made a gateway in the form of a Gothic arch, by setting up a whale's jaw bones. We bought a heifer with her first calf, and had a little garden on the hillside, to supply us with potatoes and green sauce for our fish. Our parlor, small and neat, was ornamented with our two profiles in one gilt frame, and with shells and pretty pebbles on the mantelpiece, selected from the sea's treasury of such things on Nahant Beach. On the desk, beneath the looking glass, lay the Bible, which I had begun to read aloud at the book of Genesis, and the singing book that Susan used for her evening psalm. Except the almanac, we had no other literature. All that I heard of books, was when an Indian history, or tale of shipwreck, was

sold by a pedler or wandering subscription man to some
one in the village, and read through its owner's nose to a
slumberous auditory. Like my brother fishermen, I
grew into the belief that all human erudition was collected in our pedagogue, whose green spectacles and
solemn phiz, as he passed to his little school house, amid
a waste of sand, might have gained him a diploma from
any college in New England. In truth I dreaded him.
When our children were old enough to claim his care,
you remember, Susan, how I frowned, though you were
pleased, at this learned man's encomiums on their profi-
ciency. I feared to trust them even with the alphabet ; it
was the key to a fatal treasure.

But I loved to lead them by their little hands along
the beach, and point to nature in the vast and the
minute, the sky, the sea, the green earth, the pebbles and
the shells. Then did I discourse of the mighty works
and co-extensive goodness of the Deity, with the simple
wisdom of a man whose mind had profited by lonely
days upon the deep, and his heart by the strong and
pure affections of his evening home. Sometimes my
voice lost itself in a tremulous depth ; for I felt His eye
upon me as I spoke. Once, while my wife and all of us
were gazing at ourselves in the mirror left by the tide in
a hollow of the sand, I pointed to the pictured heaven
below, and bade her observe how religion was strewn
every where in our path ; since even a casual pool of
water recalled the idea of that home whither we were
travelling, to rest forever with our children. Suddenly,
your image, Susan, and all the little faces made up of
yours and mine, seemed to fade away and vanish around
me, leaving a pale visage like my own of former days
within the frame of a large looking glass. Strange
illusion !

My life glided on, the past appearing to mingle with
the present and absorb the future, till the whole lies

before me at a glance. My manhood has long been waning with a stanch decay; my earlier contemporaries, after lives of unbroken health, are all at rest, without having known the weariness of later age; and now, with a wrinkled forehead and thin white hair as badges of my dignity, I have become the patriarch, the Uncle of the village. I love that name; it widens the circle of my sympathies; it joins all the youthful to my household, in the kindred of affection.

Like uncle Parker, whose rheumatic bones were dashed against Egg Rock, full forty years ago, I am a spinner of long yarns. Seated on the gunwale of a dory, or on the sunny side of a boat house, where the warmth is grateful to my limbs, or by my own hearth, when a friend or two are there, I overflow with talk, and yet am never tedious. With a broken voice I give utterance to much wisdom. Such, Heaven be praised! is the vigor of my faculties, that many a forgotten usage, and traditions ancient in my youth, and early adventures of myself or others, hitherto effaced by things more recent, acquire new distinctness in my memory. I remember the happy days when the haddock were more numerous on all the fishing grounds than sculpins in the surf; when the deep-water cod swam close in shore, and the dogfish, with his poisonous horn, had not learned to take the hook. I can number every equinoctial storm, in which the sea has overwhelmed the street, flooded the cellars of the village, and hissed upon our kitchen hearth. I give the history of the great whale that was landed on Whale Beach, and whose jaws, being now my gateway, will last for ages after my coffin shall have passed beneath them. Thence it is an easy digression to the halibut, scarcely smaller than the whale, which ran out six cod lines, and hauled my dory to the mouth of Boston Harbor, before I could touch him with the gaff.

If melancholy accidents be the theme of conversation,

I tell how a friend of mine was taken out of his boat by an enormous shark; and the sad, true tale of a young man on the eve of marriage, who had been nine days missing, when his drowned body floated into the very pathway, on Marblehead Neck, that had often led him to the dwelling of his bride; as if the dripping corpse would have come where the mourner was. With such awful fidelity did that lover return to fulfil his vows! Another favorite story is of a crazy maiden, who conversed with angels and had the gift of prophecy, and whom all the village loved and pitied, though she went from door to door accusing us of sin, exhorting to repentance, and foretelling our destruction by flood or earthquake. If the young men boast their knowledge of the ledges and sunken rocks, I speak of pilots, who knew the wind by its scent and the wave by its taste, and could have steered blindfold to any port between Boston and Mount Desert, guided only by the rote of the shore; the peculiar sound of the surf on each island, beach, and line of rocks, along the coast. Thus do I talk, and all my auditors grow wise, while they deem it pastime.

I recollect no happier portion of my life, than this, my calm old age. It is like the sunny and sheltered slope of a valley, where, late in the autumn, the grass is greener than in August, and intermixed with golden dandelions, that have not been seen till now, since the first warmth of the year. But with me, the verdure and the flowers are not frostbitten in the midst of winter. A playfulness has revisited my mind; a sympathy with the young and gay; an unpainful interest in the business of others; a light and wandering curiosity; arising, perhaps, from the sense that my toil on earth is ended, and the brief hour till bedtime may be spent in play. Still, I have fancied that there is a depth of feeling and reflection, under this superficial levity, peculiar to one who has lived long, and is soon to die.

Show me any thing that would make an infant smile, and you shall behold a gleam of mirth over the hoary ruin of my visage. I can spend a pleasant hour in the sun, watching the sports of the village children, on the edge of the surf; now they chase the retreating wave far down over the wet sand; now it steals softly up to kiss their naked feet; now it comes onward with threatening front, and roars after the laughing crew, as they scamper beyond its reach. Why should not an old man be merry too, when the great sea is at play with those little children? I delight, also, to follow in the wake of a pleasure party of young men and girls, strolling along the beach after an early supper at the Point. Here, with handkerchiefs at nose, they bend over a heap of eel grass, entangled in which is a dead skate, so oddly accoutred with two legs and a long tail, that they mistake him for a drowned animal. A few steps farther, the ladies scream, and the gentlemen make ready to protect them against a young shark of the dogfish kind, rolling with lifelike motion in the tide that has thrown him up. Next, they are smit with wonder at the black shells of a wagon load of live lobsters, packed in rockweed for the country market. And when they reach the fleet of dories, just hauled ashore after the day's fishing, how do I laugh in my sleeve, and sometimes roar outright, at the simplicity of these young folks and the sly humor of the fishermen! In winter, when our village is thrown into a bustle by the arrival of perhaps a score of country dealers, bargaining for frozen fish, to be transported hundreds of miles, and eaten fresh in Vermont or Canada, I am a pleased but idle spectator in the throng. For I launch my boat no more.

When the shore was solitary, I have found a pleasure that seemed even to exalt my mind, in observing the sports or contentions of two gulls, as they wheeled and hovered about each other, with hoarse screams, one moment flapping on the foam of the wave, and then soaring aloft, till their white bosoms melted into the upper sunshine. In the calm of the summer sunset, I drag my aged limbs, with a little ostentation of activity, because I am so old, up to the rocky brow of the hill. There I see the white sails of many a vessel, outward bound or homeward from afar, and the black trail of a vapor behind the eastern steamboat; there, too, is the sun, going down, but not in gloom, and there the illimitable ocean mingling with the sky, to remind me of Eternity.

But sweetest of all is the hour of cheerful musing and pleasant talk, that comes between the dusk and the lighted candle, by my glowing fireside. And never, even on the first Thanksgiving night, when Susan and I sat alone with our hopes, nor the second, when a stranger had been sent to gladden us, and be the visible image of our affection, did I feel such joy as now. All that belong to me are here; Death has taken none, nor Disease kept them away, nor Strife divided them from their parents or each other; with neither poverty nor riches to disturb them, nor the misery of desires beyond their lot, they have kept New England's festival round the patriarch's board. For I am a patriarch! Here I sit among my descendants, in my old arm chair and immemorial corner, while the firelight throws an appropriate glory round my venerable frame. Susan! My children! Something whispers me, that this happiest hour must be the final one, and that nothing remains but to bless you all, and depart with a treasure of recollected joys to Heaven. Will you meet me there? Alas! your figures grow indistinct, fading into pictures on the air, and now to fainter outlines, while the fire is glimmering on the walls of a familiar room, and shows the book that I flung down, and the sheet that I left half written, some fifty years ago. I lift my eyes to the looking glass, and perceive myself alone, unless those be the mermaid's features, retiring into the depths of the mirror, with a tender and melancholy smile.

Ah! one feels a chillness, not bodily, but about the heart, and, moreover, a foolish dread of looking behind him, after these pastimes. I can imagine precisely how a magician would sit down in gloom and terror, after dismissing the shadows that had personated dead or distant people, and stripping his cavern of the unreal splendor which had changed it to a palace. And now for a moral to my reverie. Shall it be, that, since fancy can create so bright a dream of happiness, it were better to dream on from youth to age, than to awake and strive doubtfully for something real! O, the slight tissue of a dream can no more preserve us from the stern reality of misfortune, than a robe of cobweb could repel the wintry blast. Be this the moral, then. In chaste and warm affections, humble wishes, and honest toil for some useful end, there is health for the mind, and quiet for the heart, the prospect of a happy life, and the fairest hope of Heaven.

THE AMBITIOUS GUEST.

ONE September night, a family had gathered round their hearth, and piled it high with the driftwood of mountain streams, the dry cones of the pine, and the splintered ruins of great trees, that had come crashing down the precipice. Up the chimney roared the fire, and brightened the room with its broad blaze. The faces of the father and mother had a sober gladness; the children laughed; the eldest daughter was the image of Happiness at seventeen; and the aged grandmother, who sat knitting in the warmest place, was the image of Happiness grown old. They had found the "herb, heart's ease," in the bleakest spot of all New England. This family were situated in the Notch of the White Hills, where the wind was sharp throughout the year, and pitilessly cold in the winter—giving their cottage all its fresh inclemency, before it descended on the valley of the Saco. They dwelt in a cold spot and a dangerous one; for a mountain towered above their heads, so steep, that the stones would often rumble down its sides, and startle them at midnight.

The daughter had just uttered some simple jest, that filled them all with mirth, when the wind came through the Notch and seemed to pause before their cottage— rattling the door, with a sound of wailing and lamentation, before it passed into the valley. For a moment, it saddened them, though there was nothing unusual in the tones. But the family were glad again, when they perceived that the latch was lifted by some traveller, whose footsteps had been unheard amid the dreary blast, which heralded his approach, and wailed as he was entering, and went moaning away from the door.

Though they dwelt in such a solitude, these people held daily converse with the world. The romantic pass of the Notch is a great artery, through which the life-blood of internal commerce is continually throbbing, between Maine, on one side, and the Green Mountains and the shores of the St. Lawrence on the other. The stage coach always drew up before the door of the cottage. The wayfarer, with no companion but his staff, paused here to exchange a word, that the sense of loneliness might not utterly overcome him, ere he could pass through the cleft of the mountain, or reach the first house in the valley. And here the teamster, on his way to Portland market, would put up for the night ; and, if a bachelor, might sit an hour beyond the usual bedtime, and steal a kiss from the mountain maid, at parting. It was one of those primitive taverns, where the traveller pays only for food and lodging, but meets with a homely kindness beyond all price. When the footsteps were heard, therefore, between the outer door and the inner one, the whole family rose up, grandmother, children, and all, as if about to welcome some one who belonged to them, and whose fate was linked with theirs.

The door was opened by a young man. His face at first wore the melancholy expression, almost despondency, of one who travels a wild and bleak road, at nightfall and alone, but soon brightened up, when he saw the kindly warmth of his reception. He felt his heart spring forward to meet them all, from the old woman, who wiped a chair with her apron, to the little child that held out its arms to him. One glance and smile placed the stranger on a footing of innocent familiarity with the eldest daughter.

"Ah, this fire is the right thing !" cried he; "especially when there is such a pleasant circle round it. I am quite benumbed ; for the Notch is just like the pipe of a great pair of bellows ; it has blown a terrible blast in my face, all the way from Bartlett."

"Then you are going towards Vermont?" said the master of the house, as he helped to take a light knapsack off the young man's shoulders.

"Yes ; to Burlington, and far enough beyond," replied he. "I meant to have been at Ethan Crawford's tonight ; but a pedestrian lingers along such a road as this. It is no matter ; for, when I saw this good fire, and all your cheerful faces, I felt as if you had kindled it on purpose for me, and were waiting my arrival. So I shall sit down among you, and make myself at home."

The frank-hearted stranger had just drawn his chair to the fire, when something like a heavy footstep was heard without, rushing down the steep side of the mountain, as with long and rapid strides, and taking such a leap, in passing the cottage, as to strike the opposite precipice. The family held their breath, because they knew the sound, and their guest held his, by instinct.

"The old mountain has thrown a stone at us, for fear we should forget him," said the landlord, recovering himself. "He sometimes nods his head, and threatens to come down ; but we are old neighbors, and agree together pretty well, upon the whole. Besides, we have a sure place of refuge, hard by, if he should be coming in good earnest."

Let us now suppose the stranger to have finished his supper of bear's meat ; and, by his natural felicity of manner, to have placed himself on a footing of kindness with the whole family, so that they talked as freely together, as if he belonged to their mountain brood. He was of a proud, yet gentle spirit—haughty and reserved among the rich and great ; but ever ready to stoop his head to the lowly cottage door, and be like a brother or son at the poor man's fireside. In the household of the Notch, he found warmth and simplicity of feeling, the pervading intelligence of New England, and a poetry of native growth, which they had gathered, when they little thought of it, from the mountain peaks and chasms, and at the very threshold of their romantic and dangerous abode. He had travelled far and alone ; his whole life, indeed, had been a solitary path ; for, with the lofty caution of his nature, he had kept himself apart from those who might otherwise have been his companions. The family, too, though so kind and hospitable, had that consciousness of unity among themselves, and separation from the world at large, which, in every domestic circle, should still keep a holy place, where no stranger may intrude. But, this evening, a prophetic sympathy impelled the refined and educated youth to pour out his heart before the simple mountaineers, and constrained them to answer him with the same free confidence. And thus it should have been. Is not the kindred of a common fate a closer tie than that of birth?

The secret of the young man's character was a high and abstracted ambition. He could have borne to live an undistinguished life, but not to be forgotten in the grave. Yearning desire had been transformed to hope ; and hope, long cherished, had become like certainty, that, obscurely as he journeyed now, a glory was to beam on all his pathway—though not, perhaps, while he was treading it. But, when posterity should gaze back into the gloom of what was now the present, they would trace the brightness of his footsteps, brightening as meaner glories faded, and confess, that a gifted one had passed from his cradle to his tomb, with none to recognize him.

"As yet," cried the stranger—his cheek glowing and

his eye flashing with enthusiasm—"as yet, I have done nothing. Were I to vanish from the earth to-morrow, none would know so much of me as you; that a nameless youth came up, at nightfall, from the valley of the Saco, and opened his heart to you in the evening, and passed through the Notch by sunrise, and was seen no more. Not a soul would ask—'Who was he?—Whither did the wanderer go?' But, I cannot die till I have achieved my destiny. Then, let Death come! I shall have built my monument!"

There was a continual flow of natural emotion, gushing forth amid abstracted reverie, which enabled the family to understand this young man's sentiments, though so foreign from their own. With quick sensibility of the ludicrous, he blushed at the ardor into which he had been betrayed.

"You laugh at me," said he, taking the eldest daughter's hand, and laughing himself. "You think my ambition as nonsensical as if I were to freeze myself to death on the top of Mount Washington, only that people might spy at me from the country round about. And truly, that would be a noble pedestal for a man's statue!"

"It is better to sit here by this fire," answered the girl, blushing, "and be comfortable aud contented, though nobody thinks about us."

"I suppose," said her father, after a fit of musing, "there is something natural in what the young man says; and if my mind had been turned that way, I might have felt just the same. It is strange, wife, how his talk has set my head running on things that are pretty certain never to come to pass."

"Perhaps they may," observed the wife. "Is the man thinking what he will do when he is a widower?"

"No, no!" cried he, repelling the idea with reproachful kindness. "When I think of your death, Esther, I think of mine, too. But I was wishing we had a good farm in Bartlett, or Bethlehem, or Littleton, or some other township round the White Mountains; but not where they could tumble on our heads. I should want to stand well with my neighbors, and be called Squire, and sent to General Court for a term or two; for a plain, honest man may do as much good there as a lawyer. And when I should be grown quite an old man, and you an old woman, so as not to be long apart, I might die happy enough in my bed, and leave you all crying around me. A slate gravestone would suit me as well as a marble one—with just my name and age, and a verse of a hymn, and something to let people know that I lived an honest man and died a Christian."

"There now!" exclaimed the stranger; "it is our nature to desire a monument, be it slate, or marble, or a pillar of granite, or a glorious memory in the universal heart of man."

"We're in a strange way to-night," said the wife with tears in her eyes. "They say it's a sign of something, when folks' minds go a wandering so. Hark to the children!"

They listened accordingly. The younger children had been put to bed in another room, but with an open door between, so that they could be heard talking busily among themselves. One and all seemed to have caught the infection from the fireside circle, and were outvying each other, in wild wishes, and childish projects of what they would do when they came to be men and women. At length, a little boy, instead of addressing his brothers and sisters, called out to his mother.

"I'll tell you what I wish, mother," cried he. "I want you and father and grandma'm, and all of us, and the stranger too, to start right away, and go and take a drink out of the basin of the Flume!"

Nobody could help laughing at the child's notion of

leaving a warm bed, and dragging them from a cheerful fire, to visit the basin of the Flume—a brook, which tumbles over the precipice, deep within the Notch. The boy had hardly spoken, when a wagon rattled along the road, and stopped a moment before the door. It appeared to contain two or three men, who were cheering their hearts with the rough chorus of a song, which resounded, in broken notes, between the cliffs, while the singers hesitated whether to continue their journey, or put up here for the night."

"Father," said the girl, "they are calling you by name."

But the good man doubted whether they had really called him, and was unwilling to show himself too solicitous of gain, by inviting people to patronize his house. He therefore did not hurry to the door; and the lash being soon applied, the travellers plunged into the Notch, still singing and laughing, though their music and mirth came back drearily from the heart of the mountain.

"There, mother!" cried the boy, again. "They'd have given us a ride to the Flume."

Again they laughed at the child's pertinacious fancy for a night ramble. But it happened, that a light cloud passed over the daughter's spirit; she looked gravely into the fire, and drew a breath that was almost a sigh. It forced its way, in spite of a little struggle to repress it. Then starting and blushing, she looked quickly round the circle, as if they had caught a glimpse into her bosom. The stranger asked what she had been thinking of.

"Nothing," answered she with a downcast smile. "Only I felt lonesome just then."

"O, I have always had a gift of feeling what is in other people's hearts," said he half seriously. "Shall I tell the secrets of yours? For I know what to think when a young girl shivers by a warm hearth, and complains of lonesomeness at her mother's side. Shall I put these feelings into words?"

" They would not be a girl's feelings any longer, if they could be put into words," replied the mountain nymph, laughing, but avoiding his eye.

All this was said apart. Perhaps a germ of love was springing in their hearts, so pure that it might blossom in Paradise, since it could not be matured on earth ; for women worship such gentle dignity as his ; and the proud, contemplative, yet kindly soul is oftenest captivated by simplicity like hers. But, while they spoke softly, and he was watching the happy sadness, the lightsome shadows, the shy yearnings of a maiden's nature, the wind, through the Notch, took a deeper and drearier sound. It seemed, as the fanciful stranger said, like the choral strain of the spirits of the blast, who in old Indian times had their dwelling among these mountains, and made their heights and recesses a sacred region. There was a wail, along the road, as if a funeral were passing. To chase away the gloom, the family threw pine branches on their fire, till the dry leaves crackled and the flame arose, discovering once again a scene of peace and humble happiness. The light hovered about them fondly, and caressed them all. There were the little faces of the children, peeping from their bed apart, and here the father's frame of strength, the mother's subdued and careful mien, the high-browed youth, the budding girl, and the good old grandam, still knitting in the warmest place. The aged woman looked up from her task, and with fingers ever busy, was the next to speak.

"Old folks have their notions," said she, "as well as young ones. You've been wishing and planning, and letting your heads run on one thing and another, till you've set my mind a wandering too. Now what should an old woman wish for, when she can go but a step or two before she comes to her grave? Children, it will haunt me night and day, till I tell you."

"What is it, mother?" cried the husband and wife at once.

Then the old woman, with an air of mystery, which drew the circle closer round the fire, informed them that she had provided her graveclothes some years before—a nice linen shroud, a cap with a muslin ruff, and every thing of a finer sort than she had worn since her wedding day. But, this evening, an old superstition had strangely recurred to her. It used to be said in her younger days, that if any thing were amiss with a corpse, if only the ruff were not smooth, or the cap did not set right, the corpse, in the coffin and beneath the clods, would strive to put up its cold hands and arrange it. The bare thought made her nervous.

"Don't talk so, grandmother!" said the girl, shuddering.

"Now,"—continued the old woman with singular earnestness, yet smiling strangely at her own folly,—"I want one of you, my children—when your mother is dressed, and in the coffin—I want one of you to hold a looking glass over my face. Who knows but I may take a glimpse at myself, and see whether all's right?"

"Old and young, we dream of graves and monuments," murmured the stranger youth. "I wonder how mariners feel when the ship is sinking, and they, unknown and undistinguished, are to be buried together in the ocean—that wide and nameless sepulchre?"

For a moment, the old woman's ghastly conception so engrossed the minds of her hearers, that a sound, abroad in the night, rising like the roar of a blast, had grown broad, deep, and terrible, before the fated group were conscious of it. The house, and all within it, trembled ; the foundations of the earth seemed to be shaken, as if this awful sound were the peal of the last trump. Young and old exchanged one wild glance, and remained an instant, pale, affrighted, without utterance, or power to move. Then the same shriek burst simultaneously from all their lips.

"The Slide ! The Slide !"

The simplest words must intimate, but not portray, the unutterable horror of the catastrophe. The victims rushed from their cottage, and sought refuge in what they deemed a safer spot—where, in contemplation of such an emergency, a sort of barrier had been reared. Alas ! they had quitted their security, and fled right into the pathway of destruction. Down came the whole side of the mountain in a cataract of ruin. Just before it reached the house, the stream broke into two branches— shivered not a window there, but overwhelmed the whole vicinity, blocked up the road, and annihilated every thing in its dreadful course. Long ere the thunder of that great Slide had ceased to roar among the mountains, the mortal agony had been endured, and the victims were at peace. Their bodies were never found.

The next morning, the light smoke was seen stealing from the cottage chimney up the mountain side. Within, the fire was yet smouldering on the hearth, and the chairs in a circle round it, as if the inhabitants had but gone forth to view the devastation of the Slide, and would shortly return to thank Heaven for their miraculous escape. All had left separate tokens, by which those, who had known the family, were made to shed a tear for each. Who has not heard their name ? The story has been told far and wide, and will forever be a legend of these mountains. Poets have sung their fate.

There were circumstances which led some to suppose

that a stranger had been received into the cottage on this awful night, and had shared the catastrophe of all its inmates. Others denied that there were sufficient grounds for such a conjecture. Woe, for the high-souled youth, with his dream of Earthly Immortality! His name and person utterly unknown; his history, his way of life, his plans, a mystery never to be solved; his death and his existence, equally a doubt! Whose was the agony of that death moment?

THE SISTER YEARS.

LAST night, between eleven and twelve o'clock, when the Old Year was leaving her final footprints on the borders of Time's empire, she found herself in possession of a few spare moments, and sat down—of all places in the world—on the steps of our new City Hall.   The wintry moonlight showed that she looked weary of body, and sad of heart, like many another wayfarer of earth.   Her garments, having been exposed to much foul weather and rough usage, were in very ill condition ; and as the hurry of her journey had never before allowed her to take an instant's rest, her shoes were so worn as to be scarcely worth the mending.   But, after trudging only a little distance farther, this poor Old Year was destined to enjoy a long, long sleep.   I forgot to mention, that when she seated herself on the steps, she deposited by her side a very capacious bandbox, in which, as is the custom among travellers of her sex, she carried a great deal of valuable property.   Besides this luggage, there was a folio book under her arm, very much resembling the annual volume of a newspaper.   Placing this volume across her knees, and resting her elbows upon it, with her forehead in her hands, the weary, bedraggled, world-worn Old Year heaved a heavy sigh, and appeared to be taking no very pleasant retrospect of her past existence.

While she thus awaited the midnight knell, that was to summon her to the innumerable sisterhood of departed Years, there came a young maiden treading lightsomely on tiptoe along the street from the direction of the Railroad Depôt. She was evidently a stranger, and perhaps had come to town by the evening train of cars. There was a smiling cheerfulness in this fair maiden's face, which bespoke her fully confident of a kind reception from the multitude of people, with whom she was soon to form acquaintance. Her dress was rather too airy for the season, and was bedizened with fluttering ribbons and other vanities, which were likely soon to be rent away by the fierce storms, or to fade in the hot sunshine, amid which she was to pursue her changeful course. But still she was a wonderfully pleasant looking figure, and had so much promise and such an indescribable hopefulness in her aspect, that hardly any body could meet her without anticipating some very desirable thing— the consummation of some long-sought good—from her kind offices. A few dismal characters there may be, here and there about the world, who have so often been trifled with by young maidens as promising as she, that they have now ceased to pin any faith upon the skirts of the New Year. But, for my own part, I have great faith in her ; and should I live to see fifty more such, still, from each of those successive sisters, I shall reckon upon receiving something that will be worth living for.

The New Year—for this young maiden was no less a personage—carried all her goods and chattels in a basket of no great size or weight, which hung upon her arm. She greeted the disconsolate Old Year with great affection, and sat down beside her on the steps of the City Hall, waiting for the signal to begin her rambles through the world. The two were own sisters, being both granddaughters of Time ; and though one looked so much older than the other, it was rather owing to hardships and trouble than to age, since there was but a twelvemonth's difference between them.

"Well, my dear sister," said the New Year, after the first salutations, "you look almost tired to death.

What have you been about during your sojourn in this part of Infinite Space?"

"O, I have it all recorded here in my Book of Chronicles," answered the Old Year, in a heavy tone. "There is nothing that would amuse you; and you will soon get sufficient knowledge of such matters from your own personal experience.   It is but tiresome reading."

Nevertheless, she turned over the leaves of the folio, and glanced at them by the light of the moon, feeling an irresistible spell of interest in her own biography, although its incidents were remembered without plea-sure.   The volume, though she termed it her Book of Chronicles, seemed to be neither more nor less than the Salem Gazette for 1838; in the accuracy of which journal this sagacious Old Year had so much confidence, that she deemed it needless to record her history with her own pen.

"What have you been doing in the political way?" asked the New Year.

"Why, my course here in the United States," said the Old Year—"though perhaps I ought to blush at the confession—my political course, I must acknowledge, has been rather vacillatory, sometimes inclining towards the Whigs—then causing the Administration party to shout for triumph—and now again uplifting what seemed the almost prostrate banner of the Opposition; so that historians will hardly know what to make of me in this respect.   But the Loco Focos—"

"I do not like these party nicknames," interrupted her sister, who seemed remarkably touchy about some points.   "Perhaps we shall part in better humor, if we avoid any political discussion."

"With all my heart," replied the Old Year, who had already been tormented half to death with squabbles of this kind.   "I care not if the names of Whig or Tory, with their interminable brawls about Banks and the Sub-

Treasury, Abolition, **Texas**, the Florida War, **and** a million of other topics—which you will learn soon **enough** for your own comfort—**I care** not, I say, if no whisper of these matters **ever reaches my ears again.** Yet **they** have occupied **so** large a share of my **attention,** that I scarcely know what else to tell you. There has indeed been a curious sort of war on **the Canada border,** where blood has streamed in the **names of Liberty and Pat-** riotism; but it must **remain for some future, perhaps far** distant Year, to tell whether or **no those holy names** have been rightfully invoked. Nothing **so much depresses** me, in my view of mortal affairs, **as to see high energies** wasted, **and** human **life and** happiness **thrown** away, for ends that appear oftentimes unwise, **and** still oftener remain unaccomplished. But the **wisest** people and the **best keep a steadfast faith that the progress of** Mankind is onward and upward, and **that the toil and anguish of** the path serve to wear away the **imperfections of the** Immortal Pilgrim, and will **be felt no more, when they** have done their office."

" Perhaps," cried the hopeful New Year—"perhaps I shall see that happy day !"

" I doubt whether it **be so close at hand," answered** the Old Year, gravely smiling. " **You will soon grow** weary of looking for that **blessed consummation, and** will turn for amusement **(as has frequently been my** own **practice) to the affairs of some sober little city,** like this of Salem. Here we sit on the steps of the new City Hall, which **has been completed under my administra-** tion ; **and it would make** you laugh **to see how the game** of politics, **of which the Capitol at Washington is the great chessboard, is here played in miniature.** Burning Ambition finds its fuel **here ;** here Patriotism speaks boldly in the **people's behalf, and virtuous Economy demands** retrenchment in the **emolument of a lamp-** lighter; here the Aldermen range their **senatorial dignity** around the Mayor's chair of state, and the Common Council feel that they have liberty in charge. In short, human weakness and strength, passion and policy, Man's tendencies, his aims and modes of pursuing them, his individual character, and his character in the mass, may be studied almost as well here as on the theatre of nations; and with this great advantage, that, be the lesson ever so disastrous, its Liliputian scope still makes the beholder smile."

"Have you done much for the improvement of the City?" asked the New Year. "Judging from what little I have seen, it appears to be ancient and timeworn."

"I have opened the Railroad," said the elder Year, "and half a dozen times a day, you will hear the bell (which once summoned the monks of a Spanish Convent to their devotions) announcing the arrival or departure of the cars. Old Salem now wears a much livelier expression than when I first beheld her. Strangers rumble down from Boston by hundreds at a time. New faces throng in Essex Street. Railroad hacks and omnibuses rattle over the pavements. There is a perceptible increase of oyster shops, and other establishments for the accommodation of a transitory diurnal multitude. But a more important change awaits the venerable town. An immense accumulation of musty prejudices will be carried off by the free circulation of society. A peculiarity of character, of which the inhabitants themselves are hardly sensible, will be rubbed down and worn away by the attrition of foreign substances. Much of the result will be good; there will likewise be a few things not so good. Whether for better or worse, there will be a probable diminution of the moral influence of wealth, and the sway of an aristocratic class, which, from an era far beyond my memory, has held firmer dominion here than in any other New England town."

The Old Year having talked away nearly all of her little remaining breath, now closed her Book of Chronicles, and was about to take her departure. But her sister detained her a while longer, by inquiring the contents of the huge bandbox, which she was so painfully lugging along with her.

"These are merely a few trifles," replied the Old Year, "which I have picked up in my rambles, and am going to deposit in the receptacle of things past and forgotten. We sisterhood of Years never carry any thing really valuable out of the world with us. Here are patterns of most of the fashions which I brought into vogue, and which have already lived out their allotted term. You will supply their place with others equally ephemeral. Here, put up in little China pots, like rouge, is a considerable lot of beautiful women's bloom, which the disconsolate fair ones owe me a bitter grudge for stealing. I have likewise a quantity of men's dark hair, instead of which I have left gray locks, or none at all. The tears of widows and other afflicted mortals, who have received comfort during the last twelve months, are preserved in some dozens of essence bottles, well corked and sealed. I have several bundles of love letters, eloquently breathing an eternity of burning passion, which grew cold and perished, almost before the ink was dry. Moreover, here is an assortment of many thousand broken promises, and other broken ware, all very light and packed into little space. The heaviest articles in my possession are a large parcel of disappointed hopes, which, a little while ago, were buoyant enough to have inflated Mr. Lauriat's balloon."

"I have a fine lot of hopes here in my basket," remarked the New Year. "They are a sweet-smelling flower—a species of rose."

"They soon lose their perfume," replied the sombre

Old Year. "What else have you brought to insure a welcome from the discontented race of mortals?"

"Why, to say the truth, little or nothing else," said her sister, with a smile — "save a few new Annuals and Almanacs, and some New Year's gifts for the children. But I heartily wish well to poor mortals, and mean to do all I can for their improvement and happiness."

"It is a good resolution," rejoined the Old Year; "and by the way, I have a plentiful assortment of good resolutions, which have now grown so stale and musty, that I am ashamed to carry them any farther. Only for fear that the City authorities would send Constable Mansfield, with a warrant after me, I should toss them into the street at once. Many other matters go to make up the contents of my bandbox; but the whole lot would not fetch a single bid, even at an auction of worn-out furniture; and as they are worth nothing either to you or any body else, I need not trouble you with a longer catalogue."

"And must I also pick up such worthless luggage in my travels?" asked the New Year.

"Most certainly — and well, if you have no heavier load to bear," replied the other. "And now, my dear sister, I must bid you farewell, earnestly advising and exhorting you to expect no gratitude nor good will from this peevish, unreasonable, inconsiderate, ill-intending, and worse-behaving world. However warmly its inhabitants may seem to welcome you, yet, do what you may, and lavish on them what means of happiness you please, they will still be complaining, still craving what it is not in your power to give, still looking forward to some other Year for the accomplishment of projects which ought never to have been formed, and which, if successful, would only provide new occasions of discontent. If these ridiculous people ever see any thing tolerable in you, it will be after you are gone forever."

"But I," cried the fresh-hearted New Year, "I shall try to leave men wiser than I find them. I will offer them freely whatever good gifts Providence permits me to distribute, and will tell them to be thankful for what they have, and humbly hopeful for more ; and surely, if they are not absolute fools, they will condescend to be happy, and will allow me to be a happy Year. For my happiness must depend on them."

"Alas for you, then, my poor sister !" said the Old Year, sighing, as she uplifted her burden. "We grand-children of Time are born to trouble. Happiness, they say, dwells in the mansions of Eternity ; but we can only lead mortals thither, step by step, with reluctant murmurings, and ourselves must perish on the threshold. But hark ! my task is done."

The clock in the tall steeple of Dr. Emerson's church struck twelve ; there was a response from Dr. Flint's, in the opposite quarter of the city ; and while the strokes were yet dropping into the air, the Old Year either flitted or faded away—and not the wisdom and might of Angels, to say nothing of the remorseful yearnings of the millions who had used her ill, could have prevailed with that departed Year to return one step. But she, in the company of Time and all her kindred, must hereafter hold a reckoning with Mankind. So shall it be, likewise, with the maidenly New Year, who, as the clock ceased to strike, arose from the steps of the City Hall, and set out rather timorously on her earthly course.

"A happy New Year !" cried a watchman, eyeing her figure very questionably, but without the least suspicion that he was addressing the New Year in person.

"Thank you kindly !" said the New Year ; and she gave the watchman one of the roses of hope from her basket. "May this flower keep a sweet smell, long after I have bidden you good by."

Then she stepped on more briskly through the silent

streets ; and such as were awake at the moment, heard her footfall, and said—"The New Year is come !" Wherever there was a knot of midnight roisterers, they quaffed her health. She sighed, however, to perceive that the air was tainted—as the atmosphere of this world must continually be—with the dying breaths of mortals who had lingered just long enough for her to bury them. But there were millions left alive, to rejoice at her coming ; and so she pursued her way with confidence, strewing emblematic flowers on the doorstep of almost every dwelling, which some persons will gather up and wear in their bosoms, and others will trample under foot. The Carrier Boy can only say further, that, early this morning, she filled his basket with New Year's addresses, assuring him that the whole City, with our new Mayor, and the Aldermen and Common Council at its head, would make a general rush to secure copies. Kind Patrons, will not you redeem the pledge of the NEW YEAR?

THERE is snow in yonder cold gray sky of the morning!
—and, through the partially frosted window panes, I
love to watch the gradual beginning of the storm. A
few feathery flakes are scattered widely through the air,
and hover downward with uncertain flight, now almost
alighting on the earth, now whirled again aloft into
remote regions of the atmosphere. These are not the
big flakes, heavy with moisture, which melt as they
touch the ground, and are portentous of a soaking rain.
It is to be, in good earnest, a wintry storm. The two or
three people, visible on the side walk, have an aspect of
endurance, a blue-nosed, frosty fortitude, which is evidently assumed in anticipation of a comfortless and
blustering day. By nightfall, or at least before the sun
sheds another glimmering smile upon us, the street and
our little garden will be heaped with mountain snow
drifts. The soil, already frozen for weeks past, is prepared to sustain whatever burden may be laid upon it;
and, to a northern eye, the landscape will lose its melancholy bleakness and acquire a beauty of its own, when
Mother Earth, like her children, shall have put on the
fleecy garb of her winter's wear. The cloud spirits are
slowly weaving her white mantle. As yet, indeed, there
is barely a rime like hoarfrost over the brown surface of
the street; the withered green of the grass plat is still
discernible; and the slated roofs of the houses do but
begin to look gray instead of black. All the snow that
has yet fallen within the circumference of my view, were

it heaped up together, would hardly equal the hillock of a grave. Thus gradually, by silent and stealthy influences, are great changes wrought. These little snow particles, which the storm spirit flings by handfuls through the air, will bury the great earth under their accumulated mass, nor permit her to behold her sister sky again for dreary months. We, likewise, shall lose sight of our mother's familiar visage, and must content ourselves with looking heavenward the oftener.

Now, leaving the storm to do his appointed office, let us sit down, pen in hand, by our fireside. Gloomy as it may seem, there is an influence productive of cheerfulness, and favorable to imaginative thought, in the atmosphere of a snowy day. The native of a southern clime may woo the muse beneath the heavy shade of summer foliage, reclining on banks of turf, while the sound of singing birds and warbling rivulets chimes in with the music of his soul. In our brief summer, I do not think, but only exist in the vague enjoyment of a dream. My hour of inspiration—if that hour ever comes —is when the green log hisses upon the hearth, and the bright flame, brighter for the gloom of the chamber, rustles high up the chimney, and the coals drop tinkling down among the growing heaps of ashes. When the casement rattles in the gust, and the snow flakes or the sleety raindrops pelt hard against the window panes, then I spread out my sheet of paper, with the certainty that thoughts and fancies will gleam forth upon it, like stars at twilight, or like violets in May—perhaps to fade so soon. However transitory their glow, they at least shine amid the darksome shadow which the clouds of the outward sky fling through the room. Blessed, therefore, and reverently welcomed by me, her true-born son, be New England's winter, which makes us one and all the nurslings of the storm, and sings a familiar lullaby even in the wildest shriek of the December blast. Now look

we forth again, and see how much of his task the storm
spirit has done.

Slow and sure ! He has the day, perchance the week,
before him, and may take his own time to accomplish
Nature's burial in snow. A smooth mantle is scarcely
yet thrown over the withered grass plat, and the dry
stalks of annuals still thrust themselves through the
white surface in all parts of the garden. The leafless
rose bushes stand shivering in a shallow snow drift,
looking, poor things ! as disconsolate as if they possessed
a human consciousness of the dreary scene. This is a
sad time for the shrubs that do not perish with the
summer ; they neither live nor die ; what they retain of
life seems but the chilling sense of death. Very sad are
the flower shrubs in midwinter ! The roofs of the houses
are now all white, save where the eddying wind has kept
them bare at the bleak corners. To discern the real
intensity of the storm, we must fix upon some distant
object,—as yonder spire,—and observe how the riotous
gust fights with the descending snow throughout the
intervening space. Sometimes the entire prospect is
obscured, then, again, we have a distinct, but transient
glimpse of the tall steeple, like a giant's ghost ; and now
the dense wreaths sweep between, as if demons were
flinging snow drifts at each other in mid air. Look
next into the street, where we have an amusing parallel
to the combat of those fancied demons in the upper
regions. It is a snow battle of schoolboys. What a
pretty satire on war and military glory might be written,
in the form of a child's story, by describing the snowball
fights of two rival schools, the alternate defeats and
victories of each, and the final triumph of one party, or
perhaps of neither ! What pitched battles, worthy to be
chanted in Homeric strains ! What storming of for-
tresses, built all of massive snow blocks ! What feats of
individual prowess, and embodied onsets of martial

8   12

enthusiasm! And when some well-contested and deci-
sive victory had put a period to the war, both armies
should unite to build a lofty monument of snow upon the
battle field, and crown it with the victor's statue, hewn of
the same frozen marble. In a few days or weeks thereafter, the passer-by would observe a shapeless mound
upon the level common ; and, unmindful of the famous
victory, would ask—"How came it there? Who reared
it? And what means it?" The shattered pedestal of
many a battle monument has provoked these questions,
when none could answer.

Turn we again to the fireside, and sit musing there,
lending our ears to the wind, till perhaps it shall seem
like an articulate voice, and dictate wild and airy matter
for the pen. Would it might inspire me to sketch out
the personification of a New England winter! And
that idea, if I can seize the snow-wreathed figures that
flit before my fancy, shall be the theme of the next
page.

How does Winter herald his approach? By the
shrieking blast of latter autumn, which is Nature's cry of
lamentation, as the destroyer rushes among the shivering
groves where she has lingered, and scatters the sear
leaves upon the tempest. When that cry is heard, the
people wrap themselves in cloaks, and shake their heads
disconsolately, saying—"Winter is at hand!" Then the
axe of the woodcutter echoes sharp and diligently in the
forest,—then the coal merchants rejoice, because each
shriek of Nature in her agony adds something to the
price of coal per ton—then the peat smoke spreads its
aromatic fragrance through the atmosphere. A few days
more ; and at eventide, the children look out of the window, and dimly perceive the flaunting of a snowy mantle
in the air. It is stern Winter's vesture. They crowd
around the hearth, and cling to their mother's gown, or
press between their father's knees, affrighted by the

hollow roaring voice, that bellows adown the wide flue of the chimney. It is the voice of Winter; and when parents and children hear it, they shudder and exclaim —"Winter is come! Cold Winter has begun his reign already!" Now, throughout New England, each hearth becomes an altar, sending up the smoke of a continued sacrifice to the immitigable deity who tyrannizes over forest, country side, and town. Wrapped in his white mantle, his staff a huge icicle, his beard and hair a wind-tossed snow drift, he travels over the land, in the midst of the northern blast; and woe to the homeless wanderer whom he finds upon his path! There he lies stark and stiff, a human shape of ice, on the spot where Winter overtook him. On strides the tyrant over the rushing rivers and broad lakes, which turn to rock beneath his footsteps. His dreary empire is established; all around stretches the desolation of the Pole. Yet not ungrateful be his New England children—for Winter is our sire, though a stern and rough one—not ungrateful even for the severities which have nourished our unyielding strength of character. And let us thank him, too, for the sleigh rides, cheered by the music of merry bells—for the crackling and rustling hearth, when the ruddy firelight gleams on hardy Manhood and the blooming cheek of Woman—for all the home enjoyments, and the kindred virtues, which flourish in a frozen soil. Not that we grieve, when, after some seven months of storm and bitter frost, Spring, in the guise of a flower-crowned virgin, is seen driving away the hoary despot, pelting him with violets by the handful, and strewing green grass on the path behind him. Often, ere he will give up his empire, old Winter rushes fiercely back, and hurls a snow drift at the shrinking form of Spring; yet, step by step, he is compelled to retreat north-ward, and spends the summer months within the Arctic circle.

Such fantasies, intermixed among graver toils of mind, have made the winter's day pass pleasantly. Meanwhile, the storm has raged without abatement, and now, as the brief afternoon declines, is tossing denser volumes to and fro about the atmosphere. On the window sill, there is a layer of snow, reaching half way up the lowest pane of glass. The garden is one unbroken bed. Along the street are two or three spots of uncovered earth, where the gust has whirled away the snow, heaping it elsewhere to the fence tops, or piling huge banks against the doors of houses. A solitary passenger is seen, now striding mid-leg deep across a drift, now scudding over the bare ground, while his cloak is swollen with the wind. And now the jingling of bells, a sluggish sound, responsive to the horse's toilsome progress through the unbroken drifts, announces the passage of a sleigh, with a boy clinging behind, and ducking his head to escape detection by the driver. Next comes a sledge, laden with wood for some unthrifty housekeeper, whom winter has surprised at a cold hearth. But what dismal equipage now struggles along the uneven street? A sable hearse, bestrewn with snow, is bearing a dead man through the storm to his frozen bed. O, how dreary is a burial in winter, when the bosom of Mother Earth has no warmth for her poor child!

Evening—the early eve of December—begins to spread its deepening veil over the comfortless scene; the fire-light gradually brightens, and throws my flickering shadow upon the walls and ceiling of the chamber; but still the storm rages and rattles against the windows. Alas! I shiver, and think it time to be disconsolate. But, taking a farewell glance at dead nature in her shroud, I perceive a flock of snow birds, skimming lightsomely through the tempest, and flitting from drift to drift, as sportively as swallows in the delightful prime of summer. Whence come they? Where do they build their nests and seek their food? Why, having airy wings, do they not follow summer around the earth, instead of making themselves the playmates of the storm, and fluttering on the dreary verge of the winter's eve? I know not whence they come, nor why : yet my spirit has been cheered by that wandering flock of snow birds.

RAMBLING on foot in the spring of my life and the summer of the year, I came one afternoon to a point which gave me the choice of three directions. Straight before me, the main road extended its dusty length to Boston; on the left a branch went towards the sea, and would have lengthened my journey a trifle of twenty or thirty miles; while, by the right-hand path, I might have gone over hills and lakes to Canada, visiting in my way the celebrated town of Stamford. On a level spot of grass, at the foot of the guide post, appeared an object, which, though locomotive on a different principle, reminded me of Gulliver's portable mansion among the Brobdignags. It was a huge covered wagon, or, more properly, a small house on wheels, with a door on one side and a window shaded by green blinds on the other. Two horses munching provender out of the baskets which muzzled them, were fastened near the vehicle; a delectable sound of music proceeded from the interior; and I immediately conjectured that this was some itinerant show, halting at the confluence of the roads to intercept such idle travellers as myself. A shower had long been climbing up the western sky, and now hung so blackly over my onward path that it was a point of wisdom to seek shelter here.

"Halloo! Who stands guard here? Is the door-keeper asleep?" cried I, approaching a ladder of two or three steps which was let down from the wagon.

The music ceased at my summons, and there appeared

at the door, not the sort of figure that I had mentally assigned to the wandering showman, but a most respectable old personage, whom I was sorry to have addressed in so free a style. He wore a snuff-colored coat and smallclothes with white top boots, and exhibited the mild dignity of aspect and manner which may often be noticed in aged schoolmasters, and sometimes in deacons, selectmen, or other potentates of that kind. A small piece of silver was my passport within his premises, where I found only one other person, hereafter to be described.

" This is a dull day for business," said the old gentleman, as he ushered me in ! " but I merely tarry here to refresh the cattle, being bound for the camp meeting at Stamford."

Perhaps the moveable scene of this narrative is still peregrinating New England, and may enable the reader to test the accuracy of my description. The spectacle— for I will not use the unworthy term of puppet show— consisted of a multitude of little people assembled on a miniature stage. Among them were artisans of every kind, in the attitudes of their toil, and a group of fair ladies and gay gentlemen standing ready for the 'dance ; a company of foot soldiers formed a line across the stage, looking stern, grim, and terrible enough, to make it a pleasant consideration that they were but three inches high ; and conspicuous above the whole was seen a Merry Andrew, in the pointed cap and motley coat of his profession. All the inhabitants of this mimic world were motionless, like the figures in a picture, or like that people who one moment were alive in the midst of their business and delights, and the next were transformed to statues, preserving an eternal semblance of labor that was ended, and pleasure that could be felt no more. Anon, however, the old gentleman turned the handle of a barrel organ, the first note of which produced a most enlivening effect upon the figures, and awoke them all to

their proper occupations and amusements.   By the selfsame impulse the tailor plied his needle, the blacksmith's
hammer descended upon the anvil, and the dancers
whirled away on feathery tiptoes ; the company of
soldiers broke into platoons, retreated from the stage,
and were succeeded by a troop of horse, who came
prancing onward with such 'a sound of trumpets and
trampling of hoofs, as might have startled Don Quixote
himself; while an old toper, of inveterate ill habits, uplifted his black bottle and took off a hearty swig.
Meantime the Merry Andrew began to caper and turn
somersets, shaking his sides, nodding his head, and
winking his eyes in as lifelike a manner as if he were
ridiculing the nonsense of all human affairs, and making
fun of the whole multitude beneath him.   At length the
old magician (for I compared the showman to Prospero,
entertaining his guests with a mask of shadows) paused
that I might give utterance to my wonder.

"What an admirable piece of work is this!" exclaimed I, lifting up my hands in astonishment.

Indeed, I liked the spectacle, and was tickled with the
old man's gravity as he presided at it, for I had none of
that foolish wisdom which proves every occupation that
is not useful in this world of vanities.   If there be a
faculty which I possess more perfectly than most men, it
is that of throwing myself mentally into situations foreign
to my own, and detecting, with a cheerful eye, the
desirable circumstances of each.   I could have envied
the life of this gray-headed showman, spent as it had
been in a course of safe and pleasurable adventure, in
driving his huge vehicle sometimes through the sands of
Cape Cod, and sometimes over the rough forest roads
of the north and east, and halting now on the green
before a village meeting house, and now in a paved
square of the metropolis.   How often must his heart
have been gladdened by the delight of children, as they

viewed these animated figures ! or his pride indulged, by haranguing learnedly to grown men on the mechanical powers which produced such wonderful effects ! or his gallantry brought into play (for this is an attribute which such grave men do not lack) by the visits of pretty maidens ! And then with how fresh a feeling must he return, at intervals, to his own peculiar home !

"I would I were assured of as happy a life as his," thought I.

Though the showman's wagon might have accommodated fifteen or twenty spectators, it now contained only himself and me, and a third person at whom I threw a glance on entering. He was a neat and trim young man of two or three and twenty ; his drab hat, and green frock coat with velvet collar, were smart, though no longer new ; while a pair of green spectacles, that seemed needless to his brisk little eyes, gave him something of a scholar-like and literary air. After allowing me a sufficient time to inspect the puppets, he advanced with a bow, and drew my attention to some books in a corner of the wagon. These he forthwith began to extol, with an amazing volubility of well-sounding words, and an ingenuity of praise that won him my heart, as being myself one of the most merciful of critics. Indeed his stock required some considerable powers of commendation in the salesman ; there were several ancient friends of mine, the novels of those happy days when my affections wavered between the Scottish Chiefs and Thomas Thumb ; besides a few of later date, whose merits had not been acknowledged by the public. I was glad to find that dear little venerable volume, the New England Primer, looking as antique as ever, though in its thousandth new edition ; a bundle of superannuated gilt picture books made such a child of me, that, partly for the glittering covers, and partly for the fairy tales within, I bought the whole ; and an assortment of ballads

and popular theatrical songs drew largely on my purse.
To balance these expenditures, I meddled neither with
sermons, nor science, nor morality, though volumes of
each were there ; nor with a Life of Franklin in the
coarsest of paper, but so showily bound that it was
emblematical of the Doctor himself, in the court dress
which he refused to wear at Paris ; nor with Webster's
Spelling Book, nor some of Byron's minor poems, nor
half-a-dozen little Testaments at twenty-five cents each.

Thus far the collection might have been swept from
some great bookstore, or picked up at an evening
auction room ; but there was one small blue-covered
pamphlet, which the pedler handed me with so peculiar
an air, that I purchased it immediately at his own price ;
and then, for the first time, the thought struck me, that I
had spoken face to face with the veritable author of a
printed book.   The literary man now evinced a great
kindness for me, and I ventured to inquire which way
he was travelling.

"O," said he, "I keep company with this old gentleman here, and we are moving now towards the camp
meeting at Stamford."

He then explained to me, that for the present season
he had rented a corner of the wagon as a bookstore,
which, as he wittily observed, was a true Circulating
Library, since there were few parts of the country where
it had not gone its rounds. I approved of the plan
exceedingly, and began to sum up within my mind the
many uncommon felicities in the life of a book pedler,
especially when his character resembled that of the individual before me.   At a high rate was to be reckoned
the daily and hourly enjoyment of such interviews as the
present, in which he seized upon the admiration of a
passing stranger, and made him aware that a man of
literary taste, and even of literary achievement, was
travelling the country in a showman's wagon.   A more

valuable, yet not infrequent triumph, might be won in his conversations with some elderly clergyman, long vegetating in a rocky, woody, watery back settlement of New England, who, as he recruited his library from the pedler's stock of sermons, would exhort him to seek a college education and become the first scholar in his class. Sweeter and prouder yet would be his sensations, when, talking poetry while he sold spelling books, he should charm the mind, and haply touch the heart of a fair country schoolmistress, herself an unhonored poetess, a wearer of blue stockings which none but himself took pains to look at. But the scene of his completest glory would be when the wagon had halted for the night, and his stock of books was transferred to some crowded bar room. Then would he recommend to the multifarious company, whether traveller from the city, or teamster from the hills, or neighboring squire, or the landlord himself, or his loutish hostler, works suited to each particular taste and capacity; proving, all the while, by acute criticism and profound remark, that the lore in his books was even exceeded by that in his brain.

Thus happily would he traverse the land; sometimes a herald before the March of Mind; sometimes walking arm in arm with awful Literature; and reaping every where a harvest of real and sensible popularity, which the secluded bookworms, by whose toil he lived, could never hope for.

"If ever I meddle with literature," thought I, fixing myself in adamantine resolution, "it shall be as a travelling bookseller."

Though it was still mid afternoon, the air had now grown dark about us, and a few drops of rain came down upon the roof of our vehicle, pattering like the feet of birds that had flown thither to rest. A sound of pleasant voices made us listen, and there soon appeared half way up the ladder the pretty person of a

young damsel, whose rosy face was so cheerful, that
even amid the gloomy light it seemed as if the sunbeams
were peeping under her bonnet. We next saw the dark
and handsome features of a young man, who, with easier
gallantry than might have been expected in the heart of
Yankee land, was assisting her into the wagon.   It
became immediately evident to us, when the two
strangers stood within the door, that they were of a
profession kindred to those of my companions ; and I
was delighted with the more than hospitable, the even
paternal kindness, of the old showman's manner, as he
welcomed them ; while the man of literature hastened to
lead the merry-eyed girl to a seat on the long bench.

"You are housed but just in time, my young friends,"
said the master of the wagon. "The sky would have
been down upon you within five minutes."

The young man's reply marked him as a foreigner,
not by any variation from the idiom and accent of good
English, but because he spoke with more caution and
accuracy, than if perfectly familiar with the language.

"We knew that a shower was hanging over us," said
he, "and consulted whether it were best to enter the
house on the top of yonder hill, but seeing your wagon
in the road—"

"We agreed to come hither," interrupted the girl, with
a smile, "because we should be more at home in a
wandering house like this."

I, meanwhile, with many a wild and undetermined
fantasy, was narrowly inspecting these two doves that
had flown into our ark. The young man, tall, agile, and
athletic, wore a mass of black shining curls clustering
round a dark and vivacious countenance, which, if it had
not greater expression, was at least more active, and
attracted readier notice, than the quiet faces of our
countrymen. At his first appearance, he had been laden
with a great mahogany box, of about two feet square, but

very light in proportion to its size, which he had immediately unstrapped from his shoulders and deposited on the floor of the wagon.

The girl had nearly as fair a complexion as our own beauties, and a brighter one than most of them; the lightness of her figure, which seemed calculated to traverse the whole world without weariness, suited well with the glowing cheerfulness of her face; and her gay attire, combining the rainbow hues of crimson, green, and a deep orange, was as proper to her lightsome aspect as if she had been born in it. This gay stranger was appropriately burdened with that mirth inspiring instrument, the fiddle, which her companion took from her hands, and shortly began the process of tuning. Neither of us — the previous company of the wagon — needed to inquire their trade; for this could be no mystery to frequenters of brigade musters, ordinations, cattle shows, commencements, and other festal meetings in our sober land : and there is a dear friend of mine, who will smile when this page recalls to his memory a chivalrous deed performed by us, in rescuing the showbox of such a couple from a mob of great double-fisted countrymen.

"Come," said I to the damsel of gay attire, "shall we visit all the wonders of the world together?"

She understood the metaphor at once; though indeed it would not much have troubled me, if she had assented to the literal meaning of my words. The mahogany box was placed in a proper position, and I peeped in through its small round magnifying window, while the girl sat by my side, and gave short descriptive sketches, as one after another the pictures were unfolded to my view. We visited together, at least our imaginations did, full many a famous city, in the streets of which I had long yearned to tread; once, I remember, we were in the harbor of Barcelona, gazing townwards; next, she bore me through the air to Sicily, and bade me look up at blazing Ætna;

then we took wing to Venice, and sat in a gondola
beneath the arch of the Rialto; and anon she sat me
down among the thronged spectators at the coronation
of Napoleon. But there was one scene, its locality she
could not tell, which charmed my attention longer than
all those gorgeous palaces and churches, because the
fancy haunted me, that I myself, the preceding summer,
had beheld just such a humble meeting house, in just
such a pine-surrounded nook, among our own green
mountains. All these pictures were tolerably executed,
though far inferior to the girl's touches of description;
nor was it easy to comprehend, how in so few sentences,
and these, as I supposed, in a language foreign to her,
she contrived to present an airy copy of each varied
scene. When we had travelled through the vast extent
of the mahogany box, I looked into my guide's face.

"Where are you going, my pretty maid?" inquired I,
in the words of an old song.

"Ah," said the gay damsel, "you might as well ask
where the summer wind is going. We are wanderers
here, and there, and every where. Wherever there is
mirth, our merry hearts are drawn to it. To-day, indeed
the people have told us of a great frolic and festival in
these parts; so perhaps we may be needed at what you
call the camp meeting at Stamford."

Then in my happy youth, and while her pleasant
voice yet sounded in my ears, I sighed; for none but
myself, I thought, should have been her companion in
a life which seemed to realize my own wild fancies,
cherished all through visionary boyhood to that hour.
To these two strangers, the world was in its golden age,
not that indeed it was less dark and sad than ever, but
because its weariness and sorrow had no community
with their ethereal nature. Wherever they might appear
in their pilgrimage of bliss, Youth would echo back their
gladness, care-stricken Maturity would rest a moment

from its toil, and Age, tottering among the graves, would
smile in withered joy for their sakes. The lonely cot,
the narrow and gloomy street, the sombre shade, would
catch a passing gleam like that now shining on ourselves,
as these bright spirits wandered by. Blessed pair, whose
happy home was throughout all the earth! I looked at
my shoulders, and thought them broad enough to sustain
those pictured towns and mountains; mine, too, was an
elastic foot, as tireless as the wing of the bird of paradise; mine was then an untroubled heart, that would
have gone singing on its delightful way.

"O maiden!" said I aloud, "why did you not come
hither alone?"

While the merry girl and myself were busy with the
showbox, the unceasing rain had driven another wayfarer
into the wagon. He seemed pretty nearly of the old
showman's age, but much smaller, leaner, and more
withered than he, and less respectably clad in a patched
suit of gray; withal, he had a thin, shrewd countenance,
and a pair of diminutive gray eyes, which peeped rather
too keenly out of their puckered sockets. This old
fellow had been joking with the showman, in a manner
which intimated previous acquaintance; but, perceiving
that the damsel and I had terminated our affairs, he
drew forth a folded document, and presented it to me.
As I had anticipated, it proved to be a circular, written
in a very fair and legible hand, and signed by several
distinguished gentlemen whom I had never heard of,
stating that the bearer had encountered every variety of
misfortune, and recommending him to the notice of all
charitable people. Previous disbursements had left me
no more than a five-dollar bill, out of which, however, I
offered to make the beggar a donation, provided he would
give me change for it. The object of my beneficence
looked keenly in my face, and discerned that I had none
of that abominable spirit, characteristic though it be, of

a full-blooded Yankee, which takes pleasure in detecting every little harmless piece of knavery.

"Why, perhaps," said the ragged old mendicant, "if the bank is in good standing, I can't say but I may have enough about me to change your bill."

"It is a bill of the Suffolk Bank," said I, "and better than the specie."

As the beggar had nothing to object, he now produced a small buff-leather bag, tied up carefully with a shoe-string. When this was opened, there appeared a very comfortable treasure of silver coins, of all sorts and sizes ; and I even fancied that I saw, gleaming among them, the golden plumage of that rare bird in our currency, the American Eagle. In this precious heap was my bank note deposited, the rate of exchange being considerably against me. His wants being thus relieved, the destitute man pulled out of his pocket an old pack of greasy cards, which had probably contributed to fill the buff-leather bag in more ways than one.

"Come," said he, "I spy a rare fortune in your face, and for twenty-five cents more, I 'll tell you what it is."

I never refuse to take a glimpse into futurity ; so, after shuffling the cards, and when the fair damsel had cut them, I dealt a portion to the prophetic beggar. Like others of his profession, before predicting the shadowy events that were moving on to meet me, he gave proof of his preternatural science, by describing scenes through which I had already passed. Here let me have credit for a sober fact. When the old man had read a page in his book of fate, he bent his keen gray eyes on mine, and proceeded to relate, in all its minute particulars, what was then the most singular event of my life. It was one which I had no purpose to disclose, till the general unfolding of all secrets ; nor would it be a much stranger instance of inscrutable knowledge, or fortunate conjecture, if the beggar were to meet me in the street

to-day, and repeat, word for word, the page which I
have here written. The fortune teller, after predicting a
destiny which time seems loath to make good, put up
his cards, secreted his treasure bag, and began to converse with the other occupants of the wagon.

"Well, old friend," said the showman, "you have
not yet told us which way your face is turned this
afternoon."

"I am taking a trip northward, this warm weather,"
replied the conjurer, "across the Connecticut first, and
then up through Vermont, and may be into Canada
before the fall. But I must stop and see the breaking up
of the camp meeting at Stamford."

I began to think that all the vagrants in New England
were converging to the camp meeting, and had made
this wagon their rendezvous by the way. The showman
now proposed, that, when the shower was over, they
should pursue the road to Stamford together, it being
sometimes the policy of these people to form a sort of
league and confederacy.

"And the young lady too," observed the gallant bibliopolist, bowing to her profoundly, "and this foreign
gentleman, as I understand, are on a jaunt of pleasure to
the same spot. It would add incalculably to my own
enjoyment, and I presume to that of my colleague and
his friend, if they could be prevailed upon to join our
party."

This arrangement met with approbation on all hands,
nor were any of those concerned more sensible of its
advantages than myself, who had no title to be included
in it. Having already satisfied myself as to the several
modes in which the four others attained felicity, I next
set my mind at work to discover what enjoyments were
peculiar to the old "Straggler," as the people of the
country would have termed the wandering mendicant
and prophet. As he pretended to familiarity with the

Devil, so I fancied that he was fitted to pursue and take delight in his way of life, by possessing some of the mental and moral characteristics, the lighter and more comic ones, of the Devil in popular stories. Among them might be reckoned a love of deception for its own sake, a shrewd eye and keen relish for human weakness and ridiculous infirmity, and the talent of petty fraud. Thus to this old man there would be pleasure even in the consciousness so insupportable to some minds, that his whole life was a cheat upon the world, and that, so far as he was concerned with the public, his little cunning had the upper hand of its united wisdom. Every day would furnish him with a succession of minute and pungent triumphs ; as when, for instance, his importunity wrung a pittance out of the heart of a miser, or when my silly good nature transferred a part of my slender purse to his plump leather bag ; or when some ostentatious gentleman should throw a coin to the ragged beggar who was richer than himself; or when, though he would not always be so decidedly diabolical, his pretended wants should make him a sharer in the scanty living of real indigence. And then what an inexhaustible field of enjoyment, both as enabling him to discern so much folly and achieve such quantities of minor mischief, was opened to his sneering spirit by his pretensions to prophetic knowledge.

All this was a sort of happiness which I could conceive of, though I had little sympathy with it. Perhaps, had I been then inclined to admit it, I might have found that the roving life was more proper to him than to either of his companions ; for Satan, to whom I had compared the poor man, has delighted, ever since the time of Job, in "wandering up and down upon the earth ;" and indeed a crafty disposition, which operates not in deeplaid plans, but in disconnected tricks, could not have an adequate scope, unless naturally impelled to a continual change of scene and society. My reflections were here interrupted.

"Another visitor!" exclaimed the old showman.

The door of the wagon had been closed against the tempest, which was roaring and blustering with prodigious fury and commotion, and beating violently against our shelter, as if it claimed all those homeless people for its lawful prey, while we, caring little for the displeasure of the elements, sat comfortably talking. There was now an attempt to open the door, succeeded by a voice, uttering some strange, unintelligible gibberish, which my companions mistook for Greek, and I suspected to be thieves' Latin. However, the showman stepped forward, and gave admittance to a figure which made me imagine, either that our wagon had rolled back two hundred years into past ages, or that the forest and its old inhabitants had sprung up around us by enchantment.

It was a red Indian, armed with his bow and arrow. His dress was a sort of cap adorned with a single feather of some wild bird, and a frock of blue cotton girded tight about him; on his breast, like orders of knighthood, hung a crescent and a circle, and other ornaments of silver; while a small crucifix betokened that our Father the Pope had interposed between the Indian and the Great Spirit, whom he had worshipped in his simplicity. This son of the wilderness, and pilgrim of the storm, took his place silently in the midst of us. When the first surprise was over, I rightly conjectured him to be one of the Penobscot tribe, parties of which I had often seen in their summer excursions down our Eastern rivers. There they paddle their birch canoes among the coasting schooners, and build their wigwam beside some roaring milldam, and drive a little trade in basket work where their fathers hunted deer. Our new visitor was probably wandering through the country towards Boston, subsisting on the careless charity of the people, while he turned his archery to profitable account by shooting at cents, which were to be the prize of his successful aim.

The Indian had not long been seated, ere our merry damsel sought to draw him into conversation. She, indeed, seemed all made up of sunshine in the month of May; for there was nothing so dark and dismal that her pleasant mind could not cast a glow over it; and the wild man, like a fir tree in his native forest, soon began to brighten into a sort of sombre cheerfulness. At length, she inquired whether his journey had any particular end or purpose.

"I go shoot at the camp meeting at Stamford," replied the Indian.

"And here are five more," said the girl, "all aiming at the camp meeting too. You shall be one of us, for we travel with light hearts; and as for me, 1 sing merry songs, and tell merry tales, and am full of merry thoughts, and I dance merrily along the road, so that there is never any sadness among them that keep me company. But, O, you would find it very dull indeed to go all the way to Stamford alone!"

My ideas of the aboriginal character led me to fear that the Indian would prefer his own solitary musings to the gay society thus offered him; on the contrary, the girl's proposal met with immediate acceptance, and seemed to animate him with a misty expectation of enjoyment. I now gave myself up to a course of thought which, whether it flowed naturally from this combination of events, or was drawn forth by a wayward fancy, caused my mind to thrill as if I were listening to deep music. I saw mankind, in this weary old age of the world, either enduring a sluggish existence amid the smoke and dust of cities, or, if they breathed a purer air, still lying down at night with no hope but to wear out to-morrow, and all the to-morrows which make up life, among the same dull scenes, and in the same wretched toil, that had darkened the sunshine of to-day.   But there were some, full of the primeval instinct, who preserved the freshness of youth to their latest years by the continual excitement of new objects, new pursuits, and new associates ; and cared little, though their birthplace might have been here in New England, if the grave should close over them in Central Asia.   Fate was summoning a parliament of these free spirits ; unconscious of the impulse which directed them to a common centre, they had come hither from far and near ; and last of all, appeared the representative of those mighty vagrants, who had chased the deer during thousands of years, and were chasing it now in the Spirit Land.   Wandering down through the waste of ages, the woods had vanished around his path ; his arm had lost somewhat of its strength, his foot of its fleetness, his mien of its wild regality, his heart and mind of their savage virtue and uncultured force ; but here, untamable to the routine of artificial life, roving now along the dusty road, as of old over the forest leaves, here was the Indian still.

"Well," said the old showman, in the midst of my meditations, "here is an honest company of us,—one, two, three, four, five, six—all going to the camp meeting at Stamford.   Now, hoping no offence, I should like to know where this young gentleman may be going ?"

I started.   How came I among these wanderers? The free mind, that preferred its own folly to another's wisdom ; the open spirit, that found companions every where ; above all, the restless impulse, that had so often made me wretched in the midst of enjoyments ; these were my claims to be of their society.

"My friends !" cried I, stepping into the centre of the wagon, "I am going with you to the camp meeting at Stamford."

"But in what capacity?" asked the old showman,

after a moment's silence. "All of us here can get our bread in some creditable way. Every honest man should have his livelihood. You, sir, as I take it, are a mere strolling gentleman."

I proceeded to inform the company, that, when Nature gave me a propensity to their way of life, she had not left me altogether destitute of qualifications for it ; though I could not deny that my talent was less respectable, and might be less profitable, than the meanest of theirs. My design, in short, was to imitate the story tellers of whom Oriental travellers have told us, and become an itinerant novelist, reciting my own extemporaneous fictions to such audiences as I could collect.

"Either this," said I, "is my vocation, or I have been born in vain."

The fortune teller, with a sly wink to the company, proposed to take me as an apprentice to one or other of his professions, either of which undoubtedly would have given full scope to whatever inventive talent I might possess. The bibliopolist spoke a few words in opposition to my plan, influenced partly, I suspect, by the jealousy of authorship, and partly by an apprehension that the *viva voce* practice would become general among novelists, to the infinite detriment of the book trade· Dreading the rejection, I solicited the interest of the merry damsel.

"Mirth," cried I, most aptly appropriating the words of L'Allegro, "to thee I sue ! Mirth, admit me of thy crew !"

"Let us indulge the poor youth," said Mirth, with a kindness which made me love her dearly, though I was no such coxcomb as to misinterpret her motives. "I have espied much promise in him. True, a shadow sometimes flits across his brow, but the sunshine is sur to follow in a moment. He is never guilty of a sad thought, but a merry one is twin born with it. We will take him with us ; and you shall see that he will set us all a-laughing before we reach the camp meeting at Stamford."

Her voice silenced the scruples of the rest, and gained me admittance into the league; according to the terms of which, without a community of goods or profits, we were to lend each other all the aid, and avert all the harm, that might be in our power. This affair settled, a marvellous jollity entered into the whole tribe of us, manifesting itself characteristically in each individual. The old showman, sitting down to his barrel organ, stirred up the souls of the pygmy people with one of the quickest tunes in the music book; tailors, blacksmiths, gentlemen, and ladies, all seemed to share in the spirit of the occasion; and the Merry Andrew played his part more facetiously than ever, nodding and winking particularly at me. The young foreigner flourished his fiddle bow with a master's hand, and gave an inspiring echo to the showman's melody. The bookish man and the merry damsel started up simultaneously to dance; the former enacting the double shuffle in a style which every body must have witnessed, ere Election week was blotted out of time; while the girl, setting her arms akimbo, with both hands at her slim waist, displayed such light rapidity of foot, and harmony of varying attitude and motion, that I could not conceive how she ever was to stop; imagining, at the moment, that Nature had made her, as the old showman had made his puppets, for no earthly purpose but to dance jigs. The Indian bellowed forth a succession of most hideous outcries, somewhat affrighting us, till we interpreted them as the war song, with which, in imitation of his ancestors, he was prefacing the assault on Stamford. The conjurer, meanwhile, sat demurely in a corner, extracting a sly enjoyment from the whole scene, and, like the facetious Merry Andrew, directing his queer glance particularly at me.

As for myself, with great exhilaration of fancy, I began to arrange and color the incidents of a tale, wherewith I proposed to amuse an audience that very evening ; for I saw that my associates were a little ashamed of me, and that no time was to be lost in obtaining a public acknowledgment of my abilities.

"Come, fellow-laborers," at last said the old showman, whom we had elected President ; "the shower is over, and we must be doing our duty by these poor souls at Stamford."

"We'll come among them in procession, with music and dancing," cried the merry damsel.

Accordingly — for it must be understood that our pilgrimage was to be performed on foot—we sallied joyously out of the wagon, each of us, even the old gentleman in his white-top boots, giving a great skip as we came down the ladder. Above our heads there was such a glory of sunshine and splendor of clouds, and such brightness of verdure below, that, as I modestly remarked at the time, Nature seemed to have washed her face, and put on the best of her jewelry, and a fresh green gown, in honor of our confederation. Casting our eyes northward, we beheld a horseman approaching leisurely, and splashing through the little puddles on the Stamford road. Onward he came, sticking up in his saddle with rigid perpendicularity, a tall, thin figure in rusty black, whom the showman and the conjurer shortly recognized to be, what his aspect sufficiently indicated, a travelling preacher of great fame among the Methodists. What puzzled us was the fact, that his face appeared turned from, instead of to, the camp meeting at Stamford. However, as this new votary of the wandering life drew near the little green space, where the guidepost and our wagon were situated, my six fellow-vagabonds and myself rushed forward and surrounded him, crying out with united voices—

"What news, what news, from the camp meeting at Stamford?"

The missionary looked down, in surprise, at as singular a knot of people as could have been selected from all his heterogeneous auditors. Indeed, considering that we might all be classified under the general head of Vagabond, there was great diversity of character among the grave old showman, the sly, prophetic beggar, the fiddling foreigner and his merry damsel, the smart bibliopolist, the sombre Indian, and myself, the itinerant novelist, a slender youth of eighteen. I even fancied that a smile was endeavoring to disturb the iron gravity of the preacher's mouth.

"Good people," answered he, "the camp meeting is broke up."

So saying, the Methodist minister switched his steed, and rode westward. Our union being thus nullified by the removal of its object, we were sundered at once to the four winds of Heaven. The fortune teller, giving a nod to all, and a peculiar wink to me, departed on his northern tour, chuckling within himself as he took the Stamford road. The old showman and his literary coadjutor were already tackling their horses to the wagon, with a design to peregrinate south-west along the sea coast. The foreigner and the merry damsel took their laughing leave, and pursued the eastern road, which I had that day trodden ; as they passed away, the young man played a lively strain, and the girl's happy spirit broke into a dance : and thus, dissolving, as it were, into sunbeams and gay music, that pleasant pair departed from my view. Finally, with a pensive shadow thrown across my mind, yet emulous of the light philosophy of my late companions, I joined myself to the Penobscot Indian, and set forth towards the distant city.

THE WHITE OLD MAID.

THE moonbeams came through two deep and narrow windows, and showed a spacious chamber, richly furnished in an antique fashion. From one lattice, the shadow of the diamond panes was thrown upon the floor; the ghostly light, through the other, slept upon a bed, falling between the heavy silken curtains, and illuminating the face of a young man. But, how quietly the slumberer lay! how pale his features! and how like a shroud the sheet was wound about his frame! Yes; it was a corpse, in its burial clothes.

Suddenly, the fixed features seemed to move with dark emotion. Strange fantasy! It was but the shadow of the fringed curtain, waving betwixt the dead face and the moonlight, as the door of the chamber opened, and a girl stole softly to the bedside. Was there delusion in the moonbeams, or did her gesture and her eye betray a gleam of triumph, as she bent over the pale corpse— pale as itself—and pressed her living lips to the cold ones of the dead? As she drew back from that long kiss, her features writhed, as if a proud heart were fighting with its anguish. Again it seemed that the features of the corpse had moved, responsive to her own. Still an illusion! The silken curtain had waved a second time betwixt the dead face and the moonlight, as another fair young girl unclosed the door, and glided, ghost-like, to the bedside. There the two maidens stood, both beautiful, with the pale beauty of the dead between them. But she, who had first entered, was proud and stately ; and the other, a soft and fragile thing.

"Away !" cried the lofty one. "Thou hadst him living ! The dead is mine !"

"Thine !" returned the other, shuddering. "Well hast thou spoken ! The dead is thine !"

The proud girl started, and stared into her face, with a ghastly look. But a wild and mournful expression passed across the features of the gentle one ; and, weak and helpless, she sank down on the bed, her head pillowed beside that of the corpse, and her hair mingling with his dark locks. A creature of hope and joy, the first draught of sorrow had bewildered her.

"Edith !" cried her rival.

Edith groaned, as with a sudden compression of the heart ; and removing her cheek from the dead youth's pillow, she stood upright, fearfully encountering the eyes of the lofty girl.

"Wilt thou betray me ?" said the latter, calmly.

"Till the dead bid me speak, I will be silent," answered Edith. "Leave us alone together ! Go, and live many years, and then return, and tell me of thy life. He, too, will be here ! Then, if thou tellest of sufferings more than death, we will both forgive thee."

"And what shall be the token ?" asked the proud girl, as if her heart acknowledged a meaning in these wild words.

"This lock of hair," said Edith, lifting one of the dark, clustering curls, that lay heavily on the dead man's brow.

The two maidens joined their hands over the bosom of the corpse, and appointed a day and hour, far, far in time to come, for their next meeting in that chamber· The statelier girl gave one deep look at the motionless countenance, and departed — yet turned again and trembled, ere she closed the door, almost believing that her dead lover frowned upon her. And Edith too! Was not her white form fading into the moonlight? Scorning her own weakness, she went forth, and perceived that a negro slave was waiting in the passage, with a wax light, which he held between her face and his own, and regarded her, as she thought, with an ugly expression of merriment. Lifting his torch on high, the slave lighted her down the staircase, and undid the portal of the mansion. The young clergyman of the town had just ascended the steps, and bowing to the lady passed in without a word.

Years, many years, rolled on ; the world seemed new again, so much older was it grown since the night when those pale girls had clasped their hands across the bosom of the corpse. In the interval, a lonely woman had passed from youth to extreme age, and was known by all the town as the "Old Maid in the Winding Sheet." A taint of insanity had affected her whole life, but so quiet, sad, and gentle, so utterly free from violence, that she was suffered to pursue her harmless fantasies unmolested by the world, with whose business or pleasures she had nought to do. She dwelt alone, and never came into the daylight, except to follow funerals. Whenever a corpse was borne along the street, in sunshine, rain, or snow, whether a pompous train, of the rich and proud, thronged after it, or few and humble were the mourners, behind them came the lonely woman, in a long, white garment, which the people called her shroud. She took no place among the kindred or the friends, but stood at the door to hear the funeral prayer, and walked in the rear of the procession, as one whose earthly charge it was to haunt the house of mourning, and be the shadow of affliction, and see that the dead were duly buried. So long had this been her custom, that the inhabitants of the town deemed her a part of every funeral, as much as the coffin pall or the very corpse itself, and augured ill of the sinner's destiny, unless the "Old Maid in the Winding Sheet" came gliding, like a ghost, behind.   Once, it is said, she affrighted a bridal party, with her pale presence, appearing suddenly in the illuminated hall, just as the priest was uniting a false maid to a wealthy man, before her lover had been dead a year.   Evil was the omen to that marriage !   Sometimes she stole forth by moonlight, and visited the graves of venerable Integrity, and wedded Love, and virgin Innocence, and every spot where the ashes of a kind and faithful heart were mouldering. Over the hillocks of those favored dead, would she stretch out her arms, with a gesture, as if she were scattering seeds ; and many believed that she brought them from the garden of Paradise ; for the graves which she had visited were green beneath the snow, and covered with sweet flowers from April to November. Her blessing was better than a holy verse upon the tombstone.   Thus wore away her long, sad, peaceful, and fantastic life, till few were so old as she, and the people of later generations wondered how the dead had ever been buried, or mourners had endured their grief, without the " Old Maid in the Winding Sheet."

Still, years went on, and still she followed funerals and was not yet summoned to her own festival of death. One afternoon, the great street of the town was all alive with business and bustle, though the sun now gilded only the upper half of the church spire, having left the housetops and loftiest trees in shadow.   The scene was cheerful and animated, in spite of the sombre shade between the high brick buildings.   Here were pompous merchants, in white wigs and laced velvet ; the bronzed faces of sea captains ; the foreign garb and air of Spanish creoles ; and the disdainful port of natives of Old England ; all contrasted with the rough aspect of one or two back settlers, negotiating sales of timber, from forests where axe had never sounded. Sometimes a lady passed, swelling roundly forth in an embroidered petticoat, balancing her steps in high-heeled shoes, and courtesying, with lofty grace, to the punctilious obeisances of the gentlemen. The life of the town seemed to have its very centre not far from an old mansion, that stood somewhat back from the pavement, surrounded by neglected grass, with a strange air of loneliness, rather deepened than dispelled by the throng so near it. Its site would have been suitably occupied by a magnificent Exchange, or a brick block, lettered all over with various signs ; or the large house itself might have made a noble tavern, with the "King's Arms" swinging before it, and guests in every chamber, instead of the present solitude. But, owing to some dispute about the right of inheritance, the mansion had been long without a tenant, decaying from year to year, and throwing the stately gloom of its shadow over the busiest part of the town. Such was the scene, and such the time, when a figure, unlike any that have been described, was observed at a distance down the street.

"I espy a strange sail yonder," remarked a Liverpool captain ; "that woman, in the long, white garment !"

The sailor seemed much struck by the object, as were several others, who, at the same moment, caught a glimpse of the figure that had attracted his notice. Almost immediately, the various topics of conversation gave place to speculations, in an undertone, on this unwonted occurrence.

"Can there be a funeral, so late this afternoon?" inquired some.

They looked for the signs of death at every door— the sexton, the hearse, the assemblage of black-clad relatives—all that makes up the woful pomp of funerals. They raised their eyes, also, to the sun-gilt spire of the church, and wondered that no clang proceeded from its bell, which had always tolled till now, when this figure appeared in the light of day. But none had heard that a corpse was to be borne to its home that afternoon, nor was there any token of a funeral, except the apparition of the " Old Maid in the Winding Sheet."

" What may this portend?" asked each man of his neighbor.

All smiled as they put the question, yet with a certain trouble in their eyes, as if pestilence, or some other wide calamity, were prognosticated by the untimely intrusion among the living, of one whose presence had always been associated with death and woe. What a comet is to the earth, was that sad woman to the town. Still she moved on, while the hum of surprise was hushed at her approach, and the proud and humble stood aside, that her white garment might not wave against them. It was a long, loose robe, of spotless purity. Its wearer appeared very old, pale, emaciated, and feeble, yet glided onward without the unsteady pace of extreme age. At one point of her course, a little rosy boy burst forth from a door, and ran, with open arms, towards the ghostly woman, seeming to expect a kiss from her blood-less lips. She made a slight pause, fixing her eye upon him with an expression of no earthly sweetness, so that the child shivered and stood awe-struck, rather than affrighted, while the Old Maid passed on. Perhaps her garment might have been polluted even by an infant's touch ; perhaps her kiss would have been death to the sweet boy, within a year.

" She is but a shadow," whispered the superstitious. " The child put forth his arms and could not grasp her robe !"

The wonder was increased, when the Old Maid passed beneath the porch of the deserted mansion, ascended the moss-covered steps, lifted the iron knocker, and gave three raps. The people could only conjecture, that some old remembrance, troubling her bewildered brain, had impelled the poor woman hither to visit the friends of her youth; all gone from their home, long since and forever, unless their ghosts still haunted it—fit company for the "Old Maid in the Winding Sheet." An elderly man approached the steps, and reverently uncovering his gray locks, essayed to explain the matter.

"None, Madam," said he, "have dwelt in this house these fifteen years agone—no, not since the death of old Colonel Fenwicke, whose funeral you may remember to have followed. His heirs, being ill agreed among themselves, have let the mansion house go to ruin."

The Old Maid looked slowly round, with a slight gesture of one hand, and a finger of the other upon her lips, appearing more shadow-like than ever, in the obscurity of the porch. But again she lifted the hammer, and gave, this time, a single rap. Could it be, that a footstep was now heard coming down the staircase of the old mansion, which all conceived to have been so long untenanted? Slowly, feebly, yet heavily, like the pace of an aged and infirm person, the step approached, more distinct on every downward stair, till it reached the portal. The bar fell on the inside; the door was opened. One upward glance towards the church spire, whence the sunshine had just faded, was the last that the people saw of the "Old Maid in the Winding Sheet."

"Who undid the door?" asked many.

This question, owing to the depth of shadow beneath the porch, no one could satisfactorily answer. Two or three aged men, while protesting against an inference which might be drawn, affirmed that the person within was a negro, and bore a singular resemblance to old Cæsar, formerly a slave in the house, but freed by death some thirty years before.

"Her summons has waked up a servant of the old family," said one, half seriously.

"Let us wait here," replied another. "More guests will knock at the door anon. But the gate of the grave-yard should be thrown open!"

Twilight had overspread the town, before the crowd began to separate, or the comments on this incident were exhausted. One after another was wending his way homeward, when a coach—no common spectacle in those days—drove slowly into the street. It was an old-fashioned equipage, hanging close to the ground, with arms on the panels, a footman behind, and a grave, corpulent coachman seated high in front—the whole giving a idea of solemn state and dignity. There was something awful in the heavy rumbling of the wheels. The coach rolled down the street, till, coming to the gateway of the deserted mansion, it drew up, and the footman sprang to the ground.

"Whose grand coach is this?" asked a very inquisitive body.

The footman made no reply, but ascended the steps of the old house, gave three raps with the iron hammer, and returned to open the coach door. An old man, possessed of the heraldic lore so common in that day, examined the shield of arms on the panel.

"Azure, a lion's head erased, between three flower-de-luces," said he; then whispered the name of the family to whom these bearings belonged. The last inheritor of its honors was recently dead, after a long residence amid the splendor of the British court, where his birth and wealth had given him no mean station. "He left no child," continued the herald, "and these arms, being in a lozenge, betoken that the coach appertains to his widow."

Further disclosures, perhaps, might have been made, had not the speaker suddenly been struck dumb, by the stern eye of an ancient lady, who thrust forth her head from the coach, preparing to descend. As she emerged,

the people saw that her dress was magnificent, and her
figure dignified, in spite of age and infirmity—a stately
ruin, but with a look at once of pride and wretchedness.
Her strong and rigid features had an awe about them,
unlike that of the white Old Maid, but as of something
evil. She passed up the steps, leaning on a gold-headed
cane; the door swung open as she ascended—and the light
of a torch glittered on the embroidery of her dress, and
gleamed on the pillars of the porch. After a momentary
pause—a glance backwards—and then a desperate effort
—she went in. The decipherer of the coat of arms had
ventured up the lowest step, and shrinking back immediately, pale and tremulous, affirmed that the torch was
held by the very image of old Cæsar.

"But such a hideous grin," added he, "was never
seen on the face of mortal man, black or white ! It will
haunt me till my dying day."

Meantime, the coach had wheeled round, with a
prodigious clatter on the pavement, and rumbled up the
street, disappearing in the twilight, while the ear still
tracked its course. Scarcely was it gone, when the
people began to question whether the coach and attendants, the ancient lady, the spectre of old Cæsar, and the
Old Maid herself, were not all a strangely combined
delusion, with some dark purport in its mystery. The
whole town was astir, so that, instead of dispersing, the
crowd continually increased, and stood gazing up at the
windows of the mansion, now silvered by the brightening
moon. The elders, glad to indulge the narrative propensity of age, told of the long-faded splendor of the family,
the entertainments they had given, and the guests, the
greatest of the land, and even titled and noble ones from
abroad, who had passed beneath that portal. These
graphic reminiscences seemed to call up the ghosts of
those to whom they referred. So strong was the impression on some of the more imaginative hearers, that two

or three were seized with trembling fits, at one and the same moment, protesting that they had distinctly heard three other raps of the iron knocker.

"Impossible !" exclaimed others. "See ! The moon shines beneath the porch, and shows every part of it, except in the narrow shade of that pillar. There is no one there !"

"Did not the door open?" whispered one of these fanciful persons.

"Didst thou see it, too?" said his companion, in a startled tone.

But the general sentiment was opposed to the idea that a third visitant had made application at the door of the deserted house. A few, however, adhered to this new marvel, and even declared that a red gleam, like that of a torch, had shone through the great front window, as if the negro were lighting a guest up the staircase. This, two, was pronounced a mere fantasy. But, at once, the whole multitude started, and each man beheld his own terror painted in the faces of all the rest.

"What an awful thing is this !" cried they.

A shriek, too fearfully distinct for doubt, had been heard within the mansion, breaking forth suddenly, and succeeded by a deep stillness, as if a heart had burst in giving it utterance. The people knew not whether to fly from the very sight of the house, or to rush trembling in, and search out the strange mystery. Amid their confusion and affright, they are somewhat reassured by the appearance of their clergyman, a venerable patriarch, and equally a saint, who had taught them and their fathers the way to Heaven, for more than the space of an ordinary lifetime. He was a reverend figure, with long, white hair upon his shoulders, a white beard upon his breast, and a back so bent over his staff, that he seemed to be looking downward, continually, as if to choose a proper grave for his weary frame. It was some time before the good old man, being deaf, and of impaired intellect, could be made to comprehend such portions of the affair as were comprehensible at all. But, when possessed of the facts, his energies assumed unexpected vigor.

"Verily," said the old gentleman, "it will be fitting that I enter the mansion house of the worthy Colonel Fenwicke, lest any harm should have befallen that true Christian woman, whom ye call the 'Old Maid in the Winding Sheet.'"

Behold, then, the venerable clergyman ascending the steps of the mansion, with a torchbearer behind him. It was the elderly man who had spoken to the Old Maid, and the same who had afterwards explained the shield of arms, and recognized the features of the negro. Like their predecessors, they gave three raps with the iron hammer.

"Old Cæsar cometh not," observed the priest. "Well I wot he no longer doth service in this mansion."

"Assuredly, then, it was something worse, in old Cæsar's likeness!" said the other adventurer.

"Be it as God wills," answered the clergyman. "See! my strength, though it be much decayed, hath sufficed to open this heavy door. Let us enter, and pass up the staircase."

Here occurred a singular exemplification of the dreamy state of a very old man's mind. As they ascended the wide flight of stairs, the aged clergyman appeared to move with caution, occasionally standing aside, and oftener bending his head, as it were in salutation, thus practising all the gestures of one who makes his way through a throng. Reaching the head of the staircase, he looked around, with sad and solemn benignity, laid aside his staff, bared his hoary locks, and was evidently on the point of commencing a prayer.

"Reverend sir," said his attendant, who conceived this a very suitable prelude to their further search, "would it not be well that the people join with us in prayer?"

"Welladay!" cried the old clergyman, staring strangely around him. "Art thou here with me, and none other? Verily, past times were present to me, and I deemed that I was to make a funeral prayer, as many a time heretofore, from the head of this staircase. Of a truth, I saw the shades of many that are gone. Yea, I have prayed at their burials, one after another, and the 'Old Maid in the Winding Sheet' hath seen them to their graves!"

Being now more thoroughly awake to their present purpose, he took his staff, and struck forcibly on the floor, till there came an echo from each deserted chamber, but no menial, to answer their summons. They therefore walked along the passage, and again paused, opposite to the great front window, through which was seen the crowd, in the shadow and partial moonlight of the street beneath. On their right hand was the open door of a chamber, and a closed one on their left. The clergyman pointed his cane to the carved oak panel of the latter.

"Within that chamber," observed he, "a whole life-time since, did I sit by the death bed of a goodly young man, who, being now at the last gasp—"

Apparently, there was some powerful excitement in the ideas which had now flashed across his mind. He snatched the torch from his companion's hand, and threw open the door with such sudden violence, that the flame was extinguished, leaving them no other light than the moonbeams, which fell through two windows into the spacious chamber. It was sufficient to discover all that could be known. In a high-backed, oaken arm chair, upright, with her hands clasped across her breast, and her head thrown back, sat the "Old Maid in the Winding Sheet." The stately dame had fallen on her knees, with her forehead on the holy knees of the Old Maid, one hand upon the floor, and the other pressed convulsively against her heart. It clutched a lock of hair, once sable, now discolored with a greenish mould. As the priest and layman advanced into the chamber, the Old Maid's features assumed such a semblance of shifting expression, that they trusted to hear the whole mystery explained by a single word. But it was only the shadow of a tattered curtain, waving betwixt the dead face and the moonlight.

"Both dead!" said the venerable man. "Then who shall divulge the secret? Methinks it glimmers to and fro in my mind, like the light and shadow across the Old Maid's face. And now 'tis gone!"

"AND so, Peter, you won't even consider of the business?" said Mr. John Brown, buttoning his surtout over the snug rotundity of his person, and drawing on his gloves. "You positively refuse to let me have this crazy old house, and the land under and adjoining, at the price named?"

"Neither at that, nor treble the sum," responded the gaunt, grizzled, and threadbare Peter Goldthwaite. "The fact is, Mr. Brown, you must find another site for your brick block, and be content to leave my estate with the present owner. Next summer, I intend to put a splendid new mansion over the cellar of the old house."

"Pho, Peter!" cried Mr. Brown, as he opened the kitchen door; "content yourself with building castles in the air, where house lots are cheaper than on earth, to say nothing of the cost of bricks and mortar. Such foundations are solid enough for your edifices; while this underneath us is just the thing for mine; and so we may both be suited. What say you, again?"

"Precisely what I said before, Mr. Brown," answered Peter Goldthwaite. "And, as for castles in the air, mine may not be as magnificent as that sort of architecture, but perhaps as substantial, Mr. Brown, as the very respectable brick block with dry goods stores, tailors' shops, and banking rooms on the lower floor, and lawyers' offices in the second story, which you are so anxious to substitute."

"And the cost, Peter, eh?" said Mr. Brown, as he

withdrew, in something of a pet. "That, I suppose, will be provided for, offhand, by drawing a check on Bubble Bank !"

John Brown and Peter Goldthwaite had been jointly known to the commercial world between twenty and thirty years before, under the firm of Goldthwaite and Brown ; which copartnership, however, was speedily dissolved by the natural incongruity of its constituent parts. Since that event, John Brown, with exactly the qualities of a thousand other John Browns, and by just such plodding methods as they used, had prospered wonderfully, and become one of the wealthiest John Browns on earth. Peter Goldthwaite, on the contrary, after innumerable schemes, which ought to have collected all the coin and paper currency of the country into his coffers, was as needy a gentleman as ever wore a patch upon his elbow. The contrast between him and his former partner may be briefly marked : for Brown never reckoned upon luck, yet always had it ; while Peter made luck the main condition of his projects, and always missed it. While the means held out his speculations had been magnificent, but were chiefly confined, of late years, to such small business as adventures in the lottery. Once, he had gone on a gold-gathering expedition, somewhere to the South, and ingeniously contrived to empty his pockets more thoroughly than ever ; while others, doubtless, were filling theirs with native bullion by the handful. More recently, he had expended a legacy of a thousand or two of dollars in purchasing Mexican scrip, and thereby became the proprietor of a province ; which, however, so far as Peter could find out, was situated where he might have had an empire for the same money,—in the clouds. From a search after this valuable real estate, Peter returned so gaunt and threadbare, that, on reaching New England, the scarecrows in the cornfields beckoned to him, as he passed by. "They

did but flutter in the wind," quoth Peter Goldthwaite.
No, Peter, they beckoned, for the scarecrows knew their
brother !

At the period of our story, his whole visible income
would not have paid the tax of the old mansion in which
we find him. It was one of those rusty, moss-grown,
many-peaked wooden houses, which are scattered about
the streets of our elder towns, with a beetle-browed
second story projecting over the foundation, as if it
frowned at the novelty around it. This old paternal
edifice, needy as he was, and though, being centrally
situated on the principal street of the town, it would
have brought him a handsome sum, the sagacious Peter
had his own reasons for never parting with, either by
auction or private sale. There seemed, indeed, to be a
fatality that connected him with his birthplace ; for,
often as he had stood on the verge of ruin, and standing
there even now, he had not yet taken the step beyond it
which would have compelled him to surrender the house
to his creditors. So here he dwelt with bad luck till
good should come.

Here, then, in his kitchen, the only room where a
spark of fire took off the chill of a November evening,
poor Peter Goldthwaite had just been visited by his rich
old partner. At the close of their interview, Peter, with
rather a mortified look, glanced downwards at his dress,
parts of which appeared as ancient as the days of Goldthwaite & Brown. His upper garment was a mixed
surtout, wofully faded, and patched with newer stuff on
each elbow ; beneath this, he wore a thread-bare black
coat, some of the silk buttons of which had been
replaced with others of a different pattern ; and lastly,
though he lacked not a pair of gray pantaloons, they
were very shabby ones, and had been partially turned
brown, by the frequent toasting of Peter's shins before
a scanty fire. Peter's person was in keeping with

his goodly apparel.   Gray-headed, hollow-eyed, pale-cheeked, and lean-bodied, he was the perfect picture of a man who had fed on windy schemes and empty hopes, till he could neither live on such unwholesome trash, nor stomach more substantial food.   But, withal, this Peter Goldthwaite, crack-brained simpleton as, perhaps, he was, might have cut a very brilliant figure in the world, had he employed his imagination in the airy business of poetry, instead of making it a demon of mischief in mercantile pursuits.   After all, he was no bad fellow, but as harmless as a child, and as honest and honorable, and as much of the gentleman which nature meant him for, as an irregular life and depressed circumstances will permit any man to be.

As Peter stood on the uneven bricks of his hearth, looking round at the disconsolate old kitchen, his eyes began to kindle with the illumination of an enthusiasm that never long deserted him.   He raised his hand, clinched it, and smote it energetically against the smoky panel over the fireplace.

"The time is come!" said he.   "With such a trea-sure at command, it were folly to be a poor man any longer.   To-morrow morning I will begin with the garret, nor desist till I have torn the house down!"

Deep in the chimney corner, like a witch in a dark cavern, sat a little old woman, mending one of the two pairs of stockings wherewith Peter Goldthwaite kept his toes from being frostbitten.   As the feet were ragged past all darning, she had cut pieces out of a cast-off flannel petticoat to make new soles.   Tabitha Porter was an old maid, upwards of sixty years of age, fifty-five of which she had sat in that same chimney-corner, such being the length of time since Peter's grandfather had taken her from the almshouse.   She had no friend but Peter, nor Peter any friend but Tabitha ; so long as Peter might have a shelter for his own head, Tabitha

would know where to shelter hers; or, being homeless
elsewhere, she would take her master by the hand, and
bring him to her native home, the almshouse.   Should it
ever be necessary, she loved him well enough to feed
him with her last morsel, and clothe him with her under
petticoat.   But Tabitha was a queer old woman, and,
though never infected with Peter's flightiness, had become so accustomed to his freaks and follies, that she
viewed them all as matters of course.   Hearing him
threaten to tear the house down, she looked quietly up
from her work.

   " Best leave the kitchen till the last, Mr. Peter," said she.
   "The sooner we have it all down the better," said
Peter Goldthwaite.   "I am tired to death of living in
this cold, dark, windy, smoky, creaking, groaning, dismal
old house.   I shall feel like a younger man, when we get
into my splendid brick mansion, as, please Heaven, we
shall, by this time next autumn.   You shall have a
room on the sunny side, old Tabby, finished and
furnished as best may suit your own notions."

   "I should like it pretty much such a room as this
kitchen," answered Tabitha.   "It will never be like
home to me, till the chimney corner gets as black with
smoke as this; and that won't be these hundred years.
How much do you mean to lay out on the house, Mr.
Peter?"

   "What is that to the purpose?" exclaimed Peter
loftily.   "Did not my great-granduncle, Peter Goldthwaite, who died seventy years ago, and whose namesake
I am, leave treasure enough to build twenty such?"

   "I can't say but he did, Mr. Peter," said Tabitha,
threading her needle.

   Tabitha well understood, that Peter had reference to
an immense hoard of the precious metals, which was
said to exist somewhere in the cellar or walls, or under
the floors, or in some concealed closet, or other out-of-

the-way nook of the house. This wealth, according to
tradition, had been accumulated by a former Peter Goldthwaite, whose character seems to have borne a remarkable similitude to that of the Peter of our story. Like
him, he was a wild projector, seeking to heap up gold by
the bushel and the cartload, instead of scraping it
together, coin by coin. Like Peter the second, too, his
projects had almost invariably failed, and, but for the
magnificent success of the final one, would have left him
with hardly a coat and pair of breeches to his gaunt and
grizzled person. Reports were various, as to the nature
of his fortunate speculation; one intimating that the
ancient Peter had made the gold by alchemy; another,
that he had conjured it out of people's pockets by the
black art; and a third, still more unaccountable, that
the devil had given him free access to the old provincial
treasury. It was affirmed, however, that some secret
impediment had debarred him from the enjoyment of his
riches, and that he had a motive for concealing them
from his heir, or, at any rate, had died without disclosing
the place of deposit. The present Peter's father had
faith enough in the story to cause the cellar to be dug
over. Peter himself chose to consider the legend as an
indisputable truth, and, amid his many troubles, had
this one consolation, that, should all other resources fail,
he might build up his fortunes by tearing his house
down. Yet, unless he felt a lurking distrust of the
golden tale, it is difficult to account for his permitting
the paternal roof to stand so long, since he had never
yet seen the moment when his predecessor's treasure
would not have found plenty of room in his own strong
box. But now was the crisis. Should he delay the
search a little longer, the house would pass from the
lineal heir, and with it the vast heap of gold, to remain
in its burial-place, till the ruin of the aged walls should
discover it to strangers of a future generation.

"Yes!" cried Peter Goldthwaite again; "to-morrow I will set about it."

The deeper he looked at the matter, the more certain of success grew Peter. His spirits were naturally so elastic, that even now, in the blasted autumn of his age, he could often compete with the spring-time gayety of other people. Enlivened by his brightening prospects, he began to caper about the kitchen like a hobgoblin, with the queerest antics of his lean limbs, and gesticulations of his starved features. Nay, in the exuberance of his feelings, he seized both of Tabitha's hands, and danced the old lady across the floor, till the oddity of her rheumatic motions set him into a roar of laughter, which was echoed back from the rooms and chambers, as if Peter Goldthwaite were laughing in every one. Finally, he bounded upward, almost out of sight, into the smoke that clouded the roof of the kitchen, and alighting safely on the floor again, endeavored to resume his customary gravity.

"To-morrow, at sunrise," he repeated, taking his lamp to retire to bed, "I 'll see whether this treasure be hid in the wall of the garret."

"And, as we 're out of wood, Mr. Peter," said Tabitha, puffing and panting with her late gymnastics, "as fast as you tear the house down, I 'll make a fire with the pieces."

Gorgeous, that night, were the dreams of Peter Goldthwaite! At one time, he was turning a ponderous key in an iron door, not unlike the door of a sepulchre, but which, being opened, disclosed a vault, heaped up with gold coin, as plentifully as golden corn in a granary. There were chased goblets also, and tureens, salvers, dinner dishes, and dish covers, of gold, or silver gilt, besides chains and other jewels, incalculably rich, though tarnished with the damps of the vault; for, of all the wealth that was irrevocably lost to man, whether buried

in the earth, or sunken in the sea, Peter Goldthwaite had
found it in this one treasure-place. Anon, he had
returned to the old house as poor as ever, and was
received at the door by the gaunt and grizzled figure of
a man, whom he might have mistaken for himself, only
that his garments were of a much elder fashion. But
the house, without losing its former aspect, had been
changed into a palace of the precious metals. The
floors, walls, and ceilings were of burnished silver ; the
doors, the window frames, the cornices, the balustrades,
and the steps of the staircase, of pure gold ; and silver,
with gold bottoms, were the chairs, and gold standing on
silver legs, the high chests of drawers, and silver the
bedsteads, with blankets of woven gold and sheets of
silver tissue. The house had evidently been transmuted
by a single touch ; for it retained all the marks that
Peter remembered, but in gold or silver, instead of
wood ; and the initials of his name, which, when a boy,
he had cut in the wooden doorpost, remained as deep in
the pillar of gold. A happy man would have been Peter
Goldthwaite, except for a certain ocular deception, which,
whenever he glanced backward, caused the house to
darken from its glittering magnificence into the sordid
gloom of yesterday.

Up, betimes, rose Peter, seized an axe, hammer, and
saw, which he had placed by his bedside, and hied him
to the garret. It was but scantily lighted up, as yet, by
the frosty fragments of a sunbeam, which began to
glimmer through the almost opaque bull's eyes of the
window. A moralizer might find abundant themes for
his speculative and impracticable wisdom in a garret.
There is the limbo of departed fashions, aged trifles of a
day, and whatever was valuable only to one generation
of men, and which passed to the garret when that
generation passed to the grave, not for safe keeping, but to
be out of the way. Peter saw piles of yellow and musty

account books, in parchment covers, wherein creditors,
long dead and buried, had written the names of dead and
buried debtors, in ink now so faded, that their moss-grown
tombstones were more legible.   He found old moth-
eaten garments all in rags and tatters, or Peter would
have put them on.   Here was a naked and rusty sword,
not a sword of service, but a gentleman's small French
rapier, which had never left its scabbard till it lost it.
Here were canes of twenty different sorts, but no gold-
headed ones, and shoe buckles of various pattern and
material, but not silver, nor set with precious stones.
Here was a large box full of shoes, with high heels and
peaked toes.   Here, on a shelf, were a multitude of phials,
half filled with old apothecaries' stuff, which, when the
other half had done its business on Peter's ancestors, had
been brought hither from the death chamber.   Here —
not to give a longer inventory of articles that will never be
put up at auction — was the fragment of a full-length
looking glass, which, by the dust and dimness of its surface, made the picture of these old things look older than
the reality.   When Peter, not knowing that there was a
mirror there, caught the faint traces of his own figure, he
partly imagined that the former Peter Goldthwaite had
come back, either to assist or impede his search for the
hidden wealth. And at that moment a strange notion glimmered through his brain, that he was the identical Peter
who had concealed the gold, and ought to know
whereabouts it lay.   This, however, he had unaccount-
ably forgotten.

"Well, Mr. Peter!" cried Tabitha, on the garret stairs.
"Have you torn the house down enough to heat the
teakettle?"

"Not yet, old Tabby," answered Peter; "but that's
soon done—as you shall see."

With the word in his mouth, he uplifted the axe, and
laid about him so vigorously, that the dust flew, the

boards crashed, and, in a twinkling, the old woman had an apron full of broken rubbish.

"We shall get our winter's wood cheap," quoth Tabitha.

The good work being thus commenced, Peter beat down all before him, smiting and hewing at the joists and timbers, unclinching spike nails, ripping and tearing away boards, with a tremendous racket, from morning till night. He took care, however, to leave the outside shell of the house untouched, so that the neighbors might not suspect what was going on.

Never, in any of his vagaries, though each had made him happy while it lasted, had Peter been happier than now. Perhaps, after all, there was something in Peter Goldthwaite's turn of mind, which brought him an inward recompense for all the external evil that it caused. If he were poor, ill clad, even hungry, and exposed, as it were, to be utterly annihilated by a precipice of impending ruin, yet only his body remained in these miserable circumstances, while his aspiring soul enjoyed the sunshine of a bright futurity. It was his nature to be always young, and the tendency of his mode of life to keep him so. Gray hairs were nothing, no, nor wrinkles, nor infirmity ; he might look old, indeed, and be somewhat disagreeably connected with a gaunt old figure, much the worse for wear ; but the true, the essential Peter, was a young man of high hopes, just entering on the world. At the kindling of each new fire, his burnt-out youth rose afresh from the old embers and ashes. It rose exulting now. Having lived thus long — not too long, but just to the right age — a susceptible bachelor, with warm and tender dreams, he resolved, so soon as the hidden gold should flash to light, to go a-wooing, and win the love of the fairest maid in town. What heart could resist him ? Happy Peter Goldthwaite !

Every evening—as Peter had long absented himself

from his former lounging-places, at insurance offices, news rooms, and bookstores, and as the honor of his company was seldom requested in private circles—he and Tabitha used to sit down sociably by the kitchen hearth. This was always heaped plentifully with the rubbish of his day's labor. As the foundation of the fire, there would be a goodly-sized backlog of red oak, which, after being sheltered from rain or damp above a century, still hissed with the heat, and distilled streams of water from each end, as if the tree had been cut down within a week or two. Next, there were large sticks, sound, black and heavy, which had lost the principle of decay, and were indestructible except by fire, wherein they glowed like red-hot bars of iron. On this solid basis Tabitha would rear a lighter structure, composed of the splinters of door panels, ornamented mouldings, and such quick combustibles, which caught like straw, and threw a brilliant blaze high up the spacious flue, making its sooty sides visible almost to the chimney top. Meantime, the gleam of the old kitchen would be chased out of the cobwebbed corners, and away from the dusky crossbeams overhead, and driven nobody could tell whither, while Peter smiled like a gladsome man, and Tabitha seemed a picture of comfortable age. All this, of course, was but an emblem of the bright fortune which the destruction of the house would shed upon its occupants.

While the dry pine was flaming and crackling, like an irregular discharge of fairy musketry, Peter sat looking and listening, in a pleasant state of excitement. But, when the brief blaze and uproar were succeeded by the dark-red glow, the substantial heat, and the deep singing sound, which were to last throughout the evening, his humor became talkative. One night, the hundredth time, he teased Tabitha to tell him something new about his great-granduncle.

11   12

"You have been sitting in that chimney corner fifty-
five years, old Tabby, and must have heard many a
tradition about him," said Peter. "Did not you tell me,
that, when you first came to the house, there was an old
woman sitting where you sit now, who had been housekeeper to the famous Peter Goldthwaite?"

"So there was, Mr. Peter," answered Tabitha; "and
she was near about a hundred years old. She used to
say, that she and old Peter Goldthwaite had often spent
a sociable evening by the kitchen fire—pretty much as
you and I are doing how, Mr. Peter."

"The old fellow must have resembled me in more
points than one," said Peter, complacently, "or he never
would have grown so rich. But, methinks, he might
have invested the money better than he did—no interest!
—nothing but good security!—and the house to be torn
down to come at it! What made him hide it so snug,
Tabby?"

"Because he could not spend it," said Tabitha; "for,
as often as he went to unlock the chest, the Old Scratch
came behind and caught his arm. The money, they say,
was paid Peter out of his purse; and he wanted Peter
to give him a deed of this house and land, which Peter
swore he would not do."

"Just as I swore to John Brown, my old partner,"
remarked Peter. "But this is all nonsense, Tabby!
I don't believe the story."

"Well, it may not be just the truth," said Tabitha;
"for some folks say, that Peter did make over the house
to the Old Scratch; and that's the reason it has always
been so unlucky to them that lived in it. And as soon
as Peter had given him the deed, the chest flew open,
and Peter caught up a handful of the gold. But, lo and
behold!—there was nothing in his fist but a parcel of
old rags."

"Hold your tongue, you silly old Tabby!" cried Peter

in great wrath. "They were as good golden guineas as ever bore the effigies of the king of England. It seems as if I could recollect the whole circumstance, and how I, or old Peter, or whoever it was, thrust in my hand, or his hand, and drew it out, all of a blaze with gold. Old rags, indeed!"

But it was not an old woman's legend that would discourage Peter Goldthwaite. All night long he slept among pleasant dreams, and awoke at daylight with a joyous throb of the heart, which few are fortunate enough to feel beyond their boyhood. Day after day, he labored hard, without wasting a moment, except at meal times, when Tabitha summoned him to the pork and cabbage, or such other sustenance as she had picked up, or Providence had sent them. Being a truly pious man, Peter never failed to ask a blessing; if the food were none of the best, then so much the more earnestly, as it was more needed;—nor to return thanks, if the dinner had been scanty, yet for the good appetite, which was better than a sick stomach at a feast. Then did he hurry back to his toil, and, in a moment, was lost to sight in a cloud of dust from the old walls, though sufficiently perceptible to the ear, by the clatter which he raised in the midst of it. How enviable is the consciousness of being usefully employed! Nothing troubled Peter; or nothing but those phantoms of the mind, which seem like vague recollections, yet have also the aspect of presentiments. He often paused, with his axe uplifted in the air, and said to himself,—"Peter Goldthwaite, did you never strike this blow before?"—or, "Peter, what need of tearing the whole house down? Think a little while, and you will remember where the gold is hidden." Days and weeks passed on, however, without any remarkable discovery. Sometimes, indeed, a lean gray rat peeped forth at the lean, gray man, wondering what devil had got into the old house, which had always been

so peaceable till now. And, occasionally, Peter sympa-
thized with the sorrows of a female mouse, who had
brought five or six pretty, little, soft, and delicate
young ones into the world, just in time to see them
crushed by its ruin. But, as yet, no treasure!

By this time, Peter, being as determined as Fate, and
as diligent as Time, had made an end with the uppermost regions, and got down to the second story, where
he was busy in one of the front chambers. It had
formerly been the state bed chamber, and was honored
by tradition as the sleeping apartment of Governor
Dudley, and many other eminent guests. The furniture
was gone. There were remnants of faded and tattered
paper hangings, but larger spaces of bare wall, ornamented
with charcoal sketches, chiefly of people's heads in profile. These being specimens of Peter's youthful genius,
it went more to his heart to obliterate them, than if they
had been pictures on a church wall by Michael Angelo.
One sketch, however, and that the best one, affected him
differently. It represented a ragged man, partly supporting himself on a spade, and bending his lean body over a
hole in the earth, with one hand extended to grasp something that he had found. But, close behind him, with a
fiendish laugh on his features, appeared a figure with
horns, a tufted tail, and a cloven hoof.

"Avaunt, Satan!" cried Peter. "The man shall have
his gold!"

Uplifting his axe, he hit the horned gentleman such a
blow on the head, as not only demolished him, but the
treasure-seeker also, and caused the whole scene to
vanish like magic. Moreover, his axe broke quite
through the plaster and laths, and discovered a cavity.

"Mercy on us, Mr. Peter, are you quarrelling with
the Old Scratch?" said Tabitha, who was seeking some
fuel to put under the dinner pot.

Without answering the old woman, Peter broke down

a further space of the wall, and laid open a small closet
or cupboard, on one side of the fireplace, about breast
high from the ground. It contained nothing but a brass
lamp, covered with verdigris, and a dusty piece of parchment. While Peter inspected the latter, Tabitha seized
the lamp, and began to rub it with her apron.

"There is no use in rubbing it, Tabitha," said Peter.
"It is not Aladdin's lamp, though I take it to be a token
of as much luck. Look here, Tabby!"

Tabitha took the parchment, and held it close to her
nose, which was saddled with a pair of iron-bound
spectacles. But no sooner had she began to puzzle over
it, than she burst into a chuckling laugh, holding both
her hands against her sides.

"You can't make a fool of the old woman!" cried she.
"This is your own handwriting, Mr. Peter! the same as
in the letter you sent me from Mexico."

"There is certainly a considerable resemblance,"
said Peter, again examining the parchment. "But you
know yourself, Tabby, that this closet must have been
plastered up before you came to the house, or I came
into the world. No, this is old Peter Goldthwaite's
writing; these columns of pounds, shillings, and pence
are his figures, denoting the amount of the treasure;
and this, at the bottom, is, doubtless, a reference to the
place of concealment. But the ink has either faded or
peeled off, so that it is absolutely illegible. What a
pity!"

"Well, this lamp is as good as new. That's some
comfort," said Tabitha.

"A lamp!" thought Peter. "That indicates light on
my researches."

For the present, Peter felt more inclined to ponder on
this discovery than to resume his labors. After Tabitha
had gone down stairs, he stood poring over the parchment at one of the front windows, which was so obscured

with dust, that the sun could barely throw an uncertain shadow of the casement across the floor. Peter forced it open, and looked out upon the great street of the town, while the sun looked in at his old house. The air, though mild, and even warm, thrilled Peter as with a dash of water.

It was the first day of the January thaw. The snow lay deep upon the housetops, but was rapidly dissolving into millions of waterdrops, which sparkled downwards through the sunshine, with the noise of a summer shower beneath the eaves. Along the street the trodden snow was as hard and solid as a pavement of white marble, and had not yet grown moist in the spring-like temperature. But, when Peter thrust forth his head, he saw that the inhabitants, if not the town, were already thawed out by this warm day, after two or three weeks of winter weather. It gladdened him,—a gladness with a sigh breathing through it,—to see the stream of ladies gliding along the slippery sidewalks, with their red cheeks set off by quilted hoods, boas, and sable capes, like roses amidst a new kind of foliage. The sleigh bells jingled too and fro continually, sometimes announcing the arrival of a sleigh from Vermont, laden with the frozen bodies of porkers, or sheep, and perhaps a deer or two; sometimes of a regular market man, with chickens, geese, and turkeys, comprising the whole colony of a barn yard; and sometimes of a farmer and his dame, who had come to town partly for the ride, partly to go a-shopping, and partly for the sale of some eggs and butter. This couple rode in an old-fashioned square sleigh, which had served them twenty winters, and stood twenty summers in the sun beside their door. Now, a gentleman and lady skimmed the snow, in an elegant car, shaped somewhat like a cockle shell. Now, a stage sleigh, with its cloth curtains thrust aside to admit the sun, dashed rapidly down the street, whirling in and out among the vehicles that obstructed its passage. Now came, round a corner, the similitude of Noah's ark, on runners, being an immense open sleigh, with seats for fifty people, and drawn by a dozen horses. This spacious receptacle was populous with merry maids and merry bachelors, merry girls and boys, and merry old folks, all alive with fun, and grinning to the full width of their mouths. They kept up a buzz of babbling voices and low laughter, and sometimes burst into a deep, joyous shout, which the spectators answered with three cheers, while a gang of roguish boys let drive their snowballs right among the pleasure party. The sleigh passed on, and, when concealed by a bend of the street, was still audible by a distant cry of merriment.

Never had Peter beheld a livelier scene than was constituted by all these accessories: the bright sun; the flashing waterdrops; the gleaming snow; the cheerful multitude; the variety of rapid vehicles; and the jingle jangle of merry bells, which made the heart dance to their music. Nothing dismal was to be seen, except that peaked piece of antiquity, Peter Goldthwaite's house, which might well look sad externally, since such a terrible consumption was preying on its insides. And Peter's gaunt figure, half visible in the projecting second story, was worthy of his house.

"Peter! How goes it, friend Peter?" cried a voice across the street, as Peter was drawing in his head. "Look out here, Peter!"

Peter looked, and saw his old partner, Mr. John Brown, on the opposite sidewalk, portly and comfortable, with his furred cloak thrown open, disclosing a handsome surtout beneath. His voice had directed the attention of the whole town to Peter Goldthwaite's window, and to the dusty scarecrow which appeared at it.

"I say, Peter," cried Mr. Brown again, "what the devil are you about there, that I hear such a racket, whenever

I pass by? You are repairing the old house, I suppose, —making a new one of it,—eh?"

"Too late for that, I am afraid, Mr. Brown," replied Peter. "If I make it new, it will be new inside and out, from the cellar upwards."

"Had not you better let me take the job?" said Mr. Brown, significantly.

"Not yet!" answered Peter, hastily shutting the window; for, ever since he had been in search of the treasure, he hated to have people stare at him.

As he drew back, ashamed of his outward poverty, yet proud of the secret wealth within his grasp, a haughty smile shone out on Peter's visage, with precisely the effect of the dim sunbeams in the squalid chamber. He endeavored to assume such a mien as his ancestor had probably worn, when he gloried in the building of a strong house for a home to many generations of his posterity. But the chamber was very dark to his snow-dazzled eyes, and very dismal too, in contrast with the living scene that he had just looked upon. His brief glimpse into the street had given him a forcible impression of the manner in which the world kept itself cheerful and prosperous, by social pleasures and an intercourse of business, while he, in seclusion, was pursuing an object that might possibly be a phantasm, by a method which most people would call madness. It is one great advantage of a gregarious mode of life, that each person rectifies his mind by other minds, and squares his conduct to that of his neighbors, so as seldom to be lost in eccentricity. Peter Goldthwaite had exposed himself to this influence, by merely looking out of the window. For a while, he doubted whether there were any hidden chest of gold, and in that case, whether it was so exceedingly wise to tear the house down, only to be convinced of its non-existence.

But this was momentary. Peter, the Destroyer, resumed the task which fate had assigned him, nor faltered again till it was accomplished. In the course of his search, he met with many things that are usually found in the ruins of an old house, and also with some that are not. What seemed most to the purpose was a rusty key, which had been thrust into a chink of the wall, with a wooden label appended to the handle, bearing the initials P. G. Another singular discovery was that of a bottle of wine, walled up in an old oven. A tradition ran in the family, that Peter's grandfather, a jovial officer in the old French war, had set aside many dozens of the precious liquor, for the benefit of topers then unborn. Peter needed no cordial to sustain his hopes, and therefore kept the wine to gladden his success. Many halfpence did he pick up, that had been lost through the cracks of the floor, and some few Spanish coins, and the half of a broken sixpence, which had doubtless been a love token. There was likewise a silver coronation medal of George the Third. But old Peter Goldthwaite's strong box fled from one dark corner to another, or otherwise eluded the second Peter's clutches, till, should he seek much further, he must burrow into the earth.

We will not follow him in his triumphant progress, step by step. Suffice it, that Peter worked like a steam engine, and finished, in that one winter, the job which all the former inhabitants of the house, with time and the elements to aid them, had only half done in a century. Except the kitchen, every room and chamber was now gutted. The house was nothing but a shell,—the apparition of a house,—as unreal as the painted edifices of a theatre. It was like the perfect rind of a great cheese, in which a mouse had dwelt and nibbled, till it was a cheese no more. And Peter was the mouse.

What Peter had torn down, Tabitha had burned up: for she wisely considered, that, without a house, they should need no wood to warm it ; and therefore economy

was nonsense. Thus the whole house might be said to
have dissolved in smoke, and flown up among the clouds,
through the great black flue of the kitchen chimney. It
was an admirable parallel to the feat of the man who
jumped down his own throat.

On the night between the last day of winter and the
first of spring, every chink and cranny had been ran-
sacked, except within the precincts of the kitchen. This
fated evening was an ugly one. A snow storm had set
in some hours before, and was still driven and tossed
about the atmosphere by a real hurricane, which fought
against the house, as if the prince of the air, in person,
were putting the final stroke to Peter's labors. The
framework being so much weakened, and the inward
props removed, it would have been no marvel, if, in some
stronger wrestle of the blast, the rotten walls of the edifice,
and all the peaked roofs, had come crashing down upon
the owner's head. He, however, was careless of the peril,
but as wild and restless as the night itself, or as the flame
that quivered up the chimney, at each roar of the tempestuous wind.

"The wine, Tabitha!" he cried. "My grandfather's
rich old wine! We will drink it now!"

Tabitha arose from her smoke-blackened bench in the
chimney corner, and placed the bottle before Peter, close
beside the old brass lamp, which had likewise been the
prize of his researches. Peter held it before his eyes, and,
looking through the liquid medium, beheld the kitchen
illuminated with a golden glory, which also enveloped
Tabitha, and gilded her silver hair, and converted her
mean garments into robes of queenly splendor. It
reminded him of his golden dream.

"Mr. Peter," remarked Tabitha, "must the wine be
drunk before the money is found?"

"The money *is* found!" exclaimed Peter, with a sort
of fierceness. "The chest is within my reach. I will

not sleep till I have turned this key in the rusty lock.
But, first of all, let us drink !"

There being no corkscrew in the house, he smote the
neck of the bottle with old Peter Goldthwaite's rusty key,
and decapitated the sealed cork at a single blow. He
then filled two little china teacups, which Tabitha had
brought from the cupboard. So clear and brilliant was
this aged wine, that it shone within the cups, and rendered
the sprig of scarlet flowers at the bottom of each more
distinctly visible than when there had been no wine
there. Its rich and delicate perfume wasted itself round
the kitchen.

"Drink, Tabitha !" cried Peter. "Blessings on the
honest old fellow who set aside this good liquor for you
and me ! And here 's to Peter Goldthwaite's memory !"

"And good cause have we to remember him," quoth
Tabitha, as she drank.

How many years, and through what changes of
fortune, and various calamity, had that bottle hoarded
up its effervescent joy to be quaffed at last by two such
boon companions ! A portion of the happiness of a
former age had been kept for them, and was now set
free in a crowd of rejoicing visions, to sport amid the
storm and desolation of the present time. Until they
have finished the bottle, we must turn our eyes elsewhere.

It so chanced, that, on this stormy night, Mr. John
Brown found himself ill at ease in his wire-cushioned
arm chair by the glowing grate of anthracite which
heated his handsome parlor. He was naturally a good
sort of a man, and kind and pitiful whenever the
misfortunes of others happened to reach his heart
through the padded vest of his own prosperity. This
evening he had thought much about his old partner,
Peter Goldthwaite, his strange vagaries, and continual
ill luck, the poverty of his dwelling at Mr. Brown's

last visit, and Peter's crazed and haggard aspect when he had talked with him at the window.

"Poor fellow!" thought Mr. John Brown. "Poor, crackbrained Peter Goldthwaite! For old acquaintance' sake, I ought to have taken care that he was comfortable this rough winter."

These feelings grew so powerful, that, in spite of the inclement weather, he resolved to visit Peter Goldthwaite immediately. The strength of the impulse was really singular. Every shriek of the blast seemed a summons, or would have seemed so, had Mr. Brown been accustomed to hear the echoes of his own fancy in the wind. Much amazed at such active benevolence, he huddled himself in his cloak, muffled his throat and ears in comforters and handkerchiefs, and thus fortified, bade defiance to the tempest. But the powers of the air had rather the best of the battle. Mr. Brown was just weathering the corner by Peter Goldthwaite's house, when the hurricane caught him off his feet, tossed him face downward into a snow bank, and proceeded to bury his protuberant part beneath fresh drifts. There seemed little hope of his reappearance earlier than the next thaw. At the same moment his hat was snatched away, and whirled aloft into some far distant region, whence no tidings have as yet returned.

Nevertheless, Mr. Brown contrived to burrow a passage through the snow drift, and, with his bare head bent against the storm, floundered onward to Peter's door. There was such a creaking, and groaning, and rattling, and such an ominous shaking throughout the crazy edifice, that the loudest rap would have been inaudible to those within. He therefore entered, without ceremony, and groped his way to the kitchen.

His intrusion, even there, was unnoticed. Peter and Tabitha stood with their backs to the door, stooping over a large chest, which apparently they had just dragged from a cavity, or concealed closet, on the left side of the chimney. By the lamp in the old woman's hand, Mr. Brown saw that the chest was barred and clamped with iron, strengthened with iron plates, and studded with iron nails, so as to be a fit receptacle in which the wealth of one century might be hoarded up for the wants of another. Peter Goldthwaite was inserting a key into the lock.

"O Tabitha!" cried he, with tremulous rapture, "how shall I endure the effulgence? The gold!—the bright, bright gold! Methinks I can remember my last glance at it, just as the iron-plated lid fell down. And ever since, being seventy years, it has been blazing in secret, and gathering its splendor against this glorious moment! It will flash upon us like the noonday sun!"

"Then shade your eyes, Mr. Peter!" said Tabitha, with somewhat less patience than usual. "But, for mercy's sake, do turn the key!"

And, with a strong effort of both hands, Peter did force the rusty key through the intricacies of the rusty lock. Mr. Brown, in the mean time, had drawn near, and thrust his eager visage between those of the other two, at the instant that Peter threw up the lid. No sudden blaze illuminated the kitchen.

"What's here?" exclaimed Tabitha, adjusting her spectacles, and holding the lamp over the open chest. "Old Peter Goldthwaite's hoard of old rags."

"Pretty much so, Tabby," said Mr. Brown, lifting a handful of the treasure.

O, what a ghost of dead and buried wealth had Peter Goldthwaite raised, to scare himself out of his scanty wits withal! Here was the semblance of an incalculable sum, enough to purchase the whole town, and build every street anew, but which, vast as it was, no sane man would have given a solid sixpence for. What then, in sober earnest, were the delusive treasures of the chest?

Why, here were old provincial bills of credit, and treasury notes, and bills of land banks, and all other bubbles of the sort, from the first issue, above a century and a half ago, down nearly to the Revolution. Bills of a thousand pounds were intermixed with parchment pennies, and worth no more than they.

"And this, then, is old Peter Goldthwaite's treasure!" said John Brown. "Your namesake, Peter, was something like yourself; and, when the provincial currency had depreciated fifty or seventy-five per cent., he bought it up, in expectation of a rise. I have heard my grandfather say, that old Peter gave his father a mortgage of this very house and land to raise cash for his silly project. But the currency kept sinking, till nobody would take it as a gift; and there was old Peter Goldthwaite, like Peter the second, with thousands in his strong box, and hardly a coat to his back. He went mad upon the strength of it. But, never mind, Peter! It is just the sort of capital for building castles in the air."

"The house will be down about our ears!" cried Tabitha, as the wind shook it with increasing violence.

"Let it fall!" said Peter, folding his arms, as he seated himself upon the chest.

"No, no, my old friend Peter," said John Brown. "I have house room for you and Tabby, and a safe vault for the chest of treasure. To-morrow we will try to come to an agreement about the sale of this old house. Real estate is well up, and I could afford you a pretty handsome price."

"And I," observed Peter Goldthwaite, with reviving spirits, "have a plan for laying out the cash to great advantage."

"Why, as to that," muttered John Brown to himself, "we must apply to the next court for a guardian to take care of the solid cash; and if Peter insists upon speculating, he may do it, to his heart's content, with old PETER GOLDTHWAITE'S TREASURE."

CHIPPINGS WITH A CHISEL.

PASSING a summer, several years since, at Edgartown, on the island of Martha's Vineyard, I became acquainted with a certain carver of tombstones, who had travelled and voyaged thither from the interior of Massachusetts, in search of professional employment. The speculation had turned out so successful, that my friend expected to transmute slate and marble into silver and gold, to the amount of at least a thousand dollars, during the few months of his sojourn at Nantucket and the Vineyard. The secluded life, and the simple and primitive spirit which still characterizes the inhabitants of those islands, especially of Martha's Vineyard, insure their dead friends a longer and dearer remembrance than the daily novelty and revolving bustle of the world can elsewhere afford to beings of the past. Yet, while every family is anxious to erect a memorial to its departed members, the untainted breath of ocean bestows such health and length of days upon the people of the isles, as would cause a melancholy dearth of business to a resident artist in that line. His own monument, recording his decease by starvation, would probably be an early specimen of his skill. Gravestones, therefore, have generally been an article of imported merchandise.

In my walks through the burial ground of Edgartown — where the dead have lain so long that the soil, once enriched by their decay, has returned to its original barrenness — in that ancient burial ground I noticed much variety of monumental sculpture. The elder stones, dated a century back or more, have borders elaborately carved with flowers, and are adorned with a multiplicity of death's heads, crossbones, scythes, hour-glasses, and other lugubrious emblems of mortality, with here and there a winged cherub to direct the mourner's spirit upward. These productions of Gothic taste must have been quite beyond the colonial skill of the day, and were probably carved in London, and brought across the ocean to commemorate the defunct worthies of this lonely isle. The more recent monuments are mere slabs of slate, in the ordinary style, without any superfluous flourishes to set off the bald inscriptions. But others—and those far the most impressive, both to my taste and feelings—were roughly hewn from the gray rocks of the island, evidently by the unskilled hands of surviving friends and relatives. On some there were merely the initials of a name; some were inscribed with misspelt prose or rhyme, in deep letters, which the moss and wintry rain of many years had not been able to obliterate. These, these were graves where loved ones slept! It is an old theme of satire, the falsehood and vanity of monumental eulogies; but when affection and sorrow grave the letters with their own painful labor, then we may be sure that they copy from the record on their hearts.

My acquaintance, the sculptor—he may share that title with Greenough, since the dauber of signs is a painter as well as Raphael—had found a ready market for all his blank slabs of marble, and full occupation in lettering and ornamenting them. He was an elderly man, a descendant of the old Puritan family of Wiggles-worth, with a certain simplicity and singleness, both of heart and mind, which, methinks, is more rarely found among us Yankees than in any other community of people. In spite of his gray head and wrinkled brow, he was quite like a child in all matters save what had some reference to his own business ; he seemed, unless my fancy misled me, to view mankind in no other relation than as people in want of tombstones ; and his literary attainments evidently comprehended very little, either of prose or poetry, which had not, at one time or other, been inscribed on slate or marble. His sole task and office among the immortal pilgrims of the tomb—the duty for which Providence had sent the old man into the world, as it were, with a chisel in his hand—was to label the dead bodies, lest their names should be forgotten at the resurrection. Yet he had not failed, within a narrow scope, to gather a few sprigs of earthly, and more than earthly, wisdom,—the harvest of many a grave.

And lugubrious as his calling might appear, he was as cheerful an old soul as health, and integrity, and lack of care could make him, and used to set to work upon one sorrowful inscription or another with that sort of spirit which impels a man to sing at his labor. On the whole, I found Mr. Wigglesworth an entertaining, and often instructive, if not an interesting character ; and partly for the charm of his society, and still more because his work has an invariable attraction for "man that is born of woman," I was accustomed to spend some hours a day at his workshop. The quaintness of his remarks, and their not unfrequent truth—a truth condensed and pointed by the limited sphere of his view—gave a raciness to his talk, which mere worldliness and general cultivation would at once have destroyed.

Sometimes we would discuss the respective merits of the various qualities of marble, numerous slabs of which were resting against the walls of the shop ; or sometimes an hour or two would pass quietly, without a word on either side, while I watched how neatly his chisel struck out letter after letter of the names of the Nortons, the Mayhews, the Luces, the Daggets, and other immemorial families of the Vineyard. Often, with an artist's pride, the good old sculptor would speak of favorite productions of his skill, which were scattered throughout the village graveyards of New England. But my chief and most instructive amusement was to witness his interviews with his customers, who held interminable consultations about the form and fashion of the desired monuments, the buried excellence to be commemorated, the anguish to be expressed, and finally, the lowest price in dollars and cents for which a marble transcript of their feelings might be obtained. Really, my mind received many fresh ideas, which, perhaps, may remain in it even longer than Mr. Wigglesworth's hardest marble will retain the deepest strokes of his chisel.

An elderly lady came to bespeak a monument for her first love, who had been killed by a whale in the Pacific Ocean no less than forty years before. It was singular that so strong an impression of early feeling should have survived through the changes of her subsequent life, in the course of which she had been a wife and a mother, and, so far as I could judge, a comfortable and happy woman. Reflecting within myself, it appeared to me that this lifelong sorrow—as, in all good faith, she deemed it —was one of the most fortunate circumstances of her history. It had given an ideality to her mind; it had kept her purer and less earthly than she would otherwise have been, by drawing a portion of her sympathies apart from earth. Amid the throng of enjoyments, and the pressure of worldly care, and all the warm materialism of this life, she had communed with a vision, and had been the better for such intercourse. Faithful to the husband of her maturity, and loving him with a far more real affection than she ever could have felt for this dream of her girlhood, there had still been an imaginative faith to the ocean-buried, so that an ordinary character had thus been elevated and refined. Her sighs had been the breath of Heaven to her soul. The good lady earnestly desired that the proposed monument should be ornamented with a carved border of marine plants, intertwined with twisted sea shells, such as were probably waving over her lover's skeleton, or strewn around it, in the far depths of the Pacific. But Mr. Wigglesworth's chisel being inadequate to the task, she was forced to content herself with a rose, hanging its head from a broken stem. After her departure, I remarked that the symbol was none of the most apt.

"And yet," said my friend the sculptor, embodying in this image the thoughts that had been passing through my own mind, "that broken rose has shed its sweet smell through forty years of the good woman's life."

It was seldom that I could find such pleasant food for contemplation as in the above instance. None of the applicants, I think, affected me more disagreeably than an old man who came, with his fourth wife hanging on his arm, to bespeak gravestones for the three former occupants of his marriage bed. I watched with some anxiety to see whether his remembrance of either were more affectionate than of the other two, but could discover no symptom of the kind. The three monuments were all to be of the same material and form, and each decorated, in bass relief, with two weeping willows, one of these sympathetic trees bending over its fellow, which was to be broken in the midst and rest upon a sepulchral urn. This, indeed, was Mr. Wigglesworth's standing emblem of conjugal bereavement. I shuddered at the gray polygamist, who had so utterly lost the holy sense of individuality in wedlock, that methought he was fain to reckon upon his fingers how many women, who had once slept by his side, were now sleeping in their graves. There was even—if I wrong him it is no great matter—a glance sidelong at his living spouse, as if he were inclined to drive a thriftier bargain by bespeaking four gravestones in a lot. I was better pleased with a rough old whaling captain, who gave directions for a broad marble slab, divided into two compartments, one of which was to contain an epitaph on his deceased wife, and the other to be left vacant, till death should engrave his own name there. As is frequently the case among the whalers of Martha's Vineyard, so much of this storm-beaten widower's life had been tossed away on distant seas, that out of twenty years of matrimony he had spent scarce three, and those at scattered intervals, beneath his own roof. Thus the wife of his youth, though she died in his and her declining age, retained the bridal dewdrops fresh around her memory.

My observations gave me the idea, and Mr. Wigglesworth confirmed it, that husbands were more faithful in setting up memorials to their dead wives than widows to their dead husbands. I was not ill natured enough to fancy that women, less than men, feel so sure of their own constancy as to be willing to give a pledge of it in marble. It is more probably the fact, that while men are able to reflect upon their lost companions as remembrances apart from themselves ; women, on the other hand, are conscious that a portion of their being has gone with the departed whithersoever he has gone. Soul clings to soul ; the living dust has a sympathy with the dust of the grave ; and, by the very strength of that sympathy, the wife of the dead shrinks the more sensitively from reminding the world of its existence. The link is already strong enough ; it needs no visible symbol. And, though a shadow walks ever by her side, and the touch of a chill hand is on her bosom, yet life, and perchance its natural yearnings, may still be warm within her, and inspire her with new hopes of happiness. Then would she mark out the grave, the scent of which would be perceptible on the pillow of the second bridal ? No— but rather level its green mound with the surrounding earth, as if, when she dug up again her buried heart, the spot had ceased to be a grave. Yet, in spite of these sentimentalities, I was prodigiously amused by an incident, of which I had not the good fortune to be a witness, but which Mr. Wigglesworth related with considerable humor. A gentlewoman of the town, receiving news of her husband's loss at sea, had bespoken a handsome slab of marble, and came daily to watch the progress of my friend's chisel. One afternoon, when the good lady and the sculptor were in the very midst of the epitaph, which the departed spirit might have been greatly comforted to read, who should walk into the workshop but the deceased himself, in substance as well as spirit! He had been picked up at sea, and stood in no present need of tombstone or epitaph.

"And how," inquired I, "did his wife bear the shock of joyful surprise?"

"Why," said the old man, deepening the grin of a death's head, on which his chisel was just then employed, "I really felt for the poor woman; it was one of my best pieces of marble—and to be thrown away on a living man!"

A comely woman, with a pretty rosebud of a daughter, came to select a gravestone for a twin daughter, who had died a month before. I was impressed with the different nature of their feelings for the dead; the mother was calm and wofully resigned, fully conscious of her loss, as of a treasure which she had not always possessed, and, therefore, had been aware that it might be taken from her; but the daughter evidently had no real knowledge of what death's doings were. Her thoughts knew, but not her heart. It seemed to me, that by the print and pressure which the dead sister had left upon the survivor's spirit, her feelings were almost the same as if she still stood side by side, and arm in arm, with the departed, looking at the slabs of marble; and once or twice she glanced around with a sunny smile, which, as its sister smile had faded forever, soon grew confusedly overshadowed. Perchance her consciousness was truer than her reflection—perchance her dead sister was a closer companion than in life. The mother and daughter talked a long while with Mr. Wigglesworth about a suitable epitaph, and finally chose an ordinary verse of ill-matched rhymes, which had already been inscribed upon innumerable tombstones. But, when we ridicule the triteness of monumental verses, we forget that Sorrow reads far deeper in them than we can, and finds a profound and individual purport in what seems so vague and inexpressive, unless interpreted by her. She makes the epitaph anew, though the selfsame words may have served for a thousand graves.

"And yet," said I afterwards to Mr. Wigglesworth, "they might have made a better choice than this. While you were discussing the subject, I was struck by at least a dozen simple and natural expressions from the lips of both mother and daughter. One of these would have formed an inscription equally original and appropriate."

"No, no," replied the sculptor, shaking his head, "there is a good deal of comfort to be gathered from these little old scraps of poetry : and so I always recommend them in preference to any new-fangled ones. And somehow they seem to stretch to suit a great grief, and shrink to fit a small one."

It was not seldom that ludicrous images were excited by what took place between Mr. Wigglesworth and his customers. A shrewd gentlewoman, who kept a tavern in the town, was anxious to obtain two or three gravestones for the deceased members of her family, and to pay for these solemn commodities by taking the sculptor to board. Hereupon a fantasy arose in my mind, of good Mr. Wigglesworth sitting down to dinner at a broad, flat tombstone, carving one of his own plump little marble cherubs, gnawing a pair of crossbones, and drinking out of a hollow death's head, or perhaps a lachrymatory vase, or sepulchral urn ; while his hostess's dead children waited on him at the ghastly banquet. On communicating this nonsensical picture to the old man, he laughed heartily, and pronounced my humor to be of the right sort.

"I have lived at such a table all my days," said he, "and eaten no small quantity of slate and marble."

"Hard fare !" rejoined I, smiling : "but you seemed to have found it excellent of digestion, too."

A man of fifty, or thereabouts, with a harsh, unpleasant countenance, ordered a stone for the grave of his bitter enemy, with whom he had waged warfare half a lifetime, to their mutual misery and ruin. The secret of this phenomenon was, that hatred had become the sustenance and enjoyment of the poor wretch's soul ; it had supplied the place of all kindly affections ; it had been really a bond of sympathy between himself and the man who shared the passion ; and when its object died, the unappeasable foe was the only mourner for the dead. He expressed a purpose of being buried side by side with his enemy.

"I doubt whether their dust will mingle," remarked the old sculptor to me; for often there was an earthliness in his conceptions.

"O yes," replied I, who had mused long upon the incident ; "and when they rise again, these bitter foes may find themselves dear friends. Methinks what they mistook for hatred was but love under a mask."

A gentleman of antiquarian propensities provided a memorial for an Indian of Chabbiquidick, one of the few of untainted blood remaining in that region, and said to be an hereditary chieftain, descended from the sachem who welcomed Governor Mayhew to the Vineyard. Mr. Wigglesworth exerted his best skill to carve a broken bow and scattered sheaf of arrows, in memory of the hunters and warriors whose race was ended here; but he likewise sculptured a cherub, to denote that the poor Indian had shared the Christian's hope of immortality.

"Why," observed I, taking a perverse view of the winged boy and the bow and arrows, "it looks more like Cupid's tomb than an Indian chief's!"

"You talk nonsense," said the sculptor, with the offended pride of art; he then added with his usual good nature, "How can Cupid die when there are such pretty maidens in the Vineyard?"

"Very true," answered I—and for the rest of the day I though of other matters than tombstones.

At our next meeting I found him chiselling an open book upon a marble headstone, and concluded that it was meant to express the erudition of some black-letter clergyman of the Cotton Mather school. It turned out, however, to be emblematical of the scriptural knowledge of an old woman who had never read anything but her Bible; and the monument was a tribute to her piety and good works from the Orthodox church, of which she had been a member. In strange contrast with this Christian woman's memorial, was that of an infidel, whose gravestone, by his own direction, bore an avowal of his belief that the spirit within him would be extinguished like a flame, and that the nothingness whence he sprang would receive him again. Mr. Wigglesworth consulted me as to the propriety of enabling a dead man's dust to utter this dreadful creed.

"If I thought," said he, "that a single mortal would read the inscription without a shudder, my chisel should never cut a letter of it. But when the grave speaks such falsehoods, the soul of man will know the truth by its own horror."

"So it will," said I, struck by the idea: "the poor infidel may strive to preach blasphemies from his grave;

but it will be only another method of impressing the soul with a consciousness of immortality."

There was an old man by the name of Norton, noted throughout the island for his great wealth, which he had accumulated by the exercise of strong and shrewd faculties, combined with a most penurious disposition. This wretched miser, conscious that he had not a friend to be mindful of him in his grave, had himself taken the needful precautions for posthumous remembrance, by bespeaking an immense slab of white marble, with a long epitaph in raised letters, the whole to be as magnificent as Mr. Wigglesworth's skill could make it. There was something very characteristic in this contrivance to have his money's worth even from his own tombstone, which, indeed, afforded him more enjoyment in the few months that he lived thereafter, than it probably will in a whole century, now that it is laid over his bones. This incident reminds me of a young girl, a pale, slender, feeble creature, most unlike the other rosy and healthful damsels of the Vineyard, amid whose brightness she was fading away. Day after day did the poor maiden come to the sculptor's shop, and pass from one piece of marble to another, till at last she pencilled her name upon a slender slab, which, I think, was of a more spotless white than all the rest. I saw her no more, but soon afterwards found Mr. Wigglesworth cutting her virgin name into the stone which she had chosen.

"She is dead—poor girl," said he, interrupting the tune which he was whistling, "and she chose a good piece of stuff for her headstone. Now which of these slabs would you like best to see your own name upon?"

"Why, to tell you the truth, my good Mr. Wigglesworth," replied I, after a moment's pause—for the abruptness of the question had somewhat startled me,—" to be quite sincere with you, I care little or nothing about a stone for my own grave, and am somewhat inclined to

scepticism as to the propriety of erecting monuments at
all over the dust that once was human. The weight of
these heavy marbles, though unfelt by the dead corpse
of the enfranchised soul, presses drearily upon the spirit
of the survivor, and causes him to connect the idea of
death with the dungeonlike imprisonment of the tomb,
instead of with the freedom of the skies. Every gravestone that you ever made is the visible symbol of a mistaken system. Our thoughts should soar upward with
the butterfly—not linger with the exuviæ that confined
him. In truth and reason, neither those whom we call
the living, and still less the departed, have anything to
do with the grave."

"I never heard anything so heathenish!" said Mr.
Wigglesworth, perplexed and displeased at sentiments
which controverted all his notions and feelings, and
implied the utter waste, and worse, of his whole life's
labor—"would you forget your dead friends the moment
they are under the sod?"

"They are not under the sod," I rejoined; "then why
should I mark the spot where there is no treasure hidden!
Forget them? No! But to remember them aright, I
would forget what they have cast off. And to gain the
truer conception of DEATH, I would forget the GRAVE!"

But still the good old sculptor murmured, and stumbled,
as it were, over the gravestones amid which he had
walked through life. Whether he were right or wrong,
I had grown the wiser from our companionship and from
my observations of nature and character, as displayed by
those who came, with their old griefs or their new ones,
to get them recorded upon his slabs of marble. And yet,
with my gain of wisdom, I had likewise gained perplexity;
for there was a strange doubt in my mind, whether the
dark shadowing of this life, the sorrows and regrets, have
not as much real comfort in them—leaving religious influences out of the question—as what we term life's joys.

ONE day, in the sick chamber of Father Ephraim, who
had been forty years the presiding elder over the Shaker
settlement at Goshen, there was an assemblage of several
of the chief men of the sect. Individuals had come from
the rich establishment at Lebanon, from Canterbury,
Harvard, and Alfred, and from all the other localities,
where this strange people have fertilized the rugged hills
of New England by their systematic industry. An elder
was likewise there, who had made a pilgrimage of a
thousand miles from a village of the faithful in Ken-
tucky, to visit his spiritual kindred, the children of the
sainted Mother Ann. He had partaken of the homely
abundance of their tables, had quaffed the far-famed
Shaker cider, and had joined in the sacred dance, every
step of which is believed to alienate the enthusiast from
earth, and bear him onward to heavenly purity and bliss.
His brethren of the north had now courteously invited
him to be present on an occasion, when the concurrence
of every eminent member of their community was
peculiarly desirable.

The venerable Father Ephraim sat in his easy chair,
not only hoary headed and infirm with age, but worn
down by a lingering disease, which, it was evident,
would very soon transfer his patriarchal staff to other
hands. At his footstool stood a man and woman, both
clad in the Shaker garb.

"My brethren," said Father Ephraim to the surrounding elders, feebly exerting himself to utter these few

words, " here are the son and daughter to whom I would commit the trust, of which Providence is about to lighten my weary shoulders. Read their faces, I pray you, and say whether the inward movement of the spirit hath guided my choice aright."

Accordingly, each elder looked at the two candidates with a most scrutinizing gaze. The man, whose name was Adam Colburn, had a face sunburnt with labor in the fields, yet intelligent, thoughtful, and traced with cares enough for a whole lifetime, though he had barely reached middle age. There was something severe in his aspect, and a ridigity throughout his person, character-istics that caused him generally to be taken for a school-master; which vocation, in fact, he had formerly exercised for several years. The woman, Martha Pierson, was somewhat above thirty, thin and pale, as a Shaker sister almost invariable is, and not entirely free from that corpse-like appearance which the garb of the sisterhood is so well calculated to impart.

"This pair are still in the summer of their years," observed the elder from Harvard, a shrewd old man. "I would like better to see the hoarfrost of autumn on their heads. Methinks, also, they will be exposed to peculiar temptations, on account of the carnal desires which have heretofore subsisted between them."

"Nay, brother," said the elder from Canterbury, "the hoarfrost, and the blackfrost, hath done its work on Brother Adam and Sister Martha, even as we sometimes discern its traces in our cornfields, while they are yet green. And why should we question the wisdom of our venerable Father's purpose, although this pair in their early youth have loved one another as the world's people love? Are there not many brethren and sisters among us, who have lived long together in wedlock, yet, adopting our faith, find their hearts purified from all but spiritual affection?"

Whether or no the early loves of Adam and Martha had rendered it inexpedient that they should now preside together over a Shaker village, it was certainly most singular that such should be the final result of many warm and tender hopes. Children of neighboring families, their affection was older even than their school-days ; it seemed an innate principle, interfused among all their sentiments and feelings, and not so much a distinct remembrance, as connected with their whole volume of remembrances. But, just as they reached a proper age for their union, misfortunes had fallen heavily on both, and made it necessary that they should resort to personal labor for a bare subsistence. Even under these circumstances, Martha Pierson would probably have consented to unite her fate with Adam Colburn's, and, secure of the bliss of mutual love, would patiently have awaited the less important gifts of fortune. But Adam, being of a calm and cautious character, was loath to relinquish the advantages which a single man possesses for raising himself in the world. Year after year, therefore, their marriage had been deferred. Adam Colburn had followed many vocations, had travelled far, and seen much of the world and of life. Martha had earned her bread sometimes as a seamstress, sometimes as help to a farmer's wife, sometimes as schoolmistress of the village children, sometimes as a nurse or watcher of the sick, thus acquiring a varied experience, the ultimate use of which she little anticipated. But nothing had gone prosperously with either of the lovers ; at no subsequent moment would matrimony have been so prudent a measure, as when they had first parted, in the opening bloom of life, to seek a better fortune. Still they had held fast their mutual faith. Martha might have been the wife of a man, who sat among the senators of his native state, and Adam could have won the hand, as he had unintentionally won the heart, of a rich and comely widow. But neither of them desired good fortune, save to share it with the other.

At length that calm despair which occurs only in a strong and somewhat stubborn character, and yields to no second spring of hope, settled down on the spirit of Adam Colburn. He sought an interview with Martha, and proposed that they should join the Society of Shakers. The converts of this sect are oftener driven within its hospitable gates by worldly misfortune than drawn thither by fanaticism, and are received without inquisition as to their motives. Martha, faithful still, had placed her hand in that of her lover, and accompanied him to the Shaker village. Here the natural capacity of each, cultivated and strengthened by the difficulties of their previous lives, had soon gained them an important rank in the Society, whose members are generally below the ordinary standard of intelligence. Their faith and feelings had, in some degree, become assimilated to those of their fellow-worshippers. Adam Colburn gradually acquired reputation, not only in the management of the temporal affairs of the Society, but as a clear and efficient preacher of their doctrines. Martha was not less distinguished in the duties proper to her sex. Finally, when the infirmities of Father Ephraim had admonished him to seek a successor in his patriarchal office, he thought of Adam and Martha, and proposed to renew, in their persons, the primitive form of Shaker government, as established by Mother Ann. They were to be the Father and Mother of the village. The simple ceremony, which would constitute them such, was now to be performed.

" Son Adam, and daughter Martha," said the venerable Father Ephraim, fixing his aged eyes piercingly upon them, "if ye can conscientiously undertake this charge, speak, that the brethren may not doubt of your fitness."

" Father," replied Adam, speaking with the calmness

of his character, " I came to your village a disappointed
man, weary of the world, worn out with continual trouble,
seeking only a security against evil fortune, as I had no
hope of good. Even my wishes of worldly success were
almost dead within me. I came hither as a man might
come to a tomb, willing to lie down in its gloom and
coldness, for the sake of its peace and quiet. There was
but one earthly affection in my breast, and it had grown
calmer since my youth ; so that I was satisfied to bring
Martha to be my sister in our new abode. We are
brother and sister ; nor would I have it otherwise. And
in this peaceful village I have found all that I hoped for,
—all that I desire. I will strive, with my best strength,
for the spiritual and temporal good of our community.
My conscience is not doubtful in this matter. I am
ready to receive the trust."

"Thou hast spoken well, son Adam," said the Father.
"God will bless thee in the office which I am about to
resign."

"But our sister !" observed the elder from Harvard ;
"hath she not likewise a gift to declare her sentiments?"

Martha started, and moved her lips, as if she would
have made a formal reply to this appeal. But, had
she attempted it, perhaps the old recollections, the
long-repressed feelings of childhood, youth, and woman-
hood might have gushed from her heart, in words that
it would have been profanation to utter there.

"Adam has spoken," said she hurriedly ; his sentiments are likewise mine."

But while speaking these few words, Martha grew so
pale, that she looked fitter to be laid in her coffin, than
to stand in the presence of Father Ephraim and the
elders ; she shuddered, also, as if there were something
awful or horrible in her situation and destiny. It
required, indeed, a more than feminine strength of nerve
to sustain the fixed observance of men so exalted and

famous throughout the sect as these were. They had
overcome their natural sympathy with human frailties
and affections. One, when he joined the Society, had
brought with him his wife and children, but never, from
that hour, had spoken a fond word to the former, or taken
his best-loved child upon his knee. Another, whose
family refused to follow him, had been enabled,—such
was his gift of holy fortitude,—to leave them to the mercy
of the world. The youngest of the elders, a man of
about fifty, had been bred from infancy in a Shaker
village, and was said never to have clasped a woman's
hand in his own, and to have no conception of a closer
tie than the cold fraternal one of the sect. Old Father
Ephraim was the most awful character of all. In his
youth he had been a dissolute libertine, but was converted by Mother Ann herself, and had partaken of the
wild fanaticism of the early Shakers. Tradition whispered,
at the firesides of the village, that Mother Ann had been
compelled to sear his heart of flesh with a red-hot iron,
before it could be purified from earthly passions.

However that might be, poor Martha had a woman's
heart, and a tender one, and it quailed within her as
she looked round at those strange old men, and from
them to the calm features of Adam Colburn. But
perceiving that the elders eyed her doubtfully, she
gasped for breath, and again spoke.

"With what strength is left me by my many troubles,"
said she, "I am ready to undertake this charge, and
to do my best in it."

"My children, join your hands," said Father Ephraim.

They did so. The elders stood up around, and the
Father feebly raised himself to a more erect position,
but continued sitting in his great chair.

"I have bidden you to join your hands," said he, "not
in earthly affection, for ye have cast off its chains forever; but as brother and sister in spiritual love, and

helpers of one another in your allotted task. Teach unto others the faith which ye have received. Open wide your gates,—I deliver you the keys thereof,— open them wide to all who will give up the iniquities of the world, and come hither to lead lives of purity and peace. Receive the weary ones, who have known the vanity of earth,—receive the little children, that they may never learn that miserable lesson. And a blessing be upon your labors ; so that the time may hasten on, when the mission of Mother Ann shall have wrought its full effect,—when children shall no more be born and die, and the last survivor of mortal race, some old and weary man like me, shall see the sun go down, nevermore to rise on a world of sin and sorrow ! "

The aged Father sank back exhausted, and the sur-rounding elders deemed, with good reason, that the hour was come, when the new heads of the village must enter on their patriarchal duties. In their attention to Father Ephraim, their eyes were turned from Martha Pierson, who grew paler and paler, unnoticed even by Adam Col-burn. He, indeed, had withdrawn his hand from hers, and folded his arms with a sense of satisfied ambition. But paler and paler grew Martha by his side, till, like a corpse in its burial clothes, she sank down at the feet of her early lover ; for, after many trials firmly borne, her heart could endure the weight of its desolate agony no longer.

NIGHT SKETCHES.

BENEATH AN UMBRELLA.

PLEASANT is a rainy winter's day within doors! The best study for such a day, or the best amusement,—call it which you will,—is a book of travels, describing scenes the most unlike that sombre one which is mistily presented through the windows. I have experienced, that fancy is then most successful in imparting distinct shapes and vivid colors to the objects which the author has spread upon his page, and that his words become magic spells to summon up a thousand varied pictures. Strange landscapes glimmer through the familiar walls of the room, and outlandish figures thrust themselves almost within the sacred precincts of the hearth. Small as my chamber is, it has space enough to contain the ocean-like circumference of an Arabian desert, its parched sands tracked by the long line of a caravan, with the camels patiently journeying through the heavy sunshine. Though my ceiling be not lofty, yet I can pile up the mountains of Central Asia beneath it, till their summits shine far above the clouds of the middle atmosphere. And, with my humble means, a wealth that is not taxable, I can transport hither the magnificent merchandise of an Oriental bazaar, and call a crowd of purchasers from distant countries to pay a fair profit for the precious articles which are displayed on all sides. True it is, however, that amid the bustle of traffic, or whatever else may seem to be going on around me, the raindrops will occasionally be heard to patter against my window panes,

which look forth upon one of the quietest streets in a
New England town. After a time, too, the visions vanish,
and will not appear again at my bidding. Then, it
being nightfall, a gloomy sense of unreality depresses my
spirits, and impels me to venture out, before the clock
shall strike bedtime, to satisfy myself that the world is
not entirely made up of such shadowy materials as have
busied me throughout the day. A dreamer may dwell
so long among fantasies, that the things without him will
seem as unreal as those within.

When eve has fairly set in, therefore, I sally forth,
tightly buttoning my shaggy overcoat, and hoisting my
umbrella, the silken dome of which immediately resounds
with the heavy drumming of the invisible raindrops.
Pausing on the lowest doorstep, I contrast the warmth
and cheerfulness of my deserted fireside with the drear
obscurity and chill discomfort into which I am about to
plunge. Now come fearful auguries, innumerable as the
drops of rain. Did not my manhood cry shame upon me,
I should turn back within doors, resume my elbow chair,
my slippers, and my book, pass such an evening of sluggish
enjoyment as the day has been, and go to bed inglorious.
The same shivering reluctance, no doubt, has quelled, for
a moment, the adventurous spirit of many a traveller,
when his feet, which were destined to measure the earth
around, were leaving their last tracks in the home paths.

In my own case, poor human nature may be allowed a
few misgivings. I look upward, and discern no sky, not
even an unfathomable void, but only a black, impenetrable nothingness, as though heaven and all its lights
were blotted from the system of the universe. It is as if
nature were dead, and the world had put on black, and
the clouds were weeping for her. With their tears upon
my cheek, I turn my eyes earthward, but find little consolation here below. A lamp is burning dimly at the
distant corner, and throws just enough of light along the

street to show, and exaggerate by so faintly showing, the perils and difficulties which beset my path. Yonder dingily white remnant of a huge snow bank,—which will yet cumber the sidewalk till the latter days of March,— over or through that wintry waste must I stride onward. Beyond, lies a certain Slough of Despond, a concoction of mud and liquid filth, ankle-deep, leg-deep, neck-deep,—in a word, of unknown bottom,—on which the lamplight does not even glimmer, but which I have occasionally watched, in the gradual growth of its horrors, from morn till nightfall. Should I flounder into its depths, farewell to upper earth ! And hark ! how roughly resounds the roaring of a stream, the turbulent career of which is partially reddened by the gleam of the lamp, but elsewhere brawls noisily through the densest gloom. O, should I be swept away in fording that impetuous and unclean torrent, the coroner will have a job with an unfortunate gentleman, who would fain end his troubles any where but in a mud puddle !

Pshaw ! I will linger not another instant at arm's length from these dim terrors, which grow more obscurely formidable the longer I delay to grapple with them. Now for the onset ! And lo ! with little damage, save a dash of rain in the face and breast, a splash of mud high up the pantaloons, and the left boot full of ice-cold water, behold me at the corner of the street. The lamp throws down a circle of red light around me ; and, twinkling onward from corner to corner, I discern other beacons marshalling my way to a brighter scene. But this is a lonesome and dreary spot. The tall edifices bid gloomy defiance to the storm, with their blinds all closed, even as a man winks when he faces a spattering gust. How loudly tinkles the collected rain down the tin spouts ! The puffs of wind are boisterous, and seem to assail me from various quarters at once. I have often observed that this corner is a haunt and loitering-place for those winds which have no work to do upon the deep, dashing

ships against our iron-bound shores ; nor in the forest,
tearing up the sylvan giants with half a rood of soil at their
vast roots. Here they amuse themselves with lesser freaks
of mischief. See, at this moment, how they assail yonder
poor woman, who is passing just within the verge of the
lamplight! One blast struggles for her umbrella, and turns
it wrong side outward ; another whisks the cape of her cloak
across her eyes ; while a third takes most unwarrantable
liberties with the lower part of her attire. Happily, the
good dame is no gossamer, but a figure of rotundity and
fleshly substance ; else would these aerial tormentors
whirl her aloft, like a witch upon a broomstick, and set
her down, doubtless, in the filthiest kennel hereabout.

From hence I tread upon firm pavements into the
centre of the town. Here there is almost as brilliant an
illumination as when some great victory has been won,
either on the battle field or at the polls. Two rows of
shops, with windows down nearly to the ground, cast a
glow from side to side, while the black night hangs overhead like a canopy, and thus keeps the splendor from
diffusing itself away. The wet sidewalks gleam with a
broad sheet of red light. The raindrops glitter, as if the
sky were pouring down rubies. The spouts gush with
fire. Methinks the scene is an emblem of the deceptive
glare, which mortals throw around their footsteps in the
moral world, thus bedazzling themselves, till they forget
the impenetrable obscurity that hems them in, and that
can be dispelled only by radiance from above. And after
all, it is a cheerless scene, and cheerless are the wanderers
in it. Here comes one who has so long been familiar with
tempestuous weather that he takes the bluster of the storm
for a friendly greeting, as if it should say, " How fare ye,
brother?" He is a retired sea captain, wrapped in some
nameless garment of the pea-jacket order, and is now
laying his course towards the Marine Insurance Office,
there to spin yarns of gale and shipwreck with a crew of

old sea dogs like himself. The blast will put in its word among their hoarse voices, and be understood by all of them. Next I meet an unhappy slipshod gentleman, with a cloak flung hastily over his shoulders, running a race with boisterous winds, and striving to glide between the drops of rain. Some domestic emergency or other has blown this miserable man from his warm fireside, in quest of a doctor! See that little vagabond,—how carelessly he has taken his stand right underneath a spout, while staring at some object of curiosity in a shop window! Surely the rain is his native element; he must have fallen with it from the clouds, as frogs are supposed to do.

Here is a picture, and a pretty one. A young man and a girl, both enveloped in cloaks and huddled beneath the scanty protection of a cotton umbrella. She wears rubber overshoes; but he is in his dancing pumps; and they are on their way, no doubt, to some cotillon party, or subscription ball at a dollar a head, refreshments included. Thus they struggle against the gloomy tempest, lured onward by a vision of festal splendor. But, ah! a most lamentable disaster. Bewildered by the red, blue, and yellow meteors in an apothecary's window, they have stepped upon a slippery remnant of ice, and are precipitated into a confluence of swollen floods, at the corner of two streets. Luckless lovers! Were it my nature to be other than a looker-on in life, I would attempt your rescue. Since that may not be, I vow, should you be drowned, to weave such a pathetic story of your fate, as shall call forth tears enough to drown you both anew. Do ye touch bottom, my young friends? Yes; they emerge like a water nymph and a river deity, and paddle hand in hand out of the depths of the dark pool. They hurry homeward, dripping, disconsolate, abashed, but with love too warm to be chilled by the cold water. They have stood a test which proves too strong for many. Faithful, though over head and ears in trouble!

Onward I go, deriving a sympathetic joy or sorrow from the varied aspect of mortal affairs, even as my figure catches a gleam from the lighted windows, or is blackened by an interval of darkness. Not that mine is altogether a chameleon spirit, with no hue of its own. Now I pass into a more retired street, where the dwellings of wealth and poverty are intermingled, presenting a range of strongly contrasted pictures. Here, too, may be found the golden mean. Through yonder casement I discern a family circle,—the grandmother, the parents, and the children,—all flickering, shadow-like, in the glow of a wood fire. Bluster, fierce blast, and beat, thou wintry rain, against the window panes! Ye cannot damp the enjoyment of that fireside. Surely my fate is hard, that I should be wandering homeless here, taking to my bosom night, and storm, and solitude, instead of wife and children. Peace, murmurer! Doubt not that darker guests are sitting round the hearth, though the warm blaze hides all but blissful images. Well, here is still a brighter scene. A stately mansion, illuminated for a ball, with cut-glass chandeliers and alabaster lamps in every room, and sunny landscapes hanging round the walls. See! a coach has stopped, whence emerges a slender beauty, who, canopied by two umbrellas, glides within the portal, and vanishes amid lightsome thrills of music. Will she ever feel the night wind and the rain? Perhaps,—perhaps! And will Death and Sorrow ever enter that proud mansion? As surely as the dancers will be gay within its halls to-night. Such thoughts sadden, yet satisfy my heart; for they teach me that the poor man, in this mean, weather-beaten hovel, without a fire to cheer him, may call the rich his brother, brethren by Sorrow, who must be an inmate of both their households,—brethren by Death, who will lead them both to other homes.

Onward, still onward, I plunge into the night. Now

have I reached the utmost limits of the town, where the last lamp struggles feebly with the darkness, like the farthest star that stands sentinel on the borders of uncreated space. It is strange what sensations of sublimity may spring from a very humble source. Such are suggested by this hollow roar of a subterranean cataract, where the mighty stream of a kennel precipitates itself beneath an iron grate, and is seen no more on earth. Listen a while to its voice of mystery; and fancy will magnify it, till you start, and smile at the illusion. And now another sound, — the rumbling of wheels, — as the mail coach, outward bound, rolls heavily off the pavements, and splashes through the mud and water of the road. All night long, the poor passengers will be tossed to and fro between drowsy watch and troubled sleep, and will dream of their own quiet beds, and awake to find themselves still jolting onward. Happier my lot, who will straightway hie me to my familiar room, and toast myself comfortably before the fire, musing, and fitfully dozing, and fancying a strangeness in such sights as all may see. But first let me gaze at this solitary figure, who comes hitherward with a tin lantern, which throws the circular pattern of its punched holes on the ground about him. He passes fearlessly into the unknown gloom, whither I will not follow him.

This figure shall supply me with a moral, wherewith, for lack of a more appropriate one, I may wind up my sketch. He fears not to tread the dreary path before him, because his lantern, which was kindled at the fireside of his home, will light him back to that same fireside again. And thus we, night wanderers through a stormy and dismal world, if we bear the lamp of Faith, enkindled at a celestial fire, it will surely lead us home to that Heaven whence its radiance was borrowed.

ENDICOTT AND THE RED CROSS.

AT noon of an autumnal day, more than two centuries ago, the English colors were displayed by the standard bearer of the Salem trainband, which had mustered for martial exercise under the orders of John Endicott. It was a period, when the religious exiles were accustomed often to buckle on their armor, and practise the handling of their weapons of war. Since the first settlement of New England, its prospects had never been so dismal. The dissensions between Charles the First and his subjects were then, and for several years afterwards, confined to the floor of Parliament. The measures of the King and ministry were rendered more tyrannically violent by an opposition, which had not yet acquired sufficient confidence in its own strength, to resist royal injustice with the sword. The bigoted and haughty primate, Laud, Archbishop of Canterbury, controlled the religious affairs of the realm, and was consequently invested with powers which might have wrought the utter ruin of the two Puritan colonies, Plymouth and Massachusetts. There is evidence on record, that our forefathers perceived their danger, but were resolved that their infant country should not fall without a struggle, even beneath the giant strength of the King's right arm.

Such was the aspect of the times, when the folds of the English banner, with the Red Cross in its field, were flung out over a company of Puritans. Their leader, the famous Endicott, was a man of stern and resolute countenance, the effect of which was heightened by a grizzled beard that swept the upper portion of his breastplate. This piece of armor was so highly polished, that the whole surrounding scene had its image in the glittering steel. The central object in the mirrored picture, was an edifice of humble architecture, with neither steeple nor bell to proclaim it,—what nevertheless it was,—the house of prayer. A token of the perils of the wilderness was seen in the grim head of a wolf, which had just been slain within the precincts of the town, and, according to the regular mode of claiming the bounty, was nailed on the porch of the meeting-house. The blood was still plashing on the doorstep. There happened to be visible, at the same noontide hour, so many other characteristics of the times and manners of the Puritans, that we must endeavor to represent them in a sketch, though far less vividly than they were reflected in the polished breastplate of John Endicott.

In close vicinity to the sacred edifice appeared that important engine of Puritanic authority, the whipping post—with the soil around it well trodden by the feet of evil doers, who had there been disciplined. At one corner of the meeting-house was the pillory, and at the other the stocks ; and, by a singular good fortune for our sketch, the head of an Episcopalian and suspected Catholic was grotesquely incased in the former machine; while a fellow-criminal, who had boisterously quaffed a health to the king, was confined by the legs in the latter. Side by side, on the meeting-house steps, stood a male and a female figure. The man was a tall, lean, haggard personification of fanaticism, bearing on his breast this label,— A WANTON GOSPELLER, — which betokened that he had dared to give interpretations of Holy Writ, unsanctioned by the infallible judgment of the civil and religious rulers. His aspect showed no lack of zeal to maintain his heterodoxies, even at the stake.   The woman wore a cleft stick on her tongue, in appropriate retribution for having wagged that unruly member against the elders of the church ; and her countenance and gestures gave much cause to apprehend, that, the moment the stick should be removed, a repetition of the offence would demand new ingenuity in chastising it.

The above-mentioned individuals had been sentenced to undergo their various modes of ignominy for the space of one hour at noonday.   But among the crowd were several, whose punishment would be lifelong ; some, whose ears had been cropped, like those of puppy dogs ; others, whose cheeks had been branded with the initials of their misdemeanors ; one, with his nostrils slit and seared ; and another, with a halter about his neck, which he was forbidden ever to take off, or to conceal beneath his garments.   Methinks he must have been grievously tempted to affix the other end of the rope to some convenient beam or bough.   There was likewise a young woman, with no mean share of beauty, whose doom it was to wear the letter A on the breast of her gown, in the eyes of all the world and her own children.   And even her own children knew what that initial signified. Sporting with her infamy, the lost and desperate creature had embroidered the fatal token in scarlet cloth, with golden thread and the nicest art of needlework ; so that the capital A might have been thought to mean Admirable, or anything rather than Adulteress.

Let not the reader argue, from any of these evidences of iniquity, that the times of the Puritans were more vicious than our own, when, as we pass along the very street of this sketch, we discern no badge of infamy on man or woman.   It was the policy of our ancestors to search out even the most secret sins, and expose them to shame, without fear or favor, in the broadest light of the noonday sun.   Were such the custom now, perchance we might find materials for a no less piquant sketch than the above.

Except the malefactors whom we have described, and the diseased or infirm persons, the whole male population of the town, between sixteen years and sixty, were seen in the ranks of the trainband. A few stately savages, in all the pomp and dignity of the primeval Indian, stood gazing at the spectacle. Their flint-headed arrows were but childish weapons, compared with the matchlocks of the Puritans, and would have rattled harmlessly against the steel caps and hammered iron breastplates, which enclosed each soldier in an individual fortress. The valiant John Endicott glanced with an eye of pride at his sturdy followers, and prepared to renew the martial toils of the day.

"Come, my stout hearts!" quoth he, drawing his sword. "Let us show these poor heathen that we can handle our weapons like men of might. Well for them, if they put us not to prove it in earnest!"

The iron-breasted company straightened their line, and each man drew the heavy but of his matchlock close to his left foot, thus awaiting the orders of the captain. But, as Endicott glanced right and left along the front, he discovered a personage at some little distance, with whom it behooved him to hold a parley. It was an elderly gentleman, wearing a black cloak and band, and a high-crowned hat, beneath which was a velvet skullcap, the whole being the garb of a Puritan minister. This reverend person bore a staff which seemed to have been recently cut in the forest, and his shoes were bemired as if he had been travelling on foot through the swamps of the wilderness. His aspect was perfectly that of a pilgrim, heightened also by an apostolic dignity. Just as Endicott perceived him, he laid aside his staff, and stooped to drink at a bubbling fountain, which gushed into the sunshine about a score of yards from the corner of the meeting-house. But, ere the good man drank, he turned his face heavenward in thankfulness, and then, holding back his gray beard with one hand, he scooped up his simple draught in the hollow of the other.

"What, ho! good Mr. Williams," shouted Endicott. "You are welcome back again to our town of peace. How does our worthy Governor Winthrop? And what news from Boston?"

"The Governor hath his health, worshipful Sir," answered Roger Williams, now resuming his staff, and drawing near. "And, for the news, here is a letter, which, knowing I was to travel hitherward to-day, his Excellency committed to my charge. Belike it contains tidings of much import; for a ship arrived yesterday from England."

Mr. Williams, the minister of Salem, and of course known to all the spectators, had now reached the spot where Endicott was standing under the banner of his company, and put the Governor's epistle into his hand. The broad seal was impressed with Winthrop's coat of arms. Endicott hastily unclosed the letter, and began to read; while, as his eye passed down the page, a wrathful change came over his manly countenance. The blood glowed through it, till it seemed to be kindling with an internal heat; nor was it unnatural to suppose that his breastplate would likewise become red hot, with the angry fire of the bosom which it covered. Arriving at the conclusion, he shook the letter fiercely in his hand, so that it rustled as loud as the flag above his head.

"Black tidings these, Mr. Williams," said he; "blacker never came to New England. Doubtless you know their purport?"

"Yea, truly," replied Roger Williams; "for the Governor consulted, respecting this matter, with my brethren in the ministry at Boston ; and my opinion was likewise asked. And his Excellency entreats you by me, that the news be not suddenly noised abroad, lest the people be stirred up unto some outbreak, and thereby give the King and the Archbishop a handle against us."

"The Governor is a wise man—a wise man, and a meek and moderate," said Endicott, setting his teeth grimly. "Nevertheless, I must do according to my own best judgment. There is neither man, woman, nor child in New England, but has a concern as dear as life in these tidings ; and if John Endicott's voice be loud enough, man, woman, and child shall hear them. Soldiers, wheel into a hollow square ! Ho, good people ! Here are news for one and all of you."

The soldiers closed in around their captain ; and he and Roger Williams stood together under the banner of the Red Cross ; while the women and the aged men pressed forward, and the mothers held up their children to look Endicott in the face. A few taps of the drum gave signal for silence and attention.

"Fellow - soldiers, — fellow - exiles," began Endicott, speaking under strong excitement, yet powerfully restraining it, "wherefore did ye leave your native country? Wherefore, I say, have we left the green and fertile fields, the cottages, or, perchance, the old gray halls, where we were born and bred, the churchyards where our forefathers lie buried? Wherefore have we come hither to set up our own tombstones in a wilderness? A howling wilderness it is! The wolf and the bear meet us within halloo of our dwellings. The savage lieth in wait for us in the dismal shadow of the woods. The stubborn roots of the trees break our ploughshares, when we would till the earth. Our children cry for bread, and we must dig in the sands of the sea shore to satisfy them. Wherefore, I say again, have we sought this country of a

rugged soil and wintry sky? Was it not for the enjoyment of our civil rights? Was it not for liberty to
worship God according to our conscience?"

"Call you this liberty of conscience?" interrupted a
voice on the steps of the meeting-house.

It was the Wanton Gospeller. A sad and quiet smile
flitted across the mild visage of Roger Williams. But
Endicott, in the excitement of the moment, shook his
sword wrathfully at the culprit — an ominous gesture
from a man like him.

"What hast thou to do with conscience, thou knave?"
cried he. "I said liberty to worship God, not license to
profane and ridicule him. Break not in upon my speech;
or I will lay thee neck and heels till this time to-morrow!
Hearken to me, friends, nor heed that accursed rhap-
sodist. As I was saying, we have sacrificed all things,
and have come to a land whereof the old world hath
scarcely heard, that we might make a new world unto
ourselves, and painfully seek a path from hence to
heaven. But what think ye now? This son of a Scotch
tyrant—this grandson of a Papistical and adulterous
Scotch woman, whose death proved that a golden crown
doth not always save an anointed head from the
block——"

"Nay, brother, nay," interposed Mr. Williams; "thy
words are not meet for a secret chamber, far less for a
public street."

"Hold thy peace, Roger Williams!" answered Endicott, imperiously. "My spirit is wiser than thine for
the business now in hand. I tell ye, fellow-exiles, that
Charles of England, and Laud, our bitterest persecutor,
arch-priest of Canterbury, are resolute to pursue us even
hither. They are taking counsel, saith this letter, to
send over a governor general, in whose breast shall be
deposited all the law and equity of the land. They are
minded, also, to establish the idolatrous forms of English

Episcopacy ; so that, when Laud shall kiss the Pope's toe, as cardinal of Rome, he may deliver New England, bound hand and foot, into the power of his master !"

A deep groan from the auditors,—a sound of wrath, as well as fear and sorrow,—responded to this intelligence.

"Look ye to it, brethren," resumed Endicott, with increasing energy. "If this king and this arch-prelate have their will, we shall briefly behold a cross on the spire of this tabernacle which we have builded, and a high altar within its walls, with wax tapers burning round it at noonday. We shall hear the sacring bell, and the voices of the Romish priests saying the mass. But think ye, Christian men, that these abominations may be suffered without a sword drawn ? without a shot fired ? without blood spilt, yea, on the very stairs of the pulpit ? No,—be ye strong of hand, and stout of heart ! Here we stand on our own soil, which we have bought with our goods, which we have won with our swords, which we have cleared with our axes, which we have tilled with the sweat of our brows, which we have sanctified with our prayers to the God that brought us hither ! Who shall enslave us here ? What have we to do with this mitred prelate,—with this crowned king ? What have we to do with England ?"

Endicott gazed round at the excited countenances of the people, now full of his own spirit, and then turned suddenly to the standard bearer, who stood close behind him.

"Officer, lower your banner !" said he.

The officer obeyed ; and, brandishing his sword, Endicott thrust it through the cloth, and, with his left hand, rent the Red Cross completely out of the banner. He then waved the tattered ensign above his head.

"Sacrilegious wretch !" cried the high-churchman in the pillory, unable longer to restrain himself ; "thou hast rejected the symbol of our holy religion !"

"Treason, treason!" roared the royalist in the stocks. "He hath defaced the King's banner!"

"Before God and man, I will avouch the deed," answered Endicott. "Beat a flourish, drummer!—shout, soldiers and people!—in honor of the ensign of New England. Neither Pope nor Tyrant hath part in it now!"

With a cry of triumph, the people gave their sanction to one of the boldest exploits which our history records. And, forever honored be the name of Endicott! We look back through the mist of ages, and recognize, in the rending of the Red Cross from New England's banner, the first omen of that deliverance which our fathers consummated, after the bones of the stern Puritan had lain more than a century in the dust.

THE LILY'S QUEST.

AN APOLOGUE.

Two lovers, once upon a time, had planned a little summer house, in the form of an antique temple, which it was their purpose to consecrate to all manner of refined and innocent enjoyments. There they would hold pleasant intercourse with one another, and the circle of their familiar friends ; there they would give festivals of delicious fruit ; there they would hear lightsome music, intermingled with the strains of pathos which make joy more sweet ; there they would read poetry and fiction, and permit their own minds to flit away in daydreams and romance ; there, in short—for why should we shape out the vague sunshine of their hopes ?—there all pure delights were to cluster like roses among the pillars of the edifice, and blossom ever new and spontaneously. So, one breezy and cloudless afternoon, Adam Forrester and Lilias Fay set out upon a ramble over the wide estate which they were to possess together, seeking a proper site for their Temple of Happiness. They were themselves a fair and happy spectacle, fit priest and priestess for such a shrine ; although, making poetry of the pretty name of Lilias, Adam Forrester was wont to call her Lily, because her form was as fragile, and her cheek almost as pale.

As they passed, hand in hand, down the avenue of drooping elms, that led from the portal of Lilias Fay's paternal mansion, they seemed to glance like winged

creatures through the strips of sunshine, and to scatter
brightness where the deep shadows fell. But, setting
forth at the same time with this youthful pair, there was
a dismal figure, wrapped in a black velvet cloak that
might have been made of a coffin pall, and with a sombre
hat, such as mourners wear, drooping its broad brim over
his heavy brows. Glancing behind them, the lovers well
knew who it was that followed, but wished from their
hearts that he had been elsewhere, as being a companion
so strangely unsuited to their joyous errand. It was a
near relative of Lilias Fay, an old man by the name of
Walter Gascoigne, who had long labored under the
burden of a melancholy spirit, which was sometimes
maddened into absolute insanity, and always had a tinge
of it. What a contrast between the young pilgrims of
bliss and their unbidden associate! They looked as if
moulded of Heaven's sunshine, and he of earth's gloomiest
shade; they flitted along like Hope and Joy, roaming
hand in hand through life; while his darksome figure
stalked behind, a type of all the woful influences which
life could fling upon them. But the three had not gone
far, when they reached a spot that pleased the gentle
Lily, and she paused.

"What sweeter place shall we find than this?" said
she. "Why should we seek farther for the site of our
Temple?"

It was indeed a delightful spot of earth, though undistinguished by any very prominent beauties, being merely
a nook in the shelter of a hill, with the prospect of a
distant lake in one direction, and of a church spire in
another. There were vistas and pathways, leading onward and onward into the green woodlands, and vanishing away in the glimmering shade. The Temple, if
erected here, would look towards the west; so that
the lovers could shape all sorts of magnificent dreams
out of the purple, violet, and gold of the sunset sky; and

few of their anticipated pleasures were dearer than this sport of fantasy.

"Yes," said Adam Forrester, "we might seek all day, and find no lovelier spot. We will build our Temple here."

But their sad old companion, who had taken his stand on the very site which they proposed to cover with a marble floor, shook his head and frowned; and the young man and the Lily deemed it almost enough to blight the spot, and desecrate it for their airy Temple, that his dismal figure had thrown its shadow there. He pointed to some scattered stones, the remnants of a former structure, and to flowers such as young girls delight to nurse in their gardens, but which had now relapsed into the wild simplicity of nature.

"Not here!" cried old Walter Gascoigne. "Here, long ago, other mortals built their Temple of Happiness. Seek another site for yours!"

"What!" exclaimed Lilias Fay. "Have any ever planned such a Temple save ourselves?"

"Poor child!" said her gloomy kinsman. "In one shape or other every mortal has dreamed your dream."

Then he told the lovers, how—not, indeed an antique Temple—but a dwelling had once stood there, and that a dark-clad guest had dwelt among its inmates, sitting forever at the fireside, and poisoning all their household mirth. Under this type, Adam Forrester and Lilias saw that the old man spake of Sorrow. He told of nothing that might not be recorded in the history of almost every household; and yet his hearers felt as if no sunshine ought to fall upon a spot where human grief had left so deep a stain; or, at least, that no joyous Temple should be built there.

"This is very sad," said the Lily, sighing.

"Well, there are lovelier spots than this," said Adam

Forrester, soothingly — "spots which sorrow has not blighted."

So they hastened away, and the melancholy Gascoigne followed them, looking as if he had gathered up all the gloom of the deserted spot, and was bearing it as a burden of inestimable treasure. But still they rambled on, and soon found themselves in a rocky dell, through the midst of which ran a streamlet, with ripple and foam, and a continual voice of inarticulate joy. It was a wild retreat, walled on either side with gray precipices, which would have frowned somewhat too sternly, had not a profusion of green shrubbery rooted itself into their crevices, and wreathed gladsome foliage around their solemn brows. But the chief joy of the dell was in the little stream, which seemed like the presence of a blissful child, with nothing earthly to do, save to babble merrily and disport itself, and make every living soul its play-fellow, and throw the sunny gleams of its spirit upon all.

"Here, here is the spot!" cried the two lovers with one voice, as they reached a level space on the brink of a small cascade. "This glen was made on purpose for our Temple!"

"And the glad song of the brook will be always in our ears," said Lilias Fay.

"And its long melody shall sing the bliss of our life-time," said Adam Forrester.

"Ye must build no Temple here!" murmured their dismal companion.

And there again was the old lunatic, standing just on the spot where they meant to rear their lightsome dome, and looking like the embodied symbol of some great woe, that, in forgotten days, had happened there. And, alas! there had been woe, nor that alone. A young man, more than a hundred years before, had lured hither a girl that loved him, and on this spot had murdered her, and washed his bloody hands in the stream which sung so merrily. And ever since, the victims death shrieks were often heard to echo between the cliffs.

"And see!" cried old Gascoigne, "is the stream yet pure from the stain of the murderer's hands?"

"Methinks it has a tinge of blood," faintly answered the Lily; and, being as slight as the gossamer, she trembled and clung to her lover's arm, whispering, "let us flee from this dreadful vale!"

"Come, then," said Adam Forrester, as cheerily as he could; "we shall soon find a happier spot."

They set forth again, young Pilgrims on that quest which millions—which every child of Earth—has tried in turn. And were the Lily and her lover to be more fortunate than all those millions? For a long time it seemed not so. The dismal shape of the old lunatic still glided behind them; and for every spot that looked lovely in their eyes, he had some legend of human wrong or suffering, so miserably sad, that his auditors could never afterwards connect the idea of joy with the place where it had happened. Here, a heart-broken woman, kneeling to her child, had been spurned from his feet; here, a desolate old creature had prayed to the evil one, and had received a fiendish malignity of soul in answer to her prayer; here, a new-born infant, sweet blossom of life, had been found dead, with the impress of its mother's fingers round its throat; and here, under a shattered oak, two lovers had been stricken by lightning, and fell blackened corpses in each other's arms. The dreary Gascoigne had a gift to know whatever evil and lamentable thing had stained the bosom of Mother Earth; and when his funereal voice had told the tale it appeared like a prophecy of future woe, as well as a tradition of the past. And now, by their sad demeanor, you would have fancied that the pilgrim lovers were seeking, not a temple of earthly joy, but a tomb for themselves and their posterity.

"Where in this world," exclaimed Adam Forrester, despondingly, "shall we build our Temple of Happiness?"

"Where in this world, indeed!" repeated Lilias Fay: and being faint and weary, the more so by the heaviness of her heart, the Lily drooped her head and sat down on the summit of a knoll, repeating, "Where in this world shall we build our Temple?"

"Ah! have you already asked yourselves that question?" said their companion, his shaded features growing even gloomier with the smile that dwelt on them; "yet there is a place, even in this world, where ye may build it."

While the old man spoke, Adam Forrester and Lilias had carelessly thrown their eyes around, and perceived that the spot where they had chanced to pause possessed a quiet charm, which was well enough adapted to their present mood of mind. It was a small rise of ground, with a certain regularity of shape, that had perhaps been bestowed by art; and a group of trees, which almost surrounded it, threw their pensive shadows across and far beyond, although some softened glory of the sunshine found its way there. The ancestral mansion, wherein the lovers would dwell together, appeared on one side, and the ivied church, where they were to worship, on another. Happening to cast their eyes on the ground, they smiled, yet with a sense of wonder, to see that a pale lily was growing at their feet.

"We will build our Temple here," said they, simultaneously, and with an indescribable conviction, that they had at last found the very spot.

Yet, while they uttered this exclamation, the young man and the Lily turned an apprehensive glance at their dreary associate, deeming it hardly possible that some tale of earthly affliction should not make those precincts loathsome, as in every former case. The old man stood just behind them, so as to form the chief figure in the group, with his sable cloak muffling the lower part of his visage, and his sombre hat overshadowing his brows. But he gave no word of dissent from their purpose; and an inscrutable smile was accepted by the lovers as a token that here had been no footprint of guilt or sorrow to desecrate the site of their Temple of Happiness.

In a little time longer, while summer was still in its prime, the fairy structure of the Temple arose on the summit of the knoll, amid the solemn shadows of the trees, yet often gladdened with bright sunshine. It was built of white marble, with slender and graceful pillars, supporting a vaulted dome; and beneath the centre of this dome, upon a pedestal, was a slab of dark-veined marble, on which books and music might be strewn. But there was a fantasy among the people of the neighborhood, that the edifice was planned after an ancient mausoleum, and was intended for a tomb, and that the central slab of dark-veined marble was to be inscribed with the names of buried ones. They doubted, too, whether the form of Lilias Fay could appertain to a creature of this earth, being so very delicate, and growing every day more fragile, so that she looked as if the summer breeze should snatch her up, and waft her heavenward. But still she watched the daily growth of the Temple; and so did old Walter Gascoigne, who now made that spot his continual haunt, leaning whole hours together on his staff, and giving as deep attention to the work as though it had been indeed a tomb. In due time it was finished, and a day appointed for a simple rite of dedication.

On the preceding evening, after Adam Forrester had taken leave of his mistress, he looked back towards the portal of her dwelling, and felt a strange thrill of fear;

for he imagined that, as the setting sunbeams faded from her figure, she was exhaling away, and that something of her ethereal substance was withdrawn with each lessening gleam of light. With his farewell glance, a shadow had fallen over the portal, and Lilias was invisible. His foreboding spirit deemed it an omen at the time ; and so it proved ; for the sweet earthly form, by which the Lily had been manifested to the world, was found lifeless, the next morning, in the Temple, with her head resting on her arms, which were folded upon the slab of dark-veined marble. The chill winds of the earth had long since breathed a blight into this beautiful flower, so that a loving hand had now transplanted it, to blossom brightly in the garden of Paradise.

But alas, for the Temple of Happiness ! In his unutterable grief, Adam Forrester had no purpose more at heart than to convert this Temple of many delightful hopes into a tomb, and bury his dead mistress there. And lo ! a wonder ! Digging a grave beneath the Temple's marble floor, the sexton found no virgin earth, such as was meet to receive the maiden's dust, but an ancient sepulchre, in which were treasured up the bones of generations that had died long ago. Among those forgotten ancestors was the Lily to be laid. And when the funeral procession brought Lilias thither in her coffin, they beheld old Walter Gascoigne standing beneath the dome of the Temple, with his cloak of pall, and face of darkest gloom ; and wherever that figure might take its stand, the spot would seem a sepulchre. He watched the mourners as they lowered the coffin down.

"And so," said he to Adam Forrester, with the strange smile in which his insanity was wont to gleam forth, "you have found no better foundation for your happiness than on a grave !"

But as the Shadow of Affliction spoke, a vision of Hope and Joy had its birth in Adam's mind, even from the old man's taunting words; for then he knew what was betokened by the parable in which the Lily and himself had acted; and the mystery of Life and Death was opened to him.

"Joy! joy!" he cried, throwing his arms towards Heaven, "on a grave be the site of our Temple; and now our happiness is for Eternity!"

With those words, a ray of sunshine broke through the dismal sky, and glimmered down into the sepulchre; while, at the same moment, the shape of old Walter Gascoigne stalked drearily away, because his gloom, symbolic of all earthly sorrow, might no longer abide there, now that the darkest riddle of humanity was read.

FOOTPRINTS ON THE SEA SHORE.

IT must be a spirit much unlike my own, which can keep itself in health and vigor without sometimes stealing from the sultry sunshine of the world, to plunge into the cool bath of solitude. At intervals, and not infrequent ones, the forest and the ocean summon me— one with the roar of its waves, the other with the murmur of its boughs—forth from the haunts of men. But I must wander many a mile, ere I could stand beneath the shadow of even one primeval tree, much less be lost among the multitude of hoary trunks, and hidden from earth and sky by the mystery of darksome foliage. Nothing is within my daily reach more like a forest than the acre or two of woodland near some suburban farm-house. When, therefore, the yearning for seclusion becomes a necessity within me, I am drawn to the sea shore, which extends its line of rude rocks and seldom trodden sands for leagues around our bay. Setting forth at my last ramble, on a September morning, I bound myself with a hermit's vow to interchange no thoughts with man or woman, to share no social pleasure, but to derive all that day's enjoyment from shore, and sea, and sky,—from my soul's communion with these, and from fantasies, and recollections, or anticipated realities. Surely here is enough to feed a human spirit for a single day. Farewell, then, busy world ! Till your evening lights shall shine along the street,— till they gleam upon my sea-flushed face, as I tread homeward,—free me from your ties, and let me be a peaceful outlaw.

Highways and cross paths are hastily traversed, and, clambering down a crag, I find myself at the extremity of a long beach. How gladly does the spirit leap forth, and suddenly enlarge its sense of being to the full extent of the broad, blue, sunny deep! A greeting and a homage to the Sea! I descend over its margin, and dip my hand into the wave that meets me, and bathe my brow. That far-resounding roar is Ocean's voice of welcome. His salt breath brings a blessing along with it. Now let us pace together—the reader's fancy arm in arm with mine—this noble beach, which extends a mile or more from that craggy promontory to yonder rampart of broken rocks. In front, the sea ; in the rear, a precipitous bank, the grassy verge of which is breaking away, year after year, and flings down its tufts of verdure upon the barrenness below. The beach itself is a broad space of sand, brown and sparkling, with hardly any pebbles intermixed. Near the water's edge there is a wet margin, which glistens brightly in the sunshine, and reflects objects like a mirror ; and as we tread along the glistening border, a dry spot flashes around each footstep, but grows moist again, as we lift our feet. In some spots, the sand receives a complete impression of the sole— square toe and all ; elsewhere it is of such marble firmness, that we must stamp heavily to leave a print even of the iron-shod heel. Along the whole of this extensive beach gambols the surf wave ; now it makes a feint of dashing onward in a fury, yet dies away with a meek murmur, and does but kiss the strand ; now, after many such abortive efforts, it rears itself up in an unbroken line, heightening as it advances, without a speck of foam on its green crest. With how fierce a roar it flings itself forward, and rushes far up the beach !

As I threw my eyes along the edge of the surf, I remember that I was startled, as Robinson Crusoe might have been, by the sense that human life was within the

magic circle of my solitude. Afar off in the remote
distance of the beach, appearing like sea nymphs or
some airier things, such as might tread upon the feathery
spray, was a group of girls. Hardly had I beheld them,
when they passed into the shadow of the rocks and
vanished. To comfort myself—for truly I would fain
have gazed a while longer—I made acquaintance with a
flock of beach birds. These little citizens of the sea and
air preceded me by about a stone's throw along the
strand, seeking, I suppose, for food upon its margin.
Yet, with a philosophy which mankind would do well to
imitate, they drew a continual pleasure from their toil
for a subsistence. The sea was each little bird's great
playmate. They chased it downward as it swept back,
and again ran up swiftly before the impending wave,
which sometimes overtook them and bore them off their
feet. But they floated as lightly as one of their own
feathers on the breaking crest. In their airy flutterings,
they seemed to rest on the evanescent spray. Their
images,—long-legged little figures, with gray backs and
snowy bosoms,—were seen as distinctly as the realities
in the mirror of the glistening strand. As I advanced,
they flew a score or two of yards, and, again alighting,
recommenced their dalliance with the surf wave; and
thus they bore me company along the beach, the types
of pleasant fantasies, till, at its extremity, they took wing
over the ocean, and were gone. After forming a friend-
ship with these small surf spirits, it is really worth a sigh,
to find no memorial of them, save their multitudinous
little tracks in the sand.

When we have paced the length of the beach, it is
pleasant, and not unprofitable, to retrace our steps, and
recall the whole mood and occupation of the mind during
the former passage. Our tracks, being all discernible,
will guide us with an observing consciousness through
every unconscious wandering of thought and fancy.

Here we followed the surf in its reflux, to pick up a shell which the sea seemed loath to relinquish. Here we found a seaweed, with an immense brown leaf, and trailed it behind us by its long snake-like stalk. Here we seized a live horseshoe by the tail, and counted the many claws of the queer monster. Here we dug into the sand for pebbles, and skipped them upon the surface of the water. Here we wet our feet while examining a jelly fish, which the waves, having just tossed it up, now sought to snatch away again. Here we trod along the brink of a fresh-water brooklet, which flows across the beach, becoming shallower and more shallow, till at last it sinks into the sand, and perishes in the effort to bear its little tribute to the main. Here some vagary appears to have bewildered us; for our tracks go round and round, and are confusedly intermingled, as if we had found a labyrinth upon the level beach. And here, amid our idle pastime, we sat down upon almost the only stone that breaks the surface of the sand, and were lost in an unlooked-for and overpowering conception of the majesty and awfulness of the great deep. Thus, by tracking our footprints in the sand, we track our own nature in its wayward course, and steal a glance upon it, when it never dreams of being so observed. Such glances always make us wiser.

This extensive beach affords room for another pleasant pastime. With your staff you may write verses—love verses, if they please you best—and consecrate them with a woman's name. Here, too, may be inscribed thoughts, feelings, desires, warm outgushings from the heart's secret places, which you would not pour upon the sand without the certainty that, almost ere the sky has looked upon them, the sea will wash them out. Stir not hence till the record be effaced. Now—for there is room enough on your canvas—draw huge faces—huge as that of the Sphinx on Egyptian sands—and fit them with bodies of corresponding immensity, and legs which might stride half way to yonder island. Child's play becomes magnificent on so grand a scale. But, after all, the most fascinating employment is simply to write your name in the sand. Draw the letters gigantic, so that two strides may barely measure them, and three for the long strokes! Cut deep, that the record may be permanent! Statesmen and warriors, and poets, have spent their strength in no better cause than this. Is it accomplished? Return, then, in an hour or two, and seek for this mighty record of a name. The sea will have swept over it, even as time rolls its effacing waves over the names of statesmen, and warriors, and poets. Hark, the surf wave laughs at you!

Passing from the beach, I begin to clamber over the crags, making my difficult way among the ruins of a rampart, shattered and broken by the assaults of a fierce enemy. The rocks rise in every variety of attitude; some of them have their feet in the foam, and are shagged half way upward with seaweed; some have been hollowed almost into caverns by the unwearied toil of the sea, which can afford to spend centuries in wearing away a rock, or even polishing a pebble. One huge rock ascends in monumental shape, with a face like a giant's tombstone, on which the veins resemble inscriptions, but in an unknown tongue. We will fancy them the forgotten characters of an antediluvian race; or else that Nature's own hand has here recorded a mystery, which, could I read her language, would make mankind the wiser and the happier. How many a thing has troubled me with that same idea! Pass on, and leave it unexplained. Here is a narrow avenue, which might seem to have been hewn through the very heart of an enormous crag, affording passage for the rising sea to thunder back and forth, filling it with tumultuous foam, and then leaving its floor of black pebbles bare and glistening. In this chasm there was once an intersecting vein of softer stone, which the waves have gnawed away piecemeal, while the granite walls remain entire on either side. How sharply, and with what harsh clamor, does the sea rake back the pebbles, as it momentarily withdraws into its own depths! At intervals, the floor of the chasm is left nearly dry; but anon, at the outlet, two or three great waves are seen struggling to get in at once; two hit the walls athwart, while one rushes straight through, and all three thunder, as if with rage and triumph. They heap the chasm with a snow drift of foam and spray. While watching this scene, I can never rid myself of the idea, that a monster, endowed with life and fierce energy, is striving to burst his way through the narrow pass. And what a contrast, to look through the stormy chasm, and catch a glimpse of the calm bright sea beyond!

Many interesting discoveries may be made among these broken cliffs. Once, for example, I found a dead seal, which a recent tempest had tossed into the nook of the rocks, where his shaggy carcass lay rolled in a heap of eel grass, as if the sea monster sought to hide himself from my eye. Another time, a shark seemed on the point of leaping from the surf to swallow me; nor did I, wholly without dread, approach near enough to ascertain that the maneater had already met his own death from some fishermen in the bay. In the same ramble, I encountered a bird—a large gray bird—but whether a loon, or a wild goose, or the identical albatross of the Ancient Mariner, was beyond my ornithology to decide. It reposed so naturally on a bed of dry seaweed, with its head beside its wing, that I almost fancied it alive, and trod softly lest it should suddenly spread its wings skyward. But the sea bird would soar among the clouds no more, nor ride upon its native waves; so I drew near, and pulled out one of its mottled tail feathers for a remembrance. Another day, I discovered an immense bone, wedged into a chasm of the rocks; it was at least ten feet long, curved like a cimeter, bejewelled with barnacles and small shell-fish, and partly covered with a growth of seaweed. Some leviathan of some former ages had used this ponderous mass as a jawbone. Curiosities of a minuter order may be observed in a deep reservoir, which is replenished with water at every tide, but becomes a lake among the crags, save when the sea is at its height. At the bottom of this rocky basin grow marine plants, some of which tower high beneath the water, and cast a shadow in the sunshine. Small fishes dart to and fro, and hide themselves among the seaweed; there is also a solitary crab, who appears to lead the life of a hermit, communing with none of the others denizens of the place; and likewise several five-fingers—for I know no other name than that which children give them. If your imagination be at all accustomed to such freaks, you may look down into the depths of this pool, and fancy it the mysterious depth of ocean. But where are the hulks and scattered timbers of sunken ships?—where the treasures that old Ocean hoards? — where the corroded cannon? — where the corpses and skeletons of seamen who went down in storm and battle?

On the day of my last ramble (it was a September day, yet as warm as summer), what should I behold as I approached the above described basin but three girls sitting on its margin, and—yes, it is veritably so—laving their snowy feet in the sunny water! These, these are the warm realities of those three visionary shapes that flitted from me on the beach. Hark! their merry voices, as they toss up the water with their feet! They have not seen me. I must shrink behind this rock, and steal away again.

In honest truth, vowed to solitude as I am, there is something in this encounter that makes the heart flutter

with a strangely pleasant sensation. I know these girls
to be realities of flesh and blood, yet, glancing at them
so briefly, they mingle like kindred creatures with the
ideal beings of my mind. It is pleasant, likewise, to
gaze down from some high crag, and watch a group of
children, gathering pebbles and pearly shells, and playing with the surf as with old Ocean's hoary beard. Nor
does it infringe upon my seclusion, to see yonder boat
at anchor off the shore, swinging dreamily to and fro,
and rising and sinking with the alternate swell; while
the crew—four gentlemen, in roundabout jackets—are
busy with their fishing lines. But, with an inward
antipathy and a headlong flight, do I eschew the presence of any meditative stroller like myself, known by
his pilgrim staff, his sauntering step, his shy demeanor,
his observant yet abstracted eye. From such a man, as
if another self had scared me, I scramble hastily over
the rocks, and take refuge in a nook which many a
secret hour has given me a right to call my own. I
would do battle for it even with the churl that should
produce the title deeds. Have not my musings melted
into its rocky walls and sandy floor, and made them a
portion of myself?

It is a recess in the line of cliffs, walled round by a
rough, high precipice, which almost encircles and shuts
in a little space of sand. In front, the sea appears as
between the pillars of a portal. In the rear, the precipice is broken and intermixed with earth, which gives
nourishment not only to clinging and twining shrubs,
but to trees, that gripe the rock with their naked roots,
and seem to struggle hard for footing and for soil enough
to live upon. These are fir trees; but oaks hang their
heavy branches from above, and throw down acorns on
the beach, and shed their withering foliage upon the
waves. At this autumnal season, the precipice is decked
with variegated splendor; trailing wreaths of scarlet

flaunt from the summit downward; tufts of yellow-
flowering shrubs, and rose bushes with their reddened
leaves and glossy seed berries, sprout from each crevice;
at every glance I detect some new light or shade of
beauty, all contrasting with the stern, gray rock. A rill
of water trickles down the cliff and fills a little cistern
near the base. I drain it at a draught, and find it fresh
and pure. This recess shall be my dining hall. And
what the feast? A few biscuits, made savory by soaking them in sea water, a tuft of samphire gathered from
the beach, and an apple for the dessert. By this time,
the little rill has filled its reservoir again; and, as I
quaff it, I thank God more heartily than for a civic
banquet, that He gives me the healthful appetite to make
a feast of bread and water.

Dinner being over, I throw myself at length upon the
sand, and, basking in the sunshine, let my mind disport
itself at will. The walls of this my hermitage have no
tongue to tell my follies, though I sometimes fancy that
they have ears to hear them, and a soul to sympathize.
There is a magic in this spot. Dreams haunt its precincts, and flit around me in broad sunlight, nor require
that sleep shall blindfold me to real objects, ere these be
visible. Here can I frame a story of two lovers, and
make their shadows live before me, and be mirrored in
the tranquil water, as they tread along the sand, leaving
no footprints. Here, should I will it, I can summon up
a single shade, and be myself her lover. Yes, dreamer,—
but your lonely heart will be the colder for such fancies.
Sometimes, too, the Past comes back, and finds me here,
and in her train come faces which were gladsome when
I knew them, yet seem not gladsome now. Would that
my hiding-place were lonelier, so that the past might not
find me! Get ye all gone, old friends, and let me listen
to the murmur of the sea,—a melancholy voice, but less
sad than yours. Of what mysteries is it telling? Of

sunken ships, and whereabouts they lie? Of islands
afar and undiscovered, whose tawny children are unconscious of other islands and of continents, and deem the
stars of heaven their nearest neighbors? Nothing of all
this. What then? Has it talked for so many ages, and
meant nothing all the while? No; for those ages find
utterance in the sea's unchanging voice, and warn the
listener to withdraw his interest from mortal vicissitudes,
and let the infinite idea of eternity pervade his soul.
This is wisdom; and, therefore, will I spend the next
half hour in shaping little boats of driftwood, and launch-
ing them on voyages across the cove, with the feather of
a seagull for a sail. If the voice of ages tell me true,
this is as wise an occupation as to build ships of five
hundred tons, and launch them forth upon the main,
bound to "far Cathay." Yet, how would the merchant
sneer at me!

And, after all, can such philosophy be true? Methinks
I could find a thousand arguments against it. Well,
then, let yonder shaggy rock, mid-deep in the surf—see!
he is somewhat wrathful,—he rages and roars and foams
—let that tall rock be my antagonist, and let me exercise
my oratory like him of Athens, who bandied words with
an angry sea and got the victory. My maiden speech is
a triumphant one; for the gentleman in seaweed has
nothing to offer in reply, save an immitigable roaring.
His voice, indeed, will be heard a long while after mine
is hushed. Once more I shout, and the cliffs reverberate
the sound. O, what joy for a shy man to feel himself so
solitary, that he may lift his voice to its highest pitch
without hazard of a listener! But hush!—be silent, my
good friend!—whence comes that stifled laughter? It
was musical,—but how should there be such music in
my solitude? Looking upwards, I catch a glimpse of
three faces, peeping from the summit of the cliff, like
angels between me and their native sky. Ah, fair girls,

you may make yourselves merry at my eloquence,—but it was my turn to smile when I saw your white feet in the pool! Let us keep each other's secrets.

The sunshine has now passed from my hermitage, except a gleam upon the sand just where it meets the sea. A crowd of gloomy fantasies will come and haunt me, if I tarry longer here, in the darkening twilight of these gray rocks. This is a dismal place in some moods of the mind. Climb we, therefore, the precipice, and pause a moment on the brink, gazing down into that hollow chamber by the deep where we have been, what few can be, sufficient to our own pastime — yes, say the word outright !—self-sufficient to our own happiness. How lonesome looks the recess now, and dreary too — like all other spots where happiness has been! There lies my shadow in the departing sunshine with its head upon the sea. I will pelt it with pebbles. A hit ! a hit ! I clap my hands in triumph, and see ! my shadow clapping its unreal hands, and claiming the triumph for itself. What a simpleton must I have been all day, since my own shadow makes a mock of my fooleries !

Homeward ! homeward ! It is time to hasten home. It is time ; it is time ; for as the sun sinks over the western wave, the sea grows melancholy, and the surf has a saddened tone. The distant sails appear astray, and not of earth, in their remoteness amid the desolate waste. My spirit wanders forth afar, but finds no resting-place, and comes shivering back. It is time that I were hence. But grudge me not the day that has been spent in seclusion, which yet was not solitude, since the great sea has been my companion, and the little sea birds my friends, and the wind has told me his secrets, and airy shapes have flitted around me in my hermitage. Such companionship works an effect upon a man's character, as if he had been admitted to the society of creatures that are not mortal. And when, at noontide, I tread the crowded streets, the influence of this day will still be felt; so that I shall walk among men kindly and as a brother, with affection and sympathy, but yet shall not melt into the indistinguishable mass of humankind. I shall think my own thoughts, and feel my own emotions, and possess my individuality unviolated.

But it is good, at the eve of such a day, to feel and know that there are men and women in the world. That feeling and that knowledge are mine at this moment; for, on the shore, far below me, the fishing party have landed from their skiff, and are cooking their scaly prey by a fire of driftwood, kindled in the angle of two rude rocks. The three visionary girls are likewise there. In the deepening twilight, while the surf is dashed near their hearth, the ruddy gleam of the fire throws a strange air of comfort over the wild cove, bestrewn as it is with pebbles and seaweed, and exposed to the " melancholy main." Moreover, as the smoke climbs up the precipice, it brings with it a savory smell from a pan of fried fish, and a black kettle of chowder, and reminds me that my dinner was nothing but bread and water, and a tuft of samphire, and an apple. Methinks the party might find room for another guest, at that flat rock which serves them for a table; and if spoons be scarce, I could pick up a clamshell on the beach. They see me now; and—the blessing of a hungry man upon him!—one of them sends up a hospitable shout—halloo, Sir Solitary! come down and sup with us! The ladies wave their handkerchiefs. Can I decline? No; and be it owned, after all my solitary joys, that this is the sweetest moment of a Day by the Sea Shore.

EDWARD FANE'S ROSEBUD.

THERE is hardly a more difficult exercise of fancy, than, while gazing at a figure of melancholy age, to re-create its youth, and, without entirely obliterating the identity of form and features, to restore those graces which time has snatched away. Some old people, especially women, so age-worn and woful are they, seem never to have been young and gay. It is easier to conceive that such gloomy phantoms were sent into the world as withered and decrepit as we behold them now, with sympathies only for pain and grief, to watch at death beds, and weep at funerals. Even the sable garments of their widowhood appear essential to their existence ; all their attributes combine to render them darksome shadows, creeping strangely amid the sunshine of human life. Yet it is no unprofitable task, to take one of these doleful creatures, and set fancy resolutely at work to brighten the dim eye, and darken the silvery locks, and paint the ashen cheek with rose color, and repair the shrunken and crazy form, till a dewy maiden shall be seen in the old matron's elbow chair. The miracle being wrought, then let the years roll back again, each sadder than the last, and the whole weight of age and sorrow settle down upon the youthful figure. Wrinkles and furrows, the handwriting of Time, may thus be deciphered, and found to contain deep lessons of thought and feeling. Such profit might be derived by a skilful observer, from my much-respected friend, the Widow Toothaker, a nurse of great repute, who has breathed the atmosphere of sick chambers and dying breaths these forty years.

See! she sits cowering over her lonesome hearth, with her gown and upper petticoat drawn upward, gathering thriftly into her person the whole warmth of the fire, which, now at nightfall, begins to dissipate the autumnal chill of her chamber. The blaze quivers capriciously in front, alternately glimmering into the chasms of her wrinkled visage, and then permitting a ghostly dimness to mar the outlines of her venerable figure. And Nurse Toothaker holds a teaspoon in her right hand, with which to stir up the contents of a tumbler in her left, whence steams a vapory fragrance, abhorred of temperance societies. Now she sips—now stirs—now sips again. Her sad old heart has need to be revived by the rich infusion of Geneva, which is mixed half and half with hot water in the tumbler. All day long she has been sitting by a death pillow, and quitted it for her home, only when the spirit of her patient left the clay, and went homeward too. But now are her melancholy meditations cheered, and her torpid blood warmed, and her shoulders lightened of at least twenty ponderous years, by a draught from the true Fountain of Youth, in a case bottle. It is strange that men should deem that fount a fable, when its liquor fills more bottles than the congress water! Sip it again, good nurse, and see whether a second draught will not take off another score of years, and perhaps ten more, and show us, in your high-backed chair, the blooming damsel who plighted troths with Edward Fane. Get you gone, Age and Widowhood! Come back, unwedded Youth! But, alas! the charm will not work. In spite of fancy's most potent spell, I can see only an old dame cowering over the fire, a picture of decay and desolation, while the November blast roars at her in the chimney, and fitful showers rush suddenly against the window.

Yet there was a time when Rose Grafton—such was the pretty maiden name of Nurse Toothaker—possessed beauty that would have gladdened this dim and dismal chamber as with sunshine. It won for her the heart of Edward Fane, who has since made so great a figure in the world, and is now a grand old gentleman, with powdered hair, and as gouty as a lord. These early lovers thought to have walked hand in hand through life. They had wept together for Edward's little sister Mary, whom Rose tended in her sickness, partly because she was the sweetest child that ever lived or died, but more for love of him. She was but three years old. Being such an infant, Death could not embody his terrors in her little corpse; nor did Rose fear to touch the dead child's brow, though chill, as she curled the silken hair around it, nor to take her tiny hand, and clasp a flower within its fingers. Afterward, when she looked through the pane of glass in the coffin lid, and beheld Mary's face, it seemed not so much like death, or life, as like a waxwork, wrought into the perfect image of a child asleep, and dreaming of its mother's smile. Rose thought her too fair a thing to be hidden in the grave, and wondered that an angel did not snatch up little Mary's coffin, and bear the slumbering babe to heaven, and bid her wake immortal. But when the sods were laid on little Mary, the heart of Rose was troubled. She shuddered at the fantasy, that, in grasping the child's cold fingers, her virgin hand had exchanged a first greeting with mortality, and could never lose the earthly taint. How many a greeting since! But as yet she was a fair young girl, with the dewdrops of fresh feeling in her bosom; and instead of Rose, which seemed too mature a name for her half-opened beauty, her lover called her Rosebud.

The rosebud was destined never to bloom for Edward Fane. His mother was a rich and haughty dame, with all the aristocratic prejudices of colonial times. She scorned Rose Grafton's humble parentage, and caused her son to break his faith, though, had she let him choose, he would have prized his Rosebud above the richest diamond. The lovers parted, and have seldom met again. Both may have visited the same mansions, but not at the same time; for one was bidden to the festal hall, and the other to the sick chamber; he was the guest of Pleasure and Prosperity, and she of Anguish. Rose, after their separation, was long secluded within the dwelling of Mr. Toothaker, whom she married with the revengeful hope of breaking her false lover's heart. She went to her bridegroom's arms with bitterer tears, they say, than young girls ought to shed at the threshold of the bridal chamber. Yet, though her husband's head was getting gray, and his heart had been chilled with an autumnal frost, Rose soon began to love him, and wondered at her own conjugal affection. He was all she had to love; there were no children.

In a year or two, poor Mr. Toothaker was visited with a wearisome infirmity, which settled in his joints, and made him weaker than a child. He crept forth about his business, and came home at dinner time and eventide, not with the manly tread that gladdens a wife's heart, but slowly, feebly, jotting down each dull footstep with a melancholy dub of his staff. We must pardon his pretty wife, if she sometimes blushed to own him. Her visitors, when they heard him coming, looked for the appearance of some old, old man; but he dragged his nerveless limbs into the parlor—and there was Mr. Toothaker! The disease increasing, he never went into the sunshine, save with a staff in his right hand and his left on his wife's shoulder, bearing heavily downward, like a dead man's hand. Thus, a slender woman, still looking maiden-like, she supported his tall, broad-chested frame along the pathway of their little garden, and

plucked the roses for her gray-haired husband, and
spoke soothingly as to an infant. His mind was palsied
with his body ; its utmost energy was peevishness. In a
few months more, she helped him up the staircase, with
a pause at every step and a longer one upon the landing-
place, and a heavy glance behind, as he crossed the
threshold of his chamber. He knew, poor man, that the
precincts of those four walls would thenceforth be his
world—his world, his home, his tomb—at once a dwelling and a burial-place, till he were borne to a darker and
a narrower one. But Rose was with him in the tomb.
He leaned upon her, in his daily passage from the bed to
the chair by the fireside, and back again from the weary
chair to the joyless bed—his bed and hers—their marriage bed ; till even this short journey ceased, and his
head lay all day upon the pillow, and hers all night
beside it. How long poor Mr. Toothaker was kept in
misery ! Death seemed to draw near the door, and
often to lift the latch, and sometimes to thrust his ugly
skull into the chamber, nodding to Rose, and pointing at
her husband, but still delayed to enter. "This bedridden
wretch cannot escape me !" quoth Death. "I will go
forth, and run a race with the swift, and fight a battle
with the strong, and come back for Toothaker at my
leisure !" O, when the deliverer came so near, in the
dull anguish of her worn-out sympathies, did she never
long to cry, "Death, come in !"

But, no ! We have no right to ascribe such a wish to
our friend Rose. She never failed in a wife's duty to her
poor sick husband. She murmured not, though a glimpse
of the sunny sky was as strange to her as him, nor
answered peevishly, though his complaining accents
roused her from her sweetest dream, only to share his
wretchedness. He knew her faith, yet nourished a
cankered jealousy ; and when the slow disease had
chilled all his heart, save one lukewarm spot, which

Death's frozen fingers were searching for, his last words
were : "What would my Rose have done for her first
love, if she has been so true and kind to a sick old man
like me!" And then his poor soul crept away, and left
the body lifeless, though hardly more so than for years
before, and Rose a widow, though in truth it was the
wedding night that widowed her. She felt glad, it must
be owned, when Mr. Toothaker was buried, because his
corpse had retained such a likeness to the man half alive,
that she hearkened for the sad murmur of his voice,
bidding her shift his pillow. But all through the next
winter, though the grave had held him many a month,
she fancied him calling from that cold bed, "Rose!
Rose! come put a blanket on my feet!"

So now the Rosebud was the Widow Toothaker. Her
troubles had come early, and, tedious as they seemed,
had passed before all her bloom was fled. She was still
fair enough to captivate a bachelor, or, with a widow's
cheerful gravity, she might have won a widower, stealing
into his heart in the very guise of his dead wife. But the
Widow Toothaker had no such projects. By her watch-
ings and continual cares, her heart had become knit to
her first husband with a constancy which changed its
very nature, and made her love him for his infirmities,
and infirmity for his sake. When the palsied old man
was gone, even her early lover could not have supplied
his place. She had dwelt in a sick chamber, and been
the companion of a half-dead wretch, till she could
scarcely breathe in a free air, and felt ill at ease with the
healthy and the happy. She missed the fragrance of the
doctor's stuff. She walked the chamber with a noiseless
footfall. If visitors came in, she spoke in soft and
soothing accents, and was startled and shocked by their
loud voices. Often, in the lonesome evening, she looked
timorously from the fireside to the bed, with almost a
hope of recognizing a ghastly face upon the pillow.

Then went her thoughts sadly to her husband's grave. If one impatient throb had wronged him in his lifetime —if she had secretly repined, because her buoyant youth was imprisoned with his torpid age—if ever, while slumbering beside him, a treacherous dream had admitted another into her heart—yet the sick man had been preparing a revenge, which the dead now claimed. On his painful pillow he had cast a spell around her ; his groans and misery had proved more captivating charms than gayety and youthful grace ; in his semblance, Disease itself had won the Rosebud for a bride ; nor could his death dissolve the nuptials. By that indissoluble bond she had gained a home in every sick chamber, and nowhere else ; there were her brethren and sisters ; thither her husband summoned her, with that voice which had seemed to issue from the grave of Toothaker. At length she recognized her destiny.

We have beheld her as the maid, the wife, the widow ; now we see her in a separate and insulated character ; she was, in all her attributes, Nurse Toothaker. And Nurse Toothaker alone, with her own shrivelled lips, could make known her experience in that capacity. What a history might she record of the great sicknesses in which she has gone hand in hand with the exterminating angel ! She remembers when the small-pox hoisted a red banner on almost every house along the street. She has witnessed when the typhus fever swept off a whole household, young and old, all but a lonely mother, who vainly shrieked to follow her last loved one. Where would be Death's triumph, if none lived to weep? She can speak of strange maladies that have broken out, as if spontaneously, but were found to have been imported from foreign lands, with rich silks and other merchandise, the costliest portion of the cargo. And once, she recollects, the people died of what was considered a new pestilence, till the doctors traced it to the ancient grave of a young girl, who thus caused many deaths a hundred years after her own burial. Strange that such black mischief should lurk in a maiden's grave! She loves to tell how strong men fight with fiery fevers, utterly refusing to give up their breath; and how consumptive virgins fade out of the world, scarcely reluctant, as if their lovers were wooing them to a far country. Tell us, thou fearful woman! tell us the death secrets! Fain would I search out the meaning of words, faintly gasped with intermingled sobs, and broken sentences, half audibly spoken between earth and the judgment seat!

An awful woman! She is the patron saint of young physicians, and the bosom friend of old ones. In the mansions where she enters, the inmates provide themselves black garments; the coffin maker follows her; and the bell tolls as she comes away from the threshold. Death himself has met her at so many a bedside, that he puts forth his bony hand to greet Nurse Toothaker. She is an awful woman! And, O! is it conceivable, that this handmaid of human infirmity and affliction—so darkly stained, so thoroughly imbued with all that is saddest in the doom of mortals—can ever again be bright and gladsome, even though bathed in the sunshine of eternity? By her long communion with woe, has she not forfeited her inheritance of immortal joy? Does any germ of bliss survive within her?

Hark! an eager knocking at Nurse Toothaker's door. She starts from her drowsy reverie, sets aside the empty tumbler and teaspoon, and lights a lamp at the dim embers of the fire. Rap, rap, rap! again; and she hurries adown the staircase, wondering which of her friends can be at death's door now, since there is such an earnest messenger at Nurse Toothaker's. Again the peal resounds, just as her hand is on the lock. "Be quick, Nurse Toothaker!" cries a man on the doorstep;

"old General Fane is taken with the gout in his stomach, and has sent for you to watch by his death bed. Make haste, for there is no time to lose!" "Fane! Edward Fane! And has he sent for me at last? I am ready! I will get on my cloak and begone. So," adds the sable-gowned, ashen-visaged, funereal old figure, "Edward Fane remembers his Rosebud!"

Our question is answered. There is a germ of bliss within her. Her long-hoarded constancy—her memory of the bliss that was—remaining amid the gloom of her after life, like a sweet-smelling flower in a coffin, is a symbol that all may be renewed. In some happier clime, the Rosebud may revive again with all the dew-drops in its bosom.

THE THREEFOLD DESTINY.

A FAIRY LEGEND.

I HAVE sometimes produced a singular and not unpleas-
ing effect, so far as my own mind was concerned, by
imagining a train of incidents, in which the spirit and
mechanism of the fairy legend should be combined with
the characters and manners of familiar life. In the
little tale which follows, a subdued tinge of the wild and
wonderful is thrown over a sketch of New England
personages and scenery, yet, it is hoped, without entirely
obliterating the sober hues of nature. Rather than a
story of events claiming to be real, it may be considered
as an allegory, such as the writers of the last century
would have expressed in the shape of an Eastern tale,
but to which I have endeavored to give a more lifelike
warmth than could be infused into those fanciful productions.

In the twilight of a summer eve, a tall, dark figure,
over which long and remote travel had thrown an
outlandish aspect, was entering a village, not in "Fairy
Londe," but within our own familiar boundaries. The
staff on which this traveller leaned had been his companion from the spot where it grew, in the jungles of
Hindostan ; the hat that overshadowed his sombre
brow had shielded him from the suns of Spain ; but his
cheek had been blackened by the red-hot wind of an
Arabian desert, and had felt the frozen breath of an
Arctic region. Long sojourning amid wild and danger-

ous men, he still wore beneath his vest the ataghan
which he had once struck into the throat of a Turkish
robber. In every foreign clime he had lost something
of his New England characteristics; and, perhaps, from
every people he had unconsciously borrowed a new
peculiarity; so that when the world wanderer again
trod the street of his native village, it is no wonder that
he passed unrecognized, though exciting the gaze and
curiosity of all. Yet, as his arm casually touched that
of a young woman, who was wending her way to an
evening lecture, she started, and almost uttered a
cry.

"Ralph Cranfield!" was the name that she half
articulated.

"Can that be my old playmate, Faith Egerton?"
thought the traveller, looking round at her figure, but
without pausing.

Ralph Cranfield, from his youth upward, had felt himself marked out for a high destiny. He had imbibed the
idea—we say not whether it were revealed to him by
witchcraft, or in a dream of prophecy, or that his brood-
ing fancy had palmed its own dictates upon him as the
oracles of a Sibyl—but he had imbibed the idea, and
held it firmest among his articles of faith, that three
marvellous events of his life were to be confirmed to
him by three signs.

The first of these three fatalities, and perhaps the one
on which his youthful imagination had dwelt most fondly,
was the discovery of the maid, who alone, of all the
maids on earth, could make him happy by her love. He
was to roam around the world till he should meet a
beautiful woman, wearing on her bosom a jewel in the
shape of a heart; whether of pearl, or ruby, or emerald,
or carbuncle, or a changeful opal, or perhaps a priceless
diamond, Ralph Cranfield little cared, so long as it were
a heart of one peculiar shape. On encountering this

lovely stranger, he was bound to address her thus :—
"Maiden, I have brought you a heavy heart.   May I
rest its weight on you?"   And if she were his fated bride
—if their kindred souls were destined to form a union
here below, which all eternity should only bind more
closely—she would reply, with her finger on the heart-
shaped jewel,—"This token, which I have worn so long,
is the assurance that you may!"

And, secondly, Ralph Cranfield had a firm belief that
there was a mighty treasure hidden somewhere in the
earth, of which the burial-place would be revealed to
none but him.   When his feet should press upon the
mysterious spot, there would be a hand before him,
pointing downward—whether carved of marble, or hewn
in gigantic dimensions on the side of a rocky precipice,
or perchance a hand of flame in empty air, he could not
tell ; but, at least, he would discern a hand, the forefinger pointing downward, and beneath it the Latin
word EFFODE—Dig!   And digging thereabouts, the
gold in coin or ingots, the precious stones, or of whatever else the treasure might consist, would be certain to
reward his toil.

The third and last of the miraculous events in the life
of this high-destined man, was to be the attainment of
extensive influence and sway over his fellow-creatures.
Whether he were to be a king, and founder of an
hereditary throne, or the victorious leader of a people
contending for their freedom, or the apostle of a purified
and regenerated faith, was left for futurity to show.   As
messengers of the sign, by which Ralph Cranfield might
recognize the summons, three venerable men were to
claim audience of him.   The chief among them, a dignified and majestic person, arrayed, it may be supposed,
in the flowing garments of an ancient sage, would be the
bearer of a wand, or prophet's rod.   With this wand, or
rod, or staff, the venerable sage would trace a certain

figure in the air, and then proceed to make known his heaven-instructed message; which, if obeyed, must lead to glorious results.

With this proud fate before him, in the flush of his imaginative youth, Ralph Cranfield had set forth to seek the maid, the treasure, and the venerable sage, with his gift of extended empire. And had he found them? Alas! it was not with the aspect of a triumphant man, who had achieved a nobler destiny than all his fellows, but rather with the gloom of one struggling against peculiar and continual adversity, that he now passed homeward to his mother's cottage. He had come back, but only for a time, to lay aside the pilgrim's staff, trusting that his weary manhood would regain somewhat of the elasticity of youth in the spot where his threefold fate had been foreshown him. There had been few changes in the village; for it was not one of those thriving places where a year's prosperity makes more than the havoc of a century's decay; but like a gray hair in a young man's head, an antiquated little town, full of old maids, and aged elms, and moss-grown dwellings. Few seemed to be the changes here. The drooping elms, indeed, had a more majestic spread; the weather-blackened houses were adorned with a denser thatch of verdant moss; and doubtless there were a few more gravestones in the burial ground, inscribed with names that had once been familiar in the village street. Yet, summing up all the mischief that ten years had wrought, it seemed scarcely more than if Ralph Cranfield had gone forth that very morning, and dreamed a daydream till the twilight, and then turned back again. But his heart grew cold, because the village did not remember him as he remembered the village.

"Here is the change!" sighed he, striking his hand upon his breast. "Who is this man of thought and care, weary with world wandering, and heavy with disappointed hopes? The youth returns not, who went forth so joyously!"

And now Ralph Cranfield was at his mother's gate, in front of the small house where the old lady, with slender but sufficient means, had kept herself comfortable during her son's long absence. Admitting himself within the enclosure, he leaned against a great, old tree, trifling with his own impatience, as people often do in those intervals when years are summed into a moment. He took a minute survey of the dwelling—its windows, brightened with the sky gleam, its doorway, with the half of a millstone for a step, and the faintly-traced path waving thence to the gate. He made friends again with his childhood's friend, the old tree against which he leaned; and glancing his eye adown its trunk, beheld something that excited a melancholy smile. It was a half-obliterated inscription—the Latin word EFFODE— which he remembered to have carved in the bark of the tree, with a whole day's toil when he had first begun to muse about his exalted destiny. It might be accounted a rather singular coincidence, that the bark, just above the inscription, had put forth an excrescence, shaped not unlike a hand, with the forefinger pointing obliquely at the word of fate. Such, at least, was its appearance in the dusky light.

"Now a credulous man," said Ralph Cranfield carelessly to himself, "might suppose that the treasure which I have sought round the world, lies buried, after all, at the very door of my mother's dwelling. That would be a jest indeed!"

More he thought not about the matter; for now the door was opened, and an elderly woman appeared on the threshold, peering into the dusk to discover who it might be that had intruded on her premises, and was standing in the shadow of her tree. It was Ralph Cranfield's mother. Pass me over their greeting, and leave the one to her joy and the other to his rest—if quiet rest be found.

But when morning broke, he arose with a troubled brow; for his sleep and his wakefulness had alike been full of dreams. All the fervor was rekinkled with which he had burned of yore to unravel the threefold mystery of his fate. The crowd of his early visions seemed to have awaited him beneath his mother's roof, and thronged riotously around to welcome his return. In the well-remembered chamber—on the pillow where his infancy had slumbered—he had passed a wilder night than ever in an Arab tent, or when he had reposed his head in the ghastly shades of a haunted forest. A shadowy maid had stolen to his bedside, and laid her finger on the scintillating heart; a hand of flame had glowed amid the darkness, pointing downward to a mystery within the earth; a hoary sage had waved his prophetic wand, and beckoned the dreamer onward to a chair of state. The same phantoms, though fainter in the daylight, still flitted about the cottage, and mingled among the crowd of familiar faces that were drawn thither by the news of Ralph Cranfield's return, to bid him welcome for his mother's sake. There they found him, a tall, dark, stately man, of foreign aspect, courteous in demeanor and mild of speech, yet with an abstracted eye, which seemed often to snatch a glance at the invisible.

Meantime the widow Cranfield went bustling about the house, full of joy that she again had somebody to love, and be careful of, and for whom she might vex and tease herself with the petty troubles of daily life. It was nearly noon when she looked forth from the door, and descried three personages of note coming along the street, through the hot sunshine and the masses of elm-tree shade. At length they reached her gate, and undid the latch.

"See, Ralph!" exclaimed she, with maternal pride, "here is Squire Hawkwood and the two other selectmen coming on purpose to see you! Now do tell them a good long story about what you have seen in foreign parts."

The foremost of the three visitors, Squire Hawkwood, was a very pompous, but excellent old gentleman, the head and prime mover in all the affairs of the village, and universally acknowledged to be one of the sagest men on earth. He wore, according to a fashion even then becoming antiquated, a three-cornered hat, and carried a silver-headed cane, the use of which seemed to be rather for flourishing in the air than for assisting the progress of his legs. His two companions were elderly and respectable yeomen, who, retaining an ante-revolutionary reverence for rank and hereditary wealth, kept a little in the Squire's rear. As they approached along the pathway, Ralph Cranfield sat in an oaken elbow chair, half unconsciously gazing at the three visitors, and enveloping their homely figures in the misty romance that pervaded his mental world.

"Here," thought he, smiling at the conceit, "here come three elderly personages, and the first of the three is a venerable sage with a staff. What if this embassy should bring me the message of my fate!"

While Squire Hawkwood and his colleagues entered, Ralph rose from his seat, and advanced a few steps to receive them; and his stately figure and dark countenance, as he bent courteously towards his guests, had a natural dignity, contrasting well with the bustling importance of the Squire. The old gentleman, according to invariable custom, gave an elaborate preliminary flourish with his cane in the air, then removed his three-cornered hat in order to wipe his brow, and finally proceeded to make known his errand.

"My colleagues and myself," began the Squire, "are

burdened with momentous duties, being jointly selectmen of this village. Our minds, for the space of three
days past, have been laboriously bent on the selection of
a suitable person to fill a most important office, and take
upon himself a charge and rule, which, wisely considered, may be ranked no lower than those of kings and
potentates. And whereas you, our native townsman,
are of good natural intellect, and well cultivated by
foreign travel, and that certain vagaries and fantasies of
your youth are doubtless long ago corrected ; taking all
these matters, I say, into due consideration, we are of
opinion that Providence hath sent you hither, at this
juncture, for our very purpose."

During this harangue, Cranfield gazed fixedly at the
speaker, as if he beheld something mysterious and
unearthly in his pompous little figure, and as if the
Squire had worn the flowing robes of an ancient sage,
instead of a square-skirted coat, flapped waistcoat, velvet
breeches and silk stockings. Nor was his wonder without sufficient cause ; for the flourish of the Squire's staff,
marvellous to relate, had described precisely the signal
in the air which was to ratify the message of the prophetic
Sage, whom Cranfield had sought around the world.

" And what," inquired Ralph Cranfield, with a tremor
in his voice, " what may this office be, which is to equal
me with kings and potentates ? "

" No less than instructor of our village school," answered Squire Hawkwood ; "the office being now vacant
by the death of the venerable Master Whitaker after a
fifty years' incumbency."

" I will consider of your proposal," replied Ralph
Cranfield, hurriedly, "and will make known my decision within three days."

After a few more words, the village dignitary and his
companions took their leave. But to Cranfield's fancy
their images were still present, and became more and

more invested with the dim awfulness of figures which had [first appeared to him in a dream, and afterwards had shown themselves in his waking moments, assuming homely aspects among familiar things. His mind dwelt upon the features of the Squire, till they grew confused with those of the visionary Sage, and one appeared but the shadow of the other. The same visage, he now thought, had looked forth upon him from the Pyramid of Cheops; the same form had beckoned to him among the colonnades of the Alhambra; the same figure had mistily revealed itself through the ascending steam of the Great Geyser. At every effort of his memory he recognized some trait of the dreamy Messenger of Destiny in this pompous, bustling, self-important, little great man of the village. Amid such musings, Ralph Cranfield sat all day in the cottage, scarcely hearing and vaguely answering his mother's thousand questions about his travels and adventures. At sunset, he roused himself to take a stroll, and, passing the aged elm tree, his eye was again caught by the semblance of a hand, pointing downward at the half-obliterated inscription.

As Cranfield walked down the street of the village, the level sunbeams threw his shadow far before him; and he fancied that, as his shadow walked among distant objects, so had there been a presentiment stalking in advance of him throughout his life. And when he drew near each object, over which his tall shadow had preceded him, still it proved to be one of the familiar recollections of his infancy and youth. Every crook in the pathway was remembered. Even the more transitory characteristics of the scene were the same as in by-gone days. A company of cows were grazing on the grassy roadside, and refreshed him with their fragrant breath. "It is sweeter," thought he, "than the perfume which was wafted to our ship from the Spice Islands." The round little figure of a child rolled from a doorway, and lay laughing almost beneath Cranfield's feet. The dark and stately man stooped down, and, lifting the infant, restored him to his mother's arms. "The children," said he to himself—and sighed, and smiled—"the children are to be my charge!" And while a flow of natural feeling gushed like a wellspring in his heart, he came to a dwelling which he could nowise forbear to enter. A sweet voice, which seemed to come from a deep and tender soul, was warbling a plaintive little air within.

He bent his head, and passed through the lowly door. As his foot sounded upon the threshold, a young woman advanced from the dusky interior of the house, at first hastily, and then with a more uncertain step, till they met face to face. There was a singular contrast in their two figures; he dark and picturesque—one who had battled with the world—whom all suns had shone upon, and whom all winds had blown on a varied course; she neat, comely, and quiet—quiet even in her agitation—as if all her emotions had been subdued to the peaceful tenor of her life. Yet their faces, all unlike as they were, had an expression that seemed not so alien—a glow of kindred feeling, flashing upward anew from half-extinguished embers.

"You are welcome home!" said Faith Egerton.

But Cranfield did not immediately answer; for his eye had been caught by an ornament in the shape of a Heart, which Faith wore as a brooch upon her bosom. The material was the ordinary white quartz; and he recollected having himself shaped it out of one of those Indian arrowheads which are so often found in the ancient haunts of the red men. It was precisely on the pattern of that worn by the visionary Maid. When Cranfield departed on his shadowy search he had bestowed this brooch, in a gold setting, as a parting gift to Faith Egerton.

17   12

"So, Faith, you have kept the Heart!" said he, at length.

"Yes," said she, blushing deeply—then more gayly, "and what else have you brought me from beyond the sea?"

"Faith?" replied Ralph Cranfield, uttering the fated words by an uncontrollable impulse, "I have brought you nothing but a heavy heart! May I rest its weight on you?"

"This token, which I have worn so long," said Faith, laying her tremulous finger on the Heart, "is the assurance that you may!"

"Faith! Faith!" cried Cranfield, clasping her in his arms, "you have interpreted my wild and weary dream!"

Yes, the wild dreamer was awake at last. To find the mysterious treasure, he was to till the earth around his mother's dwelling, and reap its products! Instead of warlike command, or regal or religious sway, he was to rule over the village children! And now the visionary Maid had faded from his fancy, and in her place he saw the playmate of his childhood! Would all, who cherish such wild wishes, but look around them, they would oftenest find their sphere of duty, of prosperity, and happiness, within those precincts, and in that station, where Providence itself has cast their lot. Happy they who read the riddle without a weary world search, or a lifetime spent in vain!

THE END.

M'Farlane & Erskine, Printers, Edinburgh.

www.ingramcontent.com/pod-product-compliance
Lightning Source LLC
Chambersburg PA
CBHW030808020726
47499CB00006B/1815